HELLBOY
ODD JOBS

From the Library of

_____

HELLBOY

ODD JOBS

Edited by
Christopher Golden

Illustrated by
Mike Mignola

DARK HORSE COMICS®

Mike Richardson ✠ *publisher*

Scott Allie ✠ *consulting editor*

Darcy Hockett ✠ *designer*

HELLBOY™: ODD JOBS

Published by Dark Horse Comics, Inc.
10956 SE Main Street
Milwaukie, OR 97222

December 1999
First edition
ISBN: 1-56971-440-1

3 5 7 9 10 8 6 4

PRINTED IN CANADA

TABLE OF CONTENTS

INTRODUCTION

I am a cartoonist. Most of my storytelling I do with pictures. I can draw a house, if I have reference, and if I do a good job, I can—maybe—convey a sense of place, mood, atmosphere, whatever. Aided by my colorist, Dave, I can show you that it's night or day, winter, summer, or fall. Not bad, but I'm not a "real" writer. A "real" writer does all these things with words alone. That's beyond me. Chris Golden asked me to contribute a story to this book, and all I could come up with was, "On a good day, Hellboy smelled like a dry-roasted peanut." I think it best that I stick to what I do. Leave the "real" writing to the professionals.

In the following pages, you'll find some stories that have the same feel as the stories in the comics. Others are radically different. Most are somewhere in between. I'm happy with them all. What I hoped for is what I got. Different takes. Different voices. That's what an anthology is supposed to be.

"The Nuckelavee" was originally something I was going to do as a comic, but I changed my mind. I wrote it up in rough plot form and gave it to Chris Golden. He, being a "real" writer, turned it into a "real" story. I want to thank him for that, and for assembling some of today's very best horror writers for this odd little project of ours. I want to thank regular *Hellboy* editor Scott Allie for all his help and patience, and for probably rewriting this introduction into something coherent. Last, a very special thank you to Gahan Wilson for providing that very special something extra.

There you go.

MIKE MIGNOLA

Mike Mignola
Portland, Oregon

MEDUSA'S REVENGE
YVONNE NAVARRO

B ecause of the danger involved, Hellboy had thought it would be best to work
by himself on this case.

Now he regretted it.

He didn't need help or research or someone else with supernatural powers—at
least not yet. What he wanted was someone to *share* what was spread out before him.

He wanted Anastasia.

Because below was a vista of paradise.

Hellboy had been a lot of places, seen more things and countries and beauty
than he could probably ever appreciate, but nothing had ever compared to this. He
stood on the highest point in the area, and lush hills covered in knee-length grasses
spotted with limestone boulders fell away both in front of and behind him.
Directly below was a cliff that led to the Aegean Sea and water that sparkled like a
blanket of diamonds stretched to an impossible horizon edged with barely visible
mountains, the farthest end of the universe and beyond where surely the gods of
former Grecian glory had stepped off this earth and left behind the puny mortals.
More water lapped at the opposite side of the narrow cliff point, while to his right,

hundreds of feet below, the tiny, whitewashed houses of fishermen—too many to count—crowded among the rocky nooks and crannies that eventually led to the boat docks and the sea. A warm, fresh breeze swirled around him, bringing with it the scents of saltwater and sunshine.

But the beauty of this tiny, unnamed island to the east of Tghira was deceptive, and the water that should have carried sound, should have bounced it up to him like a child skipping rocks across the surface of a quiet pond, brought only silence. No one fished on the short coast below, or cooked, or swept the neat sidewalks in front of the shacks crowded together; no dogs barked and chased hissing cats among the stalls of the deserted marketplace. Even the seagulls seemed to have fled, left the village to the ruin of whatever heavy hand of evil had descended upon it. It was just as well that Anastasia was several thousand miles away and tending to the intricacies of her own life. Here, he was certain, she would find only danger.

Hellboy shifted, trying to find a more comfortable spot to stand, one where the tiny pebbles and shells washed up here in the ocean storms didn't embed themselves into the bottoms of his hooves. He scratched at the stubble on his head, enjoying the heat of the sun as he peered down the hillside and tried unsuccessfully to spot movement. He had no doubt that there were still people down there somewhere, but they weren't stupid. Hiding probably, sequestered in their houses with heavy wooden bars thrown across the doors and the windows tightly shuttered, and be damned to the high summer temperatures or the desire for the cooling ocean wind. But wait—

There.

Hellboy stood up straighter, straining to see. At first it was only a speck, but the moving object closed the distance rapidly along the upper outskirts of the village, picking its way nimbly among the boulders and grasses. It took Hellboy a minute or so to realize that the thing seemed to have a purpose, and when he figured it out, he was anything but pleased: it was obviously angling toward him, following a path up the side of the cliff that would bring it right to his feet. Of course; he must be like a big, red beacon standing up here. He might as well have beat on his chest and shouted, *Here I am!* at the top of his lungs.

Another thirty or forty seconds—the object was moving *fast*—and Hellboy could finally recognize it for what it was: a horse.

A *stone* horse.

Hellboy felt no fear, only a sharp and detached sense of interest. Horse lovers worldwide would despise him for it, but he really didn't care about saving the oddity headed toward him with such single-minded purpose. It was surely beyond redemption, its flesh and heart petrified for all time, its thoughts, were he to believe what Dr. Manning had told him in his briefing at the Bureau's Fairfield, Connecticut office, turned solely to destruction.

Another twenty seconds and he could see it in full detail, watch the weird play of muscles moving along the rocky surface of its hide. This was no fire-breathing anomaly—it wasn't breathing at *all*, just moving with a sort of dead animation that reminded Hellboy of the earliest and crudest of the ancient stopmotion Willis O'Brien movies. The creature's eyes were as lifeless as the ground on which Hellboy stood and about as friendly; only the wide-open mouth portrayed its true intentions, the lips drawn back to reveal the horse's long, square teeth, a full set clearly aiming for a taste of Hellboy flesh.

"Not today," Hellboy rumbled, and planted himself more firmly.

The stone horse closed the last few feet and reared, pawing the air between them with hooves bigger and quite a bit sharper than Hellboy's own. Until he'd met it face to face, Hellboy hadn't registered how huge the horse was; raised on its hind legs, he wasn't thrilled to discover that his head came only to mid-ribcage level at the front of the moving statue.

Great, Hellboy thought. Created by a sculptor who'd liked working big.

He dodged the swipe of one hoof and backskipped as the front of the horse came down, landing heavily right where Hellboy had been standing only a second before. He swung at it and was surprised when he missed—made of rock or not, the statue was considerably faster than he expected and it danced out of range with ease. It circled to the left and came back for another try, this time at an eerily soundless charge that put its full body weight into it.

"You call this strategy?" Hellboy asked dryly, just before he threw himself sideways and out of the way. The world turned upside down as he slid and bumped his way a full twenty feet down the hillside before a rocky outcropping stopped his descent with a not-too-pleasant *thud*. There was a tremendous crash and Hellboy craned his neck to see back up the hill as he felt a vibration run through the ground. The horse statue was on its way, and any sense of surefootedness had disappeared: its own weight had gotten the better of it and the thing was rolling end over end—

Straight for him.

Hellboy yelped and clawed at the ground, found his balance at the last second, and scrambled sideways across the grass like a clumsy spider. He felt the breeze as the rock creature tumbled past and a shower of stinging, sharp-edged pebbles hit him, more gifts from the unlikely animal assassin. Trying to watch almost cost him his hold and he cussed and found it again, finally steadying himself as he saw the horse somersault a final time and crash against the boulders where the base of the cliff met the shoreline. Rock against rocks and it was all over; the thing's head shattered and the rest of it broke into four or five large pieces. Fascinated, Hellboy saw the pieces quiver for a few seconds, as though they were trying to work themselves back together before they realized a vital part was now forever missing. They stopped as Hellboy stared; from where he lay amid the rocks and grasses, the dust settling around the remains of the horse statue looked like a burial shroud, a final layer of gravel that should have remained undisturbed.

"Great," Hellboy muttered to himself as he found his footing and dusted himself off. "Chased by stone horses in the first quarter hour—what's next?"

And what *was* next? He turned back toward the village and studied it, this time crouching so he wasn't such a target to more of the reanimated objects he knew were prowling the narrow streets and alleyways. He could see movement down there now, but thankfully nothing else, man, beast, or stone, seemed to be headed up the hill toward him; for a nervous few moments he'd wondered if these statues had some kind of telepathic link to one another. For now, though, it looked like he'd be okay on that count.

Too bad Jayson Paras hadn't had the same luck.

Dr. Manning had shown Hellboy a photograph of the amateur archaeologist and pre-doctorate student of ancient mythology. Tall, strong, and young—no more than twenty-eight—with the sort of dark hair and eyes that women craved set in a rugged face tanned golden brown by the Grecian sun. Hellboy had accepted what he was in this world a long time ago, but sometimes, when he saw a man like that, he couldn't help but wonder what his existence would have been like had he been born under more human circumstances.

Be that as it may, Paras had come back from the Isle of Kárpathos, and friends, family, and colleagues had listened with skepticism to his account of this latest in a series of summer trips. He had, he claimed, found a tomb buried deep in a cave on the coast of the Sea of Crete, the entrance to which had previously been only a fable, as mythical as the secret of the gods it was meant to conceal. It was in this cave that Paras discovered—or so he insisted—the Shield of Athena, the same one on which the Greek legends declared was imprisoned the deadly head of Medusa.

If the ancient story of how the sight of Medusa would turn a person to stone was true, how Jayson Paras had found, packed up, and then transported the shield was a mystery, and one which would probably remain so for eternity. Now Paras was surely as dead as most of the people in the village; whatever procedures he had undertaken to keep the shield from being seen had failed and someone had discovered the crate and pried it open. The mystery, of course, was why that unfortunate adventurer—and the next, and the next one after that—hadn't simply become petrified until someone had gotten a clue about what was going on.

And . . . oh yeah. There were also those pesky living statues to think about.

Well, Hellboy thought, this was just like an archaeology project. He'd never find the answers if he didn't dig around a bit.

Hunkered down to keep out of sight as much as possible, Hellboy scuttled down the side of the cliff and slipped into the ocean-swept streets of the village.

The village itself was a bewildering maze, a meandering trail of streets too narrow for conventional cars and which held an unspoiled beauty that made it the better for it. Most of the houses were whitewashed or painted in creams, pale yellows, and light gray to reflect the sun; window boxes held everything from sweetly scented flowers to pungent clumps of herbs ready to be plucked and tossed into the midday cooking pots. That, Hellboy realized, was the first indication that something was dreadfully wrong here: instead of the expected smells of olive oil and goat cheese, baking bread and smoking fish, there was a faint smell of dust and decay beneath the surface. Even the goats had fled from whatever had invaded this village. The smell of death was constantly washed aside by the sometimes strong winds off the sea, but it always built up again, like the scent embedded in the trunk of a car where a mummified corpse had remained undiscovered for months.

The village was filled with stone bodies.

It wasn't hard to follow the trail, and the dead ones themselves unwittingly gave Hellboy the clues he needed to begin piecing together this incredible mythological disaster. Many of them were clumped on the steps leading to the village's tiny Greek Orthodox church, but whatever protection they'd expected to find had either not lent itself to the existing threat or simply not felt benevolent that day.

Hellboy stayed close to the buildings, still enjoying in spite of himself the high summer heat that reflected off the tile rooftops as he crept along. An hour of cautious exploring took him back to his starting point but revealed nothing. He began again, preparing himself for a slower, more thorough search, then his eyes narrowed and he paused just the other side of the church. Of all the frozen-stone bodies he'd seen in the village, those gathered here, at the bottom of the flight of stairs leading to the worn double doors, bothered him the most. It wasn't so much that they had sought help here and not found it—that was bad enough—but that there were so *many*. Why here and not, say, in front of the weathered constabulary four blocks over? Or maybe at the undersized but clean hospital at the other end of the village's main street?

Could it be, perhaps, that there was something . . . *interesting* inside?

Time to find out.

Hellboy wrapped his hand around the door handle and pulled, was surprised to feel solid resistance. Not an ordinary door lock—that would have given under his heavy tug. No, this was as if something *held* it closed on the other side, something with a solid strength on line with Hellboy's own.

Since when did a church want to keep people *out*?

Hellboy scowled and yanked harder, putting his weight into it when he felt that same resistance, then getting aggravated enough to give it his full power. The force on the other side increased, then suddenly gave way; Hellboy grunted as his body lurched backward and he tumbled down the steps, staring stupidly at what remained of the door, a chunk of ragged wood surrounding the handle, still clutched in his thick fingers. He started to automatically look toward the now gaping doorway, then remembered the dangerous legend behind the Medusa—if whatever waited for him in that doorway held the shield upon which her head had been imprisoned and Hellboy looked upon it, he could end up being made out of the same unyielding rock as had been the horse he'd destroyed on the cliffside.

Damn, Hellboy thought. This was going to be harder than he'd guessed.

He lifted one arm and slung it protectively across his eyes, then stood and lumbered back up the steps with the stone hand of his right arm held stiff in front of him like a football player, wondering how the hell he was supposed to fight something he couldn't even look at. He hit the entranceway at a dead run, then nearly fell flat when he encountered nothing to block his path. He flailed for balance then realized belatedly that in trying to stay upright he'd lowered his arm and gripped the worn wooden pews on either side of the narrow aisle. His tail swept the floor and hit something else, and when he glanced over his shoulder Hellboy saw the remains of what he assumed had been the statue trying to hold the door shut. When the wood had ripped away, the soldier figure had fallen against a stone basin containing holy water, and now its head and upper torso lay in pieces on the cold tiles of the floor. The rest of it twitched uselessly at Hellboy's feet.

The interior of the building was filled with shadows cast by the muted light bleeding through the gritty panes of the old windows. If there were electric lights, they weren't turned on; what few candles adorned the single, long room were unlit as well. Nothing moved, but Hellboy was not fooled.

More, he thought. There *have* to be more.

And indeed there were.

At the opposite end of the room was a scarred, double-wide wooden pulpit. A few rose from behind it and the rest came from between the first three rows of pews, like a hideous gray army of more than three dozen. Obviously the oldest of what the village had to offer in adornments, and in the ten or so seconds before they attacked, Hellboy made the connection: this small island off the coast of Greece had kept its secrets well and held its own heritage apart from much of what had been pilfered and appropriated by the world's museums. The stone statues that moved before him—depictions of nearly naked Greek gods and goddesses bearing everything from swords and shields to mythical serpents, were the *original* sculptures, the ones that dated back far enough, perhaps, to predate the village's solely human population when the Greek gods had walked the earth.

Back to the time of Medusa.

The village was full of stone, granite, limestone, and marble figures, but most of them remained just that. These, however—

"Medusa's victims," Hellboy said. His voice came out hoarse with amazement. "Every one of you was stupid enough to look her in the face." He shook his head in disgust. "And look what it got you."

Dead or undead, apparently they didn't have vocal cords. Hellboy's comment brought no response, and certainly didn't slow the coming charge. He started to open his mouth and say something else when the first wave of Medusa's warriors hit him.

Something drove a boulder-sized fist into his side and knocked the wind out of him, then another figure bonked him hard on the head. Hellboy sucked in air and managed to block the edge of a sword headed for the bridge of his nose—it might be just rock, but it sure would've hurt had it found its target. "Hey!" he cried. "Cut it out!"

Like they were listening.

"Well, this just sucks," Hellboy snarled as he took another teeth-rattling blow, this one on his left shoulder and nearly hard enough to make his arm go numb. "Time to *rock* and roll!"

He began to fight in earnest.

His left fist was useless against stone but his right was a fine weapon, manufactured for just this type of situation. He swung and spun, then swung again, over and over as he braced himself with his tail so the impact of his blows wouldn't knock him off his feet—the last thing he needed was to get buried under God-knows-how-much weight if these things fell on him.

Everything in a circle around him seemed to disintegrate as he battled, rocks and pebbles whizzing through the air and pelting his face and chest. He struck out again, connecting with whatever was in his way, and something exploded before he could see what it was. With a grunt he brought his stone hand up and smacked at another figure; the shoulders of a toga-draped woman crumbled beneath the blow. Hellboy was getting tired of this and angrier by the second; in about a half a minute, he was going to lose his temper and dig something out of his belt that would lay waste to the entire building.

"*Enough.*"

A single word, uttered by a voice that sounded like it had come from a throat lined with sandpaper and ground glass, and it all simply . . .

Stopped.

Hellboy blinked stupidly at the suddenly empty spaces around him, then watched what was left of the stone soldiers back off in that same, eerie silence. The remainder of the mini-army wasn't much: three or four male statues unremarkable except for their extraordinarily handsome physiques, an equal number of female, a few more figures that could have gone either way and which bore attachments that represented creatures from Grecian mythology, including the thick, delicately sculpted body of a headless serpent.

"*Come closer . . . Hellboy.*"

"Damn," Hellboy grumbled to himself. "I really *hate* it when they know my name."

Hellboy obeyed not because the voice commanded it but because he wanted to; keeping his eyes safely focused on the floor was easy because it was a necessity. The place was littered with rocks and stones from the fight—if he didn't watch where he was walking, he'd likely end up with something stuck in one of his hooves like the lion with the pebble between his paws in that stupid fairy tale. "This is as far as I'm going to go," Hellboy said flatly and stopped at the third pew from the front. "You want to tell me what's going on here?"

"*Isn't it obvious?*" the voice hissed. "*I've finally been releasssssed.*"

The last word was long and drawn out, like the sound the tongue of a snake— a very *big* snake—might make when it flicks out to taste the air.

"Pardon me for pointing this out," Hellboy retorted. "But last I heard you were missing the bottom part of your mobility."

"*But I am still powerful.*"

There was an almost amiable tone to the voice that made Hellboy's eyes narrow with suspicion. He wasn't about to say so, but it only took a quick look around to realize that he had to agree with the power part. "Must be hard when you have to depend on someone else for a ride all the time," he said blandly.

"*Perhaps. But there are always those willing to serve.*"

Hellboy glanced around, but the faces of the stone statues were just that, cold rock, totally unreadable. Were they watching him—could they tell he was considering a blind rush on the podium? Through all this, there had been no movement behind it, and Hellboy thought it was a pretty good bet that the shield with Medusa's head on it had been stashed back there before the rest of her stone cronies had surged forward to fight him. If he could leap to the podium and bring his stone hand down and over, give it one good blow, the shield—and presumably the biggest problem this picturesque Grecian village had—might be obliterated.

"*What about you, Hellboy? Would you serve?*" The voice of Medusa paused, as if contemplating. "*The other gods have long gone, and they no longer concern themselves with the puny distresses of mortals. With your special . . . talents . . . we could rule this pathetic world.*"

Hellboy looked again at the figures around him, but he was just as clueless about what was going on in their "minds" as he had been before.

"Me rule something?" He shook his head nonchalantly, hoping that whatever attention span existed in these rock-headed warriors would be drawn by that movement and away from the minute tensing of his massive leg muscles. "Nah, I never was the management type. The only thing I want to do in that respect is—"

"Rule you *out!*"

Hellboy sprang.

He rolled into the wooden podium like a bowling ball and it shattered. Too late he realized how distorted sound had been in this closed-up building with its high, peaked roof. His stone fist swiped downward at empty air and then he fell, landing facefirst on the floor hard enough to make his eyes water, tiles cool against the always over-warm red skin of his face. Something moved just out of view on his right side and Hellboy rolled and came to his feet in an instinctive fighting stance, leaning forward with his shoulders hunched and his fists up, hooves planted firmly a shoulder's width apart. But the only thing in front of him was the smooth backside of another statue, this one with most of her upper body, including the right half of her head, missing.

Damn. Where had Medusa's voice been coming from?

"*An unfortunate choice, Hellboy,*" she said, and then the fragmented statue spun, much faster than Hellboy would have ever expected—

—and he was facing the head of Medusa straight on.

His eyes met hers involuntarily and everything in him locked up and went numb. Out of his peripheral vision he saw the headless snake—boy, Medusa seemed to like her subjects without that upper appendage, didn't she?—slide heavily across the floor until it was out of sight somewhere below. The only comforting thing he could come up with was that at least with no head or mouth the damned thing couldn't eat him.

Whether his body was turning into stone or not, Hellboy could still see, and boy that Medusa woman was one *ugly* mother. Jutting cheekbones, a bulbous nose and a mouthful of tiny, pointed teeth surrounded by stretched, cracked lips were just a few of her many attributes—not a babe Hellboy would want to kiss on a dare, especially with the bristly tongue that jutted obscenely from between those deadly looking teeth. Her skin was as gray as the one-armed figure that held up her shield, and below a high, misshapen forehead her eyes were the only thing with any color in them: they were a deep red and shot through with flecks of black and yellow, like the gaze of some overhungry, hellish cat.

And then, of course, there was her fabled hair.

Snakes all right, hundreds of them, and all complete with fangs and nasty little triangular heads that writhed and hissed and snapped at everything, including each other. Too bad they didn't just bite the witch that had commandeered them to be her eternal headdress.

"*You could have ruled at my side,*" Medusa said almost mournfully. Her snakes twisted and hissed louder as she talked, as though competing with their mistress' voice. "*But now . . .*"

If she'd had a body, Hellboy thought the Medusa would have shaken her head at him in disappointment, as if judging the behavior of a bad little boy. Instead, she stared at him, her eyes filled with malice. "*What do you think of my subjects, Hellboy?*" she asked, as though he could actually answer. "*Not what I would have chosen for myself, but certainly convenient. My original prey, I gazed upon them eons ago and after all this time, they still await my bidding. Too bad they're so damaged.*"

The head smiled at him then, and if Hellboy had thought it was ghastly looking before, it was nothing compared to the way that hideous mouth now twisted up in happiness. "*But still they serve their purpose, as that fool Paras found out.*" Medusa laughed, the sound screaming into Hellboy's ears and making him want to cringe. God, he thought, have these other statues been like this for all these thousands of years—able to hear and see and think, able to *know*, but helpless to do anything about it?

Would the same thing happen to him now?

"*You see,*" Medusa continued, "*Paras thought he was being so intelligent, the way he uncrated me and so diligently kept the packing material between himself and my shield. But when he lifted me from the wooden box, it was in a place where many of my subjects were also stored—I believe you call it a museum.*" Medusa chuckled. "*He was quite surprised when the stone woman across the room came to life and rushed him. He's still there, you know, waiting for my bidding. He makes a fine statue.*"

Wait a minute, Hellboy thought. His gaze cut experimentally to the right, then to the left.

I can still move my *eyes.*

"*My body still exists, Hellboy, hidden deep in a cavern on Mt. Ídhi in Crete. And* you, *with your perfect physical body and unstoppable strength, will take me there for my reunion. I need only wait a small measure of time and then reanimate you as I have done with my more ancient subjects. You will find yourself as obedient as they, although, unfortunately, you will lack the more . . . interesting . . . aspects of your personality.*"

Hellboy barely heard her. He was concentrating on his eyes, rolling them around and around enough to make himself dizzy inside whatever weird stone covering had encased him. Made of stone? He wasn't afraid of that—he'd always had a part of him that was stone and it still functioned just fine.

Why shouldn't the rest of him do the same thing?

The Medusa's voice had taken on a dreamy, singsong quality that did nothing to make it more pleasant, but Hellboy was focusing on himself, on making the tingle he felt when he rolled his eyes spread throughout his face and neck, then on to the rest of his muscles. "*Once my head and body are rejoined, I will take my rightful place as the new owner of this world, the only god left who walks among mortals and has the power to rule them. There will be no force on earth that can stop me. I have waited thousands of years for this moment, for retribution against—*"

Hellboy flexed his arms.

Whatever Medusa had been about to say died in mid-sentence as her terrible eyes widened. Hellboy grinned, pleased to feel the stretch of his mouth, the warm air in the church as it rushed into his lungs, the movement of his own tongue against the back of his teeth when he spoke.

"Hi, honey. *I'm home!*"

He heard her hiss at him just before he leapt, then the statue that was holding her turned its back to him, protecting the shield and taking the blow that Hellboy had meant for that ancient, ugly face. The entire back of it shattered and it went down, the face and whatever power of mobility it had possessed going with it; out of the corner of one eye Hellboy saw the shield roll awkwardly away and bump against the back wall, then fall face up. He started to go after it and tripped, unused to the quadrupled weight of his new stone body. He was cumbersome and slow, but at least he wasn't as fragile as the rest of Medusa's soldiers; the only thing that seemed to be truly paralyzed—as petrified as the legends claimed—was his stone hand.

Fine. It might be inconvenient, but if it wouldn't move then he'd use it as a battering ram or something.

Hellboy hauled himself upright, then promptly hit the floor again as something twined around his feet—that damned, headless snake. He started to bat it aside then realized it was a more formidable foe than he'd assumed; it quickly coiled itself around his tail and both legs, and he found himself fighting to keep it from winding its way up his chest. He might not be lunch for the thing, but Hellboy knew the big snakes—the boas and pythons—killed by asphyxiating their prey, squeezing and holding until the trapped creature simply couldn't breathe anymore.

But he couldn't get his fingers underneath it, couldn't find a hole between the snake and his own stony skin big enough to snag a grip. The other hand was next to useless—his fingers wouldn't move at all. He scrambled around for a few more seconds, then absurdly a line from an old folk song popped into his head—

"If I had a hammer, I'd hammer in the morning . . . "

Hellboy hunched over and began to pound on the snake with jackhammer speed using his stone-dead hand.

He felt each blow all the way down to his teeth as it vibrated through the beast thrashing around him—he had to acknowledge that he might not like being *all* made of stone, but it had certainly increased his power. After five more seconds the hold loosened enough for him to think he might be able to continue breathing after all, and the next quarter minute made pieces of the snake fly in all directions, a miniexplosion of crushed stone and gravel.

He came upright and threw his arms wide, roaring like an oversized gorilla as he met the fresh onslaught of stone-faced warriors that were pouring into the church, drawn, no doubt, by some sort of telepathic command from Medusa. But it was a useless effort for them—where Medusa's power had turned them into a mini-army of fighters, it had unwittingly turned Hellboy into an undefeatable one-man machine of destruction. Again and again his double-stoned fist flashed out, dwindling their already reduced numbers.

Until, finally, it was only him and Medusa's head.

Certain that more statues were likely to come pouring into the church at any moment, Hellboy bounded over to it, then yanked back instinctively when the hair-snakes contorted wildly and bit at him. For the first time he realized how wrong he'd been in assuming that the shield was also made of stone. It wasn't; instead, he found himself looking at a living head attached to a hand-hammered disc, flesh melded onto a metal circle into which had been carved a thousand glyphs—no doubt they were ancient Grecian spells geared to destroying or continuing to imprison the head. Hellboy could never hope to decipher these markings in time to help himself, and it only took a second to realize he would never be able to break the shield . . .

So he was back to that hammer thing again.

Ignoring the repulsive knots of snakes, Hellboy bent and hefted the shield. The creatures in Medusa's hair attacked him viciously, but their long fangs couldn't penetrate the stone skin in which their mistress's own gaze had sheathed him. In his hands, the metal felt uncomfortably warm, even for Hellboy, and he had to fight the urge to toss it away before his job was done. Instead, he literally began to fight with it, punching and pounding and twisting, turning then trying to tear—*anything* that would do some measure of damage to this seemingly indestructible piece of godly armor.

Nothing.

"Damn it!" Hellboy roared. The head and hair still flailed at him, and this time the snakes had changed their tactics and were going for his eyes, the only part of him that was likely to still be vulnerable. In frustration he flung the shield back to the floor; this time it landed face down and Hellboy let his anger take control. He began to jump on it, up and down and all over again, each time bringing the stone-fortified weight of his not-inconsiderable body down fully in the center like a child stomping on a hated toy.

Beneath him, Medusa's enraged screams reached a crescendo that made his eardrums ache, but . . . did he detect a change in that awful voice, a *weakening?* And was that a *dent* he saw growing in the middle of the shield?

Another mighty pounce, and another, and more still. Somewhere inside his head Hellboy heard a brain-splitting shriek, then the shield gave way beneath him. He dropped to floor level with a grunt and stopped, staring fixedly down at a spiderweb of cracks that began to run along the backside of the armor, threading their way in a spiral pattern until they reached the outside edge. Something dark, wet, and viscous spread from beneath the shield—gods' blood perhaps, something which ordinary man was never meant to see. As Hellboy gawked, the shield suddenly trembled and the battered, uneven surface of the metal crumbled, morphing before his eyes until it became stone, Medusa's revenge turned upon herself. Even the black puddle beneath the shield hardened and began to change, lightening until all that remained was a fine powder of stone dust.

And finally, Medusa's head was silent.

Hellboy reached tentatively for one edge and flipped it rightside up. It landed against the tiled floor with a clang so out of place inside the quiet church that it made Hellboy look around guiltily to see if he'd disturbed someone. On the floor at his feet, the shield still held the face and head of Medusa, but now it was deadened and veined with chips and holes.

Still, Hellboy didn't trust it.

Against the wall was a tall, marble cross. Hellboy bounded over and picked it up, pleased at its substantial weight, then returned to stand over the shield. It was the same as it had been a moment before—

Maybe.

Or maybe not. Did he see something malevolent in the dead Medusa's eyes as she glared unseeingly up at him?

Again, maybe.

But he could take care of that.

As though he were staking some kind of perverted vampire, Hellboy upended the cross and drove it point-down into the center of Medusa's forehead.

And the shield shattered into a thousand pieces, and was no more.

It took nearly three days for the stone skin covering his own to finally slough away.

During that time, the flesh beneath it itched unmercifully and Hellboy found himself clawing at his body countless times while he waited for the process to complete itself. Each time he started to rant or feel his temper start to go, he would look around at this once-picturesque village in the Greek isles and remind himself that what he endured could, indeed, be worse.

Much, *much* worse.

Because with the destruction of Medusa's head had come the release—and resurrection—of her victims.

All those reanimated statues were also sloughing away their stone prisons, changing back to flesh bodies which had, either in battle with Hellboy or with the passage of time, lost all or a part of themselves. Returning to life with missing limbs, heads, or huge chunks knocked from parts of their bodies, the ancient figures were incomplete abominations; if they had mouths they screamed in terror and pain but they—and the strange, mythical creatures that came back to life bonded with them—would not die on their own.

And so the townsfolk—those who finally came out of hiding now that the worst was over—moved in to complete the slaughter.

The more recent victims of Medusa were returning to flesh as well, but most of them were dead or in the same shape as the ancient ones. Nothing could be done for them, and their fate was the same: faces grim with mourning, the inhabitants of the village exercised their hands at killing, then spread the bodies of old and new side by side.

The village's menfolk found Jayson Paras, resurrected from stone but still locked and wandering aimlessly in the lower level of the tiny, local museum. Ironically unscathed, the amateur archaeologist insisted he'd been sleeping and that he'd had some kind of nightmare. Everyone thought he was quite mad.

And all Paras ever talked about, from that day forward, was an image from the dream that he couldn't get out of his head.

Snakes.

JIGSAW
STEPHEN R. BISSETTE

O h, she loved to touch him, especially when he was asleep in the early morning. Guy had labored through the night shift at one job or another as long as she had known him. He came home as the night faded, quietly shedding his clothes to slide into bed, stirring Francine as he fell into sleep. This was his ritual, their ritual, and it had been so for the five years they had been living together. She was his touchstone, his vacation, his salvation, and they shared their fleeting waking hours and Sundays with no one.

That was just as she liked it. Though she tolerated his complaints whenever necessary, it gave their time together an urgency she reveled in. They had struck a unique rhythm together, apart from everyone and anyone around them, and his work schedule was instrumental in keeping the world at bay.

And when Guy slept, it was bliss.

Her bliss.

Hers alone, with him.

His scent always carried his current employment home, like a bee carrying pollen to the hive. Of late, Francine and Guy shared the musk of the hospice where they had met, stealing away from the dusk-to-dawn caverns of the ward. The hospice was their shared workplace, an easy walk from their *appartement.* Its patients were their surrogate children to care for and commiserate over, its odors theirs to cling to. The scents of their world and their bodies mingled amid the bedclothes like a shared kiss after coffee, tongues heavy with the earthy aftertaste of the waking hours.

This morning, the familiar tang of his own sweat was tinged with an unfamiliar melange of dust, detergents, and dampness she was becoming accustomed to, the clinging remnants of his janitorial duties at the *Faculte de Medecine.* It was a commute on the Metro, a weekend addition to his duties at the hospice, but they needed the money, and Guy had welcomed the additional income.

Though he bemoaned their lack of waking time together because of his work schedule, she secretly savored the dawn hour. As he lay still as a sleeping infant, it was her hour with him, alone, and no one ever disturbed it. It was her anchor and her pleasure, and it reminded her of the morning she'd first fallen for him.

Sunday mornings let her drink him in at her own pace: softly, slowly, without feeling like a thief stealing glances. She savored the glow that filtered into the bedroom, gradually illuminated his close-cropped bristle of blond hair, the smooth curve of his brow and sculpted slopes of his child-like nose, the softness of his eyelashes, his thin lips, the gentle pulsing of his throat, the rise and fall of his hairless chest. He still looked like a teenage boy.

The touch of dawn's rays invited her fingers to follow their lead.

"*Cheri . . .*"

At times, he would sleep soundly despite her whispers and gentle caress; at times, she would rouse him, and the morning would be theirs. That was wonderful, too—but when sleep veiled her touch, the hands of the clock ceased to move, he remained oblivious to Sunday church bells and the stirring of the *Boulevard Richard'lenoir* outside, and he was hers.

Hers, as ever, it seemed.

And as ever, she wondered what he was dreaming.

He could barely see the outline of the tall man who plucked his face to pieces. Blood filled his eyes, and try as he might to blink and clear them, it did no good. Without eyelids, the urge to blink only pained him. Part of him didn't care to see, really. He could feel the heat of the blood, taste it in his mouth.

How could he help it, now that his lips were gone?

Despite the chanting and the crying of the infants, he could hear the music of the cutting tools and the insistent slushy whispers of the incisions. There was a metallic sting across his hairline, the furrow of the blade gliding into his brow and deep into his remaining cheek. The cutting seemed endless, though he knew there had to be an end to it soon. How much more could they remove before his skull was picked clean?

Then he heard the cold clang of a saw, and felt its blade rest against his jaw.

The chanting faded as if on cue, followed by the inviting gurgle of running water. Its cold bite spilled over and into his wounds, across his flayed rictus grin and between his remaining teeth. He instinctively gulped at it, embraced it with the stump of his tongue, straining his neck to move toward its source until the stream of water lifted and poured into his lidless eyes, washing his vision clear for a moment.

The tall, gowned man still stood over him, bonesaw in hand, now held ceremoniously aloft.

The gown was adorned with arcane symbols, their patterns confused by the spots of dark blood and bits of flesh. Among them, though, one stood out: an arc within a square, bisected by a sword.

There were other figures behind and above him, and the sound of shrieking birds and yowling children, but only the surgeon was visible, methodically disassembling him, skin from muscle, tendon from bone, molar by molar.

The surgeon leaned in close, and muttered in a low, almost inaudible Teutonic voice:

"I will tell you of your father . . . "

He bolted awake, slamming the stumps of his horns against the headboard, inadvertently splintering it a second later as his outsized right fist flailed out. The stony knuckles shattered the dried wood like pasteboard. His tail lashed out from under the blankets, slamming against the night table, spilling lamp, phone, and note pad across the rug.

"The BPRD isn't going to keep covering the damage deposit," said the cold man reading in the chair across the room.

"Jeez," Hellboy whispered, clamping his left hand over his eyes.

"You all right?" the cold man inquired, glancing up from his book.

Hellboy touched his face tentatively, savoring the feel of bristle, brow, and the ridge of his pug nose. He shook his head to clear his mind, wincing at the vivid authenticity of the nightmare.

His tongue slid over his teeth—all in place—and lips, blessedly intact. He leaned forward, head still in hand, and cleared his throat.

"Yeah, Abe," he said, "I'm peachy."

Abraham's gills fluttered as they always did before speaking.

"Can it," Hellboy muttered, "They're just dreams—"

"Of your head being methodically flayed and sectioned."

As he placed his book in his lap, Abraham's amphibian gaze betrayed none of the concern that resonated in his voice.

"I'll call the Bureau for you," Abe offered. "Could you make out anything more this time?"

Hellboy sat up in the bed, dropping his hooves to the floor. He fumbled for the phone, pushing aside the torn lamp shade to retrieve the receiver. He busied himself for a moment tidying up the mess, twisting the bulb of the righted lamp and grunting with pleasure when the light flickered on. Turning his attention to the shattered headboard, he traced the center of impact with a blackened fingernail.

The silence hung between them, eased only by the wet suction of Abraham's breathing.

"I still can almost make out the symbols on his robe," Hellboy whispered. "But there's too much blood obscuring things. They're alchemical in nature, I'm sure. And—"

Abe's sticky breath: In. Out.

Hellboy reached down to pick up the hotel stationery pad. The ornate masthead of the *Hotel de la Cathedrale* graced the top of each sheet of paper, framed with leering gargoyles.

Hellboy paused a moment, pen poised at the thatch of hair under his lip, then drew the symbol he recalled from the gown in the dream: an arc, within a square, split by a single sword, point down. The blade was curved, disrupting the crucifixion symbol of most European inverted swords: this was not a cross. He handed it to Abe and walked to the window.

Outside, the gargoyles of the Notre Dame Cathedral met his gaze.

"There was something else. He spoke to me this time. German."

The gargoyles' eyes expressed nothing, just as Abe's lidless glare betrayed nothing.

"Big promises about . . . my father."

Abe looked away, as if pondering the curtains or the bidet.

"We're about done with the Cocteau manifestation. Manning said there was something else here in Paris," Abe stated flatly, "but he said nothing about its link to you. You're picking up more and more information, the closer we get to the source."

"There's nothing psychic about it," Hellboy grumbled. "What a pain in the ass . . . "

"Liz disagrees. So does Manning."

Hellboy glared at Abe. "And you?"

That fishy grin, betraying nothing. "Anything else you can recall?"

Hellboy touched his face again, unconsciously tracing the line of his jaw with his fingers.

"A bonesaw, the bastard had a bonesaw. Was going to take my jaw off this time."

"Watch some television," Abe said soothingly. "I'll call the BPRD once you've settled down. I'll scan and fax your drawing over, too."

Hellboy abandoned the window and moved to the bed. Kicking off the blankets, he leaned back into his pillow, his jaw clenched.

"Yeah, great, French TV," he muttered. "TF1, FR2, M6, *Le Cinque*—nothing but mindless *varietes* this time of night. The novelty has worn off. You know, I miss the British news programs Liz had us watching last weekend. They had an amusing attitude about the French."

"Until we wrap up loose ends on the Cocteau visitation, we're stuck here," Abe reminded him. "The locale has intensified your nightmares, too, which has given the Bureau reason to drag their feet a bit longer. Better start learning French, or find some SECAM videos."

"Ducky. Go soak in the tub, would you?"

"There's always the music videos I picked up in London," Abe grinned. "This Magnetoscope plays PAL as well as SECAM."

"Spare me," Hellboy muttered. Reaching for the remote, he punched the play button and resumed watching the SECAM conversions Liz had sent along of the medical channel from the satellite at home. A retinal operation, by the look of things, filmed with clinical detachment. The blessedly English-speaking narrator purred professionally, her explanations lost on Hellboy.

"Suit yourself," Abe grunted, returning to his book.

Hellboy packed his pillows against the ruined headboard and leaned back, awash in the cool light of the screen.

When it was someone else's problem, there was a certain fascination in seeing an eye so neatly breached, a perverse pleasure to be savored in the precision of the arc of the cut.

"I've still one good eye," the old man cackled. "Your *petite belle* is a saint, so mind your manners about her, Guy."

"Thomas, I meant no insult." Guy grinned.

"Don't speak of your *cheri* that way," Thomas grimaced. "I won't hear of it."

Guy and Francine each had their favorites among the patients, but Thomas was Guy's only friend among them. The old man was approaching a century in age, but few people offered him the respect his tenacity had earned. Guy was one of the few who seemed undisturbed by the old man's gruff manner, barely coherent speech, and disfigured visage. When he grimaced like this, it emphasized the puckered ridge of scar tissue where his nose had once been.

"*Pardon!*" Guy laughed, "Never again!"

It was rumored that Thomas was the last surviving fossil of the *Union des Gueles Cassees*, World War I veterans who had lost limbs and faces in the trenches, but Guy had never bothered to ask Thomas. It seemed possible; surely, teenagers had fought there, too, and the hospice bedded many veterans of later wars. Thomas never spoke of the war, any war, or the cause of his mutilation, so Guy never inquired. It seemed unimportant.

Thomas was his own man, and Guy felt a great affinity with him.

Thomas's voice dropped to a conspiratorial whisper.

"How is the new job going at the *Faculte de Medecine*?" he asked.

Guy pulled his chair closer to Thomas's bedside and leaned in to speak softly. Fraternizing so with the patients was discouraged, of course, as death was a frequent visitor to the home. Francine and Guy had been repeatedly warned not to grow too close to any of their wards. They acknowledged the cold logic of the rules, given the high mortality rate, but neither could maintain the aloof stoicism of the older nurses or the callous disregard of their more cynical workmates.

"Fine, I think," Guy whispered. "I can't tell yet if they're giving me all the shit details as an initiation, or if that's what they hired me for."

"What did you find last week sweeping up the bibliotheque?" Thomas asked, his finger crooked to urge Guy closer with his reply. "Anything of interest?"

"Nothing much," Guy whispered back. "A cloth bookmark for Francine. No one will ever miss it. Very ornate, she loves it. But you could hide anything in some of the nooks and crannies of that library."

Thomas grunted and nodded, though he couldn't hide his disappointment. Guy leaned in closer with the promise of treasure yet to be found.

"They've got me assigned to the medical archives for the rest of the season. Some rooms haven't been touched in decades, I'm told."

"Ah!" Thomas grunted with satisfaction. "If you find my arm there, bring it back for me, will you?"

There was much to despise about the hospice job—long hours, low pay; bedpans, bedsores, and constant illness; accusations and abuse from suspicious relatives or uncaring visitors vainly asserting their regard for discarded lives; the thieving of greedy siblings, adult children, and untrustworthy caregivers; the tenants' bottomless sorrow, depression, and despair; the merciless dimming of eyes, hearts, and lives. All there was to love in it were the people like Thomas who somehow retained their dignity and heart amid the remnants of so many dwindling sparks.

"Go on with you," Thomas croaked. "Steal some dinner with your *belle* before you head off to your new job. Long, long night ahead of you, *mon frere*."

Guy squeezed Thomas's lone hand, and bid him *adieu*. There were others to attend to within the remaining hour, and the long Metro ride to the *Faculte* ahead of him.

But between the two, there was a fleeting meal with Francine at the cafe on the corner, right by the Metro *Richard'lenoir* entrance. He had enough to cover their dinner and his round trip on the Metro.

Tomorrow, he would have something for Thomas.

To Abraham, the soft green of the hotel phone looked like a bar of soap perched on the expanse of Hellboy's blazing-red palm.

When Abe held the phone, it disappeared against his skin, as if he were made of the same wet-looking plastic—the same color and contours of the bathroom tub, sink, commode, and the bidet. Having memorized the visage of every Notre Dame gargoyle facing their windows, and unable to leave the room without wrapping himself up like the Invisible Man, Abe had taken to finding small pleasures in the textures of the room itself. It was a meditative art lost on his travel partner.

"Like a fish in a fish bowl," Hellboy had chuckled when Abe had tried to share his observations earlier that morning. "We're gonna kill each other if we stay cooped up in this shoe box much longer."

Hellboy's flat, stony hand was cupped around the phone like a monstrous soap dish, enhancing the illusion. His normal hand held the phone to his ear, jade within fire, as Elizabeth Sherman drove the final nail into her arguments for them to stay put in Paris another week.

"Listen, HB, Kate's on her way over to you in a day or two," Liz concluded. "That drawing from your most recent dream kicked up some dust for her, and she believes you're onto something."

"Pah," he scoffed. Abe recognized the slow sagging of Hellboy's shoulders: they would be staying longer, floundering in the fish bowl.

"All right. If the Bureau can justify the expense, there must be something to all this. When's Katie arriving?"

Abe savored the shifting of green on red, emerald plastic on flame-baked skin, as Hellboy shifted the phone to the crook of his neck and struggled with pen and pad to take down Liz's instructions.

"Yes, I'll have her call you," he growled. "No, we're not far at all from the *Palais de Justice*, and the *prefecture de police* is right down the boulevard. Later, Liz."

He hung up, returning the receiver to its cradle.

There was an inexplicably delicious completion in the coupling of smooth green on green between the sinewy scarlet left and the hammered red right hand. Abe's gaze drifted up to Hellboy's brooding brow.

"What the hell are you grinning at, fish face?"

Weary from the day at the hospice and the Metro ride, Guy shuffled his way through the halls of the *Faculte de Medecine*. He'd already lost his way twice this evening, and hoped he was finally cleaning the right room.

It was a storage room, of that there could be no doubt. He just hoped it was the correct one. He doublechecked the number on the *Directeur*'s note against the faded numbers on the door, and went to work.

It had perhaps once been used for classes, but the desks and chairs were stacked against the far wall, shrouded in cobwebs and dust. The other two walls were nothing but shelves, piled high with books, boxes, files, dirt-opaqued jars and instruments, and all manner of paraphernalia.

The high windows were blocked with crusty curtains, and partially obscured by expansive shelving that stretched from floor to ceiling. Nevertheless, the moonlight filtered through here and there, back-lighting the various beakers, scales, and specimen jars. Moonlit, the contents of some of the jars gleamed through the decades of dust that buried them, casting pale shadows and reflecting the odd glimmer of long-dead eyes, wings, teeth, fins, and embryos.

Guy fumbled for the lights, finding the switch just as the distant ringing of a church bell deepened the gloom.

Even with the lights on, the room seemed dark. Nevertheless, he had to start somewhere. The ceiling lights illuminated the topmost shelves best; besides, the scattered dirt and dust would settle onto everything. It just made sense to start with the uppermost levels and work his way down. Two stepladders were braced together at the bottom of the window shelving. He separated them and propped the sturdiest of the pair alongside the shelving, and climbed as far up as he felt safe.

In time, he had cleared two shelves. Their contents were strewn across the floor in roughly defined categories: paper, files, cardboard, instruments, and specimen jars. The latter were of some interest, though the glass was too filthy to clearly see what they contained. That would take some time, which he could indulge during another shift, after the sorting and disposal detail was further underway.

As Guy dragged the stepladder to a new location, he tipped it to avoid a clutch of specimen jars he'd just placed at the foot of the shelves. The top step clipped a box of files on the third shelf down and sent it tumbling. Guy steadied the ladder, preventing it from falling, but it was too late. Everything to the right of the toppled box of files went with it. Guy winced as something bulky hit the tiles, and glass shattered, scattering into the settling papers and files.

Something that looked like oversized escargot and black purses slid over the floor, pooling in formaldehyde that soaked into one stack of papers. Hopefully, the documents weren't too important.

Grumbling to himself, he set the ladder aside and hunkered down to pick up the mess.

A half hour later, he had the spill in order, save for the spilled specimen jar that had shattered and scattered a potpourri of shark embryos and skate egg cases in one corner, and an odd collection of gray, dessicated pieces of what appeared to be metal, rock, or some painted substance he simply couldn't identify. They were unusually lightweight, despite their appearance. Their edges were irregular, though they seemed to have been precision cut, not broken, into their odd variety of shapes.

Guy gathered the gray blocks and shards into a single corner of the floor and began to toy with them. There were well over two dozen in all, some as big as his fist, others small and smooth as marbles. Only their color was uniform, indicating their relation to one another.

Holding them up to each other to compare their contours, he found two of them seemed to fit together. With a flex of his wrist, he snapped them into place as they seemed designed to do. To his surprise, the fit was snug. He sorted through the rest and found a third which fit into place, too.

And a fourth . . .

A fifth . . .

By the tenth piece—a large marble which slipped smoothly into a rounded socket—Guy became uneasy as he began to recognize the pattern of the puzzle.

He held one of the unassembled pieces in one hand, the partially assembled mass in the other, and felt a cold shiver ripple up his neck.

The piece in his hand was a nose.

He dropped it as if it were a spider that had just landed on his palm.

He nervously gazed at the mass he held in his other hand, and let the wave of recognition wash over him: the odd, disarticulated object was a human head, somehow mummified, preserved, and jigsawed into pieces.

As his realization reeled into revulsion, he impulsively snapped his fingers open, dropping the object.

It hit the floor. One of the assembled pieces broke free, but the impact was felt in another way.

The rounded marble—an eye—opened in the dusty relic, suddenly warm with color. It was alive.

Guy scrambled to his feet as if stung by a bee. He stood frozen at an odd angle, legs akimbo, arms outstretched, as if to flee or fight. As the minutes ticked by, though, and the object simply lay still, Guy began to relax.

A head. A human head, preserved and jigsawed into pieces.

As revulsion gave way to reason, he decided it was safe to sit back down next to the object. Surely, it was some kind of teaching tool, designed to instruct anatomy students. Why else would a medical university have such an obscenity in storage?

Perhaps it was a game, a puzzle. A three-dimensional jigsaw puzzle. But the detail, the sculpting—no, it seemed to be a genuine human head. No artist could craft such an object complete with bristling brows, whiskers, and hair stubble.

Mesmerized, Guy returned to the puzzle. He fondled the strangely weightless pieces and convinced himself it was just a trick of the light that the eye seemed to glower from within.

Under the watchful gaze of the single, open orb, Guy continued to fit the metallic pieces together, solving the puzzle until the jaw and a portion of the tongue snapped into place.

There was an impossible stirring beneath his hand, and then the head began to speak to him in a soft, barely audible whisper.

"I will make of you a king . . . "

His hands spasmed open, dropping the gray mass to the floor. His every instinct was to flee, or to bring his foot down upon the dust ball and stomp it into oblivion.

Still, it whispered, with a voice dry as wasp paper.

"Restore me," it beckoned, "and I will make of you a king."

Guy closed his eyes and threw the cleaning rag over the damned thing. He sat still, praying under his breath, finally daring to take a peek once more.

The filthy rag completely covered the head. He was afraid to hold his gaze; if the rag should stir, drawn in by a breath, he would surely break down.

Holding his breath, Guy scrambled towards it on his hands and knees and looked away as he tightened the wrap. Mercifully, it made no further sound. If he heard it speak again, he knew he would scream.

Streaming with sweat, he frantically gathered up the various unassembled pieces and stuffed them into an unlabeled manila envelope among the paper debris he had thrown to the floor from the top shelf. He began to feel lightheaded, then remembered to take a breath.

He shuddered when his nervous breathing was echoed from within the rag.

Driven by fear—of staying, of discovery, of the damned thing beneath the wrap—Guy scrambled to his feet and grabbed the largest broom propped against the door.

The urge to jab at the object or just smash it swept over him again, but he instead used the broom to keep the thing as far from reach as possible as he jammed it and the unlabeled manila envelope into the far corner beneath the towers of desks and chairs.

Once it was out of sight, Guy began to calm down. He broke down the cardboard and stacked the flats against the corner where the damned thing was now hidden, as if to blot it out. Regaining some clarity of mind, he swept up the broken glass and the shark embryos, consigned them to the trash bag, and then proceeded to mop the floor.

The pungent aroma of the spilled formaldehyde should have overwhelmed everything, but all he could smell was the head, a dry odor ripe with age, mold, and spores. He coughed and gagged, shook his head, and finished the mopping.

Whenever possible, he averted his gaze from the end of the room dominated by the stacked desks and chairs. He jumped at the occasional echoes of his own breathing, couldn't put out the light or slam the door quickly enough.

He had somehow finished the cleanup, though he couldn't remember the final minutes. He continued to sweat as he left the *Faculte,* entered the Metro, and started the long ride home. As he got off at *Richard'lenoir,* he still felt anxious and afraid.

What would he say to Francine? What would he tell himself?

His heart sank as their *appartement* window came into view. The light was on inside—Francine had waited up for him. He could not simply slip into the bed and close his eyes. She would see something was wrong. He'd never kept any secrets from her. How, where would he begin?

For the first time, he noticed how badly he smelled. The stench of his sweat and the cleaning fluids was bad enough, but he could smell something else. He sniffed his hands, and shivered:

He could still smell the thing.

He was rubbing his hands against his pant legs when he staggered into the *appartement,* afraid of what he might say.

Francine looked up at him from her perch at the edge of the bed, her eyes red and swollen.

"Guy," she whispered, "Thomas is dead."

"**W**elcome to *La Table D'or*. And your friend would be —?"

"Abraham Sapien," Hellboy responded to the maitre d'. "Dr. Kate Corrigan is expecting us. Private salon."

"*Bonjour,*" Abe managed between the coils of his scarf. The flustered maitre d' gazed for only a moment, as if to penetrate the opaque shielding of Abe's mirror shades; he had no way of knowing the opacity of the lidless eyes beneath the lenses. If anything, the starched guardian of the restaurant's sanctuary seemed more disturbed by Abraham's guise in such muggy weather than he had been by Hellboy's trench-coated stature. They cut a mean rug, he and Abe, no doubt about it.

"Yes, of course," the maitre d' chirped, regaining his composure. "Your private salon is right this way—we wouldn't want to disrupt the clientele. Dr. Corrigan had requested special attention be given, and I apologize we weren't quicker to recognize your arrival."

"Lead on," Hellboy gestured, sorry he couldn't milk their entrance for a little more juice.

Abe kept his gloved hand to his face as they were led into a separate dining chamber. Kate stood to greet them, brow cocked at the maitre d'.

"What's the *soup de jour*?" Hellboy asked.

"I've ordered for us," Kate replied. "The food and wine is already here."

"Thank you, madam. If I could be of any more service—"

The evident relief on his face coaxed a smile from Hellboy, who turned to close the salon door behind the efficient clicking of the maitre d's polished shoes. Abe gasped as he slung the scarf away from his neck, quick to exchange greetings with Corrigan as he finished stripping away his disguise. Hellboy claimed his seat and managed a sip of wine before Abe was ready to join them.

"You're looking good, Kate," Hellboy cooed. He rarely saw Corrigan dressed up for dinner, every dirty-blond hair brushed into place.

Kate smiled at Hellboy and turned to Abraham. "Room comfortable at the *Hotel de la Cathedrale*?"

Abe nodded. "Your choice? Very nice. Like the big bathtub. Good color, too."

"Matches his eyes," Hellboy snorted. "Thanks for getting us out of there tonight."

"Let's get to it, shall we?" Kate began. "Was this the symbol you saw in your dream?"

"Yeah, huh," Hellboy grunted, cradling his wine goblet in his left hand. "Told you I wasn't much of an artist."

"On the contrary," Kate whispered, "I found it with nary a blind alley."

The rough arc, within a square, split by a single sword, point down: but the arc was, in the old woodcut reproductions, a serpent, split by the curving blade.

"I've traced this back to a group of alchemists who made their mark in Southern France during the late sixteenth, early seventeenth century. I need more to go on, but it's a start, and you seem to be suffering more vivid dreams the closer you've come to the source: vague memories in Connecticut, more vivid dreams en route to the U.K. and in London, a narrative pattern to the dreams and increasing specifics now that you're in Paris."

Hellboy shifted his glare to Abe. "Tattletale."

Abe shrugged, sipping his bottled water. Kate leaned across the table toward Hellboy, gingerly placing her pale hand on his rough stone fingers.

"You've had more nightmares since you've been here, haven't you?"

Abe looked away as Hellboy cleared his throat, turning his slitted eyes from the amphibian's averted gaze to Kate's open, imploring look. He swished his wine thoughtfully and then swallowed it down in a single gulp.

Bad form. No matter.

"You both know how I hate this psychic stuff," he muttered. "It's worse when it's scrambling your own noggin."

Kate closed her other hand over his massive paw.

"Tell her about the head," Abe insisted.

"I thought it was happening to you—"

"Yeah," he managed. "I've been completely sliced and diced and brazed. But now there's more. I can hear rugrats wailing, men chanting. Latin, French, Spanish, Italian. I see babies cut from throat to crotch. I smell blood."

Kate pulled a notebook from her bag and began writing.

"I can see something else," Hellboy concluded. "A head, not mine, but jigsawed, like what they've done to me there in the dream. It's been turned to stone or something. Last night it opened its eyes and spoke to me. German."

"Did it speak of your father again?" Abe asked.

Hellboy nodded, and poured a fresh glass of wine.

The morning after Thomas's death, Guy quit the invalid's hospice. He made his apologies, and fled the building. For Francine, it was a loss upon a loss, with no time to catch her breath.

Francine flinched when the *Monsieur le Directeur* used Guy as an example to all at the monthly staff meeting. He had grown too attached to one of the patients, the *Directeur* explained, an intimacy ill-advised in the medical and nursing profession. The *Directeur* gazed meaningfully at Francine, no doubt misinterpreting the tears she brushed away from her cheek.

She missed Thomas, too—but she missed Guy's attachment to the hospice even more. It created a sudden, irreparable vacuum that frightened her. For the first time, there were fissures in their life together.

Days later, he still would not speak of what had happened in the medical lab the evening that Thomas had died. He never explained the odd smell, or what had already shaken him so, before he'd learned of Thomas's passing. She had laundered the uneasy stink of that night from the bedclothes, but Guy's sleep was still restless and punctuated with inexplicable shivers.

That she planned to clock extra hours at the hospice only aggravated the unspoken rift. As if goaded to match her distance, Guy secured extra evenings at the *Faculte de Medecine*, claiming he needed to make up for the loss of once-dependable income and had to cover the additional Metro fees necessary to the longer commute.

She didn't like it; the *Faculte* was a mystery to her. She'd never laid eyes on its doors, much less its expansive halls and cluttered rooms. He'd made no friends there as yet to speak of, and rarely had any anecdotes to share. He hardly ever spoke about the university, really, dismissing it to ask instead after her favorite patients at the hospice.

It was as if her job meant more to him than his own, and she enjoyed the attention, though that attention quickly waned in the days after Thomas's death.

Through it all, a week—just a week!—passed without their sharing a waking moment together.

Ah, but Sunday remained their own. She still had him that Sunday morning. She roused him, and they made love, and he finally cried and spoke of Thomas, and she eased him back into the slumber where he was hers and hers alone, if only for a few hours.

Come Monday, they returned to work again, and the gulf between them widened.

Guy had avoided the room all week, despite the notes from the *Faculte Directeur* urging him to at least start with the cleanup of the archives.

He had dreamt of the thing in the corner all week; horrible, unspeakable dreams, in which it was his own head being cut into sections, while birds and babies cried around him. He had never dreamed of blood before in his short life. Never. Ever.

Playing the radio wherever he worked in the *Faculte*, Guy braced himself to go back.

He would go there, as soon as he was finished in the offices.

Once the *bibliotheque* was clean.

After he had swept the hall, he would do it.

He would open the door.

He would go in.

He would switch on the light.

Moving stiffly, carefully keeping his back to the wall stacked with the desks and chairs, Guy slid the more dependable looking of the two ladders over to the shelves. He was about to lift it up to brace it against the shelving supports when he heard the willowy rasping from the far corner.

Paper thin, dry as dust, a breath.

A half hour later, he reentered the room. Soaked in sweat, he stared balefully at the flats of cardboard he had stacked over the hollow beneath the desks, where he had hidden the damned object.

Again, the breath, unmistakable.

Guy began to tremble. He rubbed his face and eyes, then steeled himself for the worst. Hesitantly, he shuffled to the cardboard and carefully set it aside. He bent down, sobbing, and forced himself to reach into the darkness beneath the desk.

It was still there, beneath the filthy wrap. Guy tenderly picked the bits of dust and dirt away, and slowly peeled back the rag. Its lone eye fixed him, a reservoir of unspeakable sorrow.

Is this all he had feared?

He held it just so for a long, long time. Gradually, his breathing steadied, and he continued to unwrap the thing.

Guy cradled the head in his arms, studying its features. It was handsome, in its way, he thought. There was a coppery burnish to the skin that made it seem strong, ageless.

The eye held its gaze, and Guy met it, now unafraid.

This time, when it spoke, he did not drop it or flee.

He listened.

It promised him much he'd never had, many things he'd always wanted.

It promised him things he'd never dreamed of. Never. Ever.

It wanted so little in exchange.

As if in a dream, Guy reached for the unlabeled manila envelope he had hidden away with the object that fateful night of discovery. He reached inside, and as the head whispered to him, Guy methodically coaxed each one of the remaining gray pieces into place. As he felt the round gray piece shift into position in the socket opposite the single eye, sliding between calloused lids with a satisfying pop, he looked down with pride on his work.

The gray orb swelled into the socket and gradually moistened and glowed with the same baleful gold of the other eye.

It promised him more, and more. It needed so little.

"Feed me," it begged, "and I will make of you a king."

As it whispered, Guy nestled the head into the crook of his arm. It wanted such a trifle, and promised him so much. What could it hurt to try?

Guy unbuttoned his shirt, and lifted the head toward his chest. He tilted his own head back as he felt the dessicated lips slide over his nipple and begin to suck.

He felt weak as he stepped off at the *Richard'lenoir.* The Metro had nearly rocked him to sleep, and he felt tired, so tired. He stepped off the train and had to hold onto the pillar as the doors slid shut and the train raced on to its next destination. Fumbling with his buttons, his wrist accidentally brushed against his chest and a bolt of agony cleared his mind for a moment.

His nipples were sore, terribly sore. He dared a peek at the pinkish stains on his undershirt. He peeled one side back to wince at the raw blotchy skin beneath. Band-Aids, he needed two Band-Aids.

Suddenly aware of his surroundings again, Guy buttoned up his shirt and made his way off the platform and up the stairs to the boulevard. The morning air was crisp and helped him to focus. Above, the dawn breeze stirred the leaves of the trees. Guy took a deep breath and closed his eyes. The soft wind felt good, and the rustling leaves were soothing. He would make it to the *appartemente,* and he would be all right. Guy's head lolled, bringing his gaze to rest on the sidewalk.

There, amid the fallen leaves, was a twenty-franc note.

Guy chuckled, and bent to pick it up. Twenty francs! He stood up and admired it for a moment before folding it with care and tucking it into his shirt pocket. He patted the pocket and moved on. His step was a little surer now, and he was smiling.

As the dawn light asserted itself, something else caught Guy's eye on the sidewalk. Another note—another twenty-franc note. And another.

He nervously looked up the boulevard. Surely, there was some mistake. Finding one note was an occasion, but three was unlikely. He strained to see if someone were walking up ahead, someone the notes belonged to. Or a bank car, with its back doors swinging open. But there was no one, nothing.

Guy furtively bent down to pick up the notes. He inspected them carefully, held them up to be sure of what he was seeing. One was indeed a twenty-franc note, but the other was fifty francs. Perhaps he could take Francine out for coffee this morning, if he could stay awake, if she had time.

Further up the street, at the base of the stairway to their *appartement,* Guy found another fifty, and a one-hundred-franc note. His stride assured, he bound up the steps two at a time and made his way to bed, deciding not to disturb Francine's slumber.

Tomorrow. He would share the good news tomorrow.

"Moro—his name was Moro," Kate began. "Some sources link his name with a series of ominous events recorded in two illustrated broadsheets published here in Paris around 1650."

One slide followed another, each woodcut image executed with a primitive vigor. Hellboy stroked his sideburns, drinking in the spectacle.

"Grave robbing, necrophilia, cannibalism," Kate continued, "but no evidence of the authorities capturing or executing him, though as you can see in this second one, his accomplices were broken on *La Roue*, beheaded, and their remains were burned."

"Bummer," Hellboy whispered. "The Wheel."

Kate held the slide on screen, bringing up the room lights. Abraham was already combing through the papers she had laid on the table, thankful for the diversion from the countless hours of quarantine.

"The thread picks up in a number of Dutch texts," she said, pointing to the documents in Abe's webbed hands. "The Dutch were particularly infuriated by the Catholic persecution of the Protestants which drove a group referred to as 'the Waldenses' from the south of France to seek sanctuary in the Alps, into the valleys of Piemont which were later renamed Vaudois. Repeated attempts to exterminate this group over quite a span of time culminated in the massacre of an entire village in the mid-seventeenth century."

Kate clicked the remote on the slide projector, bringing a new image into view. The illustration was of its time, not as crude as the woodcuts they'd been looking at a moment ago. These were more accomplished drawings, still vivid with an uncanny sense of immediacy. A clutch of women and children clinging to their belongings were crowded to the left of the panel, as two soldiers brandishing swords dominated the center, directing the hapless innocents out of the frame.

"This is one of many Dutch broadsheets depicting the atrocities. Apparently the Jesuits turned up the heat, coercing village children into the Catholic fold. The alleged murder of a Catholic priest at Fenile and unspecified insults to Catholic rituals in Torre prompted more heat, with dissenters being forced out of their homes in January of 1655. When the Church authorities were informed that the exiled Waldenses had returned to their homes, orders were given and the villages were purged in April of that same year."

Abe set aside the papers to share Hellboy's careful scrutiny of the horrific images. Rape and plunder gave way to more monstrous extremes: women and children put to the sword; nude bodies roasting over raging fires with soldiers at rest alongside, eating the flesh; infants thrown onto rocks as their mothers were split with axes; children split asunder, their bodies stuffed with gunpowder; steaming objects and liquids poured into every bodily orifice; a grisly bowling match played with tiny heads before a wailing parent, bound hand and foot.

"The soldiers were a ragtag pack of mercenaries from all over Europe. French, Hungarians, Bavarians, Irish, and Spanish. Catholics one and all, promised indulgence for their efforts."

Hellboy's unflinching gaze drank it all in. "Okay, but what's Moro got to do with all this?"

"A local priest named Jean Leger survived and escaped," Kate explained, "and he was the primary source for news of the atrocities. He carefully gathered evidence from any and all eyewitnesses and survivors he could find, including prisoners released after the Treaty of Pignerol and soldiers stupid enough to boast of their crimes. The documentation is impressive, drawn from statements sworn before public notaries of the time. His work bore fruit, firing up the Dutch and Cromwell's England. John Milton wrote a passionate poem protesting the outrage . . . "

Abe read from a page of Kate's papers. His flinty, flat voice lent a strange weight to the text. "'Avenge O Lord thy slaughter'd Saints, whose bones Lie scatter'd on the Alpine mountains cold . . . '"

Hellboy turned to Kate. "And Moro?"

"Leger's diary chronicles his search for Moro. Leger claimed Moro was an alchemist, though his use of the term is tainted. I'm sure Moro was into something far, far more extreme. Leger wrote that it was Moro who had methodically conspired against the Catholics to perform blood rituals. Leger maintained Moro had murdered the Catholic priest at Fenile, and it was one of Moro's foul rituals that had sullied the Catholic church in Torre, though he could find nothing to document his claims."

Abe droned on. "'Forget not: in thy book record their groanes . . . '"

Hellboy turned from Kate to stare again at the horrors on the screen.

"'. . . Who were thy Sheep and in their ancient Fold, Slayn by the bloody Piemontese that roll'd Mother with Infant down the rocks . . . '"

A soldier pulled a fetus from a woman's womb, while two other mercenaries slid their blades down the stomachs of two other infants.

"Later entries assert that Moro conspired with the Jesuits," Kate continued, "and in fact had a hand in the hiring of the mercenaries involved in these crimes. Leger believed Moro orchestrated the atrocities—that the atrocities were rituals in and of themselves, requiring the blood of infants in vast quantities."

Abe had dropped his voice, but continued reading the Milton poem. Neither Kate or Hellboy stopped him.

"'. . . Their moans The Vales redoubled to the Hills, and they to Heaven. Their martyred blood and ashes sow O'er all the Italian fields where still doth sway the triple Tyrant . . .'"

"Blood, ashes, fire," Hellboy murmured. "Moro was up to something."

"'. . . that from these may grow A hunder'd fold, who having learnt thy way . . .'"

"Leger's diary is inconclusive," Kate said. "I found a trio of Dutch texts that claimed Moro was ultimately brought to justice on French soil under peculiar circumstances."

Abe dropped his voice even lower. "'. . . Early may fly the Babylonian wo.'"

As Abe returned the paper to the desk, Hellboy turned back to face Kate. The room's air conditioner came on as a fan in the slide projector whirred. The screen caught the subtle breezes, and the bisected infants on screen seemed to wriggle.

"How peculiar?" Hellboy asked.

Kate changed the slide, motioning to the screen. "The Catholic church apparently conspired with some unusual bedfellows, a group of alchemists associated with this symbol."

There, on the screen, was the serpent within a square, split by a crescent sword, point down.

"The Church had Moro drawn and quartered in a public place, but his head would not burn. One of the texts claimed it still lived, and spoke, promising earthly gain for any who would salvage it."

Hellboy and Abe exchanged glances and grunted.

"Moro's head was turned over to the alchemists, who apparently sectioned the head and transmuted the elements to stone before the Church tidied up by burning the alchemists alive for heresy and scattering the pieces of the head to the four corners of France."

Hellboy mustered a grim smile. "Ah, the benevolent gratitude of the Church."

Abe read Kate's features. "There's more, I see."

"Yes. Ragna Rok."

Hellboy flinched for the first time. "Great. Another kraut spook squad."

"No. *The* spook squad. World War II, Pre-Ragna Rok, our old circle of friends in the service of der Fuehrer: Klaus Werner Von Krupt, Kurtz, Haupstein—and two others who never made the cut to the big time. They believed Moro's head was an arcane artifact of great power."

"Huh. More kraut head cheese, like Von Klempt."

"Two contemporary scholars claim the Third Reich sought and found the sections of the transmuted head during the Occupation. Reportedly, Von Krupt and company converged here in Paris to collect the pieces, intent on reassembling it when the French Resistance inadvertently broke up the operation."

"Hmph," Hellboy grunted. "Probably had no idea what kind of party they crashed. Probably for the better."

Kate shut off the slide projector, shook her head, and closed her eyes, tired of talking. "There are no further records to work from yet, but I've only begun to check the local *bibliotheques*. But your dreams suggest—"

"What?" Hellboy grumbled. "We've still seen no manifestation outside of my nightmares. Nothing to put our hands on."

"Seems fair to assume something is still here," Abe concluded.

Hellboy tapped his finger to his temple. "Or here."

The head spoke to him even in his sleep now. Gone were the dreams of dissection, babies howling, and blood; the head was bathed in an ethereal light, as if it were the vision at Fatima. It spoke slowly, eloquently, of all that Guy would have and do. And as it spoke, he felt a deepening calm wash over him.

He would have no more need of money, of mortal love, of flesh. Gone forever was hunger, pain, want, work. As he listened, he heard the new truth; as he watched, its lips spoke the words, but they began to form other thoughts, other things.

Though his sleep had been restless, Guy had not touched her all morning. As Francine leaned over him tenderly and brought her hand up to his chest, he flinched. Taken aback, she rolled away from him, and slowly pulled the sheets up, careful not to wake him.

The white gauze bandages were wrapped double-layer around his chest and back. There was no tape at the back, as a doctor would do it. The wrap was uneven, favoring his right side. She could smell no disinfectant, none of the odors of a doctor's office. What had he done to himself? She felt hot tears build and spill from the corners of her eyes, slipping down into her pillow. She brought her hand to her mouth to suppress a sob, and Guy stirred and rolled over onto his back.

As she saw the blood stains, soaking into the gauze from beneath, she bit her hand.

Outside, the Sunday morning stirrings of *Boulevard Richard'lenoir* began.

He woke and left without comment. The more she had pressed him about his injuries, the more sullen and withdrawn he had become. He lied about having seen a doctor, claiming the *Faculte* doctor on duty for the night shift was drunk and had done a poor job of bandaging him up. When she asked the doctor's name, he

pulled a clean pair of pants from the armoire drawers, put them on, and dashed out of the *appartement* without another word.

Francine sat at the edge of the bed—their bed—and fought back the tears. She busied herself with making the bed, gathering their clothes for the laundry—anything —to keep the tears at bay, though the ache inside grew more and more unbearable.

His clothes stank of the *Faculte* labs. They smelled old, dry, dead. It smelled like Thomas had that morning that they'd found him, so still in his bed. Guy had smelled like that, too, ever since that night. The tears spilled anew.

She folded his work shirt over her arm. As she picked up his work pants off the floor, something drifted from his pocket and settled onto the carpet.

A leaf, neatly folded.

She picked up the leaf and turned it over curiously. It was creased and folded like a franc note, and even felt like one. Francine sat back down on the edge of the bed and set Guy's work pants in her lap. His pockets were bulging; she had to empty them to do the wash anyway.

She gingerly reached into each pocket and pulled out leaf after leaf, carefully folded. She set them down beside her on the bed, and fought the urge to count them.

"I found them this morning on the boulevard," Guy explained. "I've been finding them all week, every night."

Startled, she jumped, dropping his pants and shirt to the floor. When had he come in?

"They were everywhere on the boulevard," Guy stammered, "a-and I made sure they belonged to no one. They're mine. Ours."

She couldn't bear to look at him. Her own shame at being caught mingled with her confusion and growing dread.

"They're ours. I thought I could treat us to dinner tonight, before my shift begins," he continued.

Her eyes drifted to the floor—anywhere to avoid looking at his face, his imploring eyes— and settled on his shirt pocket. Five or six carefully folded leaves jutted up from the pocket.

He had his hand out now, with another leaf on his palm.

"See, there are still a few outside," Guy exclaimed. "I just found another, as I was going. I brought it back for you."

She absentmindedly plucked it from his hand, like the gift it was meant to be, and placed it on the bed with the others. And she began to laugh.

Now she understood: it was a joke, to make up for their moods. She began to laugh, looking to his eyes for the shared twinkle, and the laugh caught in her throat when she saw the pain and rage on his reddened face.

His words came like a torrent, slapping her time and again.

And then he was gone, leaving her alone once more.

He had hidden the head in the library. With the new attention being given to the archives since he had begun the cleanup, he was terrified someone would find his treasure, his savior. That someone would take it from him.

There were so many places to hide things in the library. Places only he went.

He unwrapped it lovingly. No more rags: he had wrapped it in one of his own shirts, his white shirt, his Sunday shirt.

As always, the eyes lolled in his direction, the mouth gaped like a fish gasping out of water. It spoke to him, showered him with promises, with predictions, with kisses. It suckled at his breast—thankfully, he could feel nothing any longer—but today it wriggled like an unhappy infant.

Guy pulled it away from his withered nipple. The skin was forever raw, but it bled no longer. The head smacked its lips, and looked up at Guy with hunger.

It spoke to him, slowly. At first, its words sickened him, he began to feel the way he had that first night. But the drone of its words, its wisdom, centered him anew, and Guy complied with its wishes. He took off his shirt and unbuttoned his trousers.

Again, it began to suckle. He guided it slowly down, down, lower . . .

The head glowered at him, and began to rise. And as it rose, the babies howled and the crows shrieked and the sky darkened. The head rose from a lake of unborn children, barely formed fetal shapes that writhed like maggots in the dirt.

From beneath the head's ragged, abbreviated throat, veins and nerves extended themselves with startling speed. They spiraled around one another like string, intertwining and swelling into rope-like limbs. The ridged protrusion of the esophagus distended itself at the center of this tapestry of extremities, thrusting down like some obscene caterpillar until the webbing of nerves, veins, and soft cartilage orchestrated itself into two arms and two legs jutting from the virgin trunk of the body.

As he managed to back away from the looming growth, one of the tendrils rippled out from the fetal torso and seized him. He struggled, but already the veins had swollen into powerful talons, digging into his red flesh. He raised his right hand to smash the grip, but another tendril entangled that arm, and another had his left.

Behind the lattice work of coalescing limbs, he could see a line of sprouts erupting from the ground. They, too, grew heads and limbs, bristling with armor, and they began to march—

The ringing of the phone mercifully cut the nightmare procession off. Hellboy fumbled for the receiver and dragged it to his pillow.

"Yeah?"

He could hear Abe stirring in the bed across from him.

"Call to Search Team One from the Bureau for Paranormal Research and Defense in Fairfield—"

"Yeah, yeah, put them on," Hellboy stammered impatiently.

Elizabeth Sherman's voice changed his mood. "HB, you all right?"

"Since it's you, Liz, I'm fine. Why the wake-up call?"

"Kate couldn't reach you earlier, contacted us with some new information on an old university not far from you, the *Faculte de Medecine*. Could you meet her there tomorrow?"

Hellboy fumbled for the pen and reached for the light. Abe groaned as he turned it on and buried his head in the sheets. Tough having no eyelids at this time of morning. Hellboy scrawled down the specs, underlining the time and street address.

"Right, the Latin Quarter. Got it. Thanks, baby."

"HB, you all right? Manning wants to know if you need any assistance—"

"Just more bad dreams, Liz. Still nothing physical. It'll be over soon." He dropped his voice as he clicked off the light and leaned back against his pillow and the shattered headboard.

"This isn't Cavendish Hall. In. Out. No one gets hurt, right?"

At the mention of Cavendish Hall, Abe pulled the sheets down and turned to look at Hellboy.

Abe kept his gaze fixed on his partner long after the call had concluded, and the steady heaving of his rusty barrel chest had slowed into the even rise and fall of slumber.

Francine waited until she saw Guy shuffle down the stairs at the Metro *Richard'lenoir*. He was on his way back to the *Faculte*; she had time, finally, to visit the *appartement* one more time and get her things out of there.

Sobbing, she timidly used her key, climbed the stairs, and entered what had been until a week ago her—their—home.

The stench was terrible. It was the same odor that had clung to him that night that Thomas had died, magnified one hundredfold. She choked and rushed to the cistern to wet her handkerchief. She held the damp cloth to her nose, taking shallow breaths.

She went to the closets, pulling out her travel bags. When she turned to the armoire, her heart sank to see her clothes and belongings already out of the drawers, rudely piled atop it.

Did he want her gone so badly?

The tears were streaming down her cheeks as she took the wet handkerchief away from her nostrils. The stink was overwhelming, but this was worse. Sobs racked her body as she struggled to refold her clothing. As she did so, she realized all of Guy's clothing was scattered here, too, and more of it was strewn on the floor and crammed behind the armoire.

Regaining her composure, she gingerly slid what was hers into the travel bags, pausing to slide open the top drawer and check if she had everything. She gasped and drew back.

The drawer was filled with leaves, precisely arranged and stacked like banknotes.

Shivering, she closed her bags and rushed out into the darkness.

Guy furtively glanced down the hall. What was the *Faculte Directeur* doing here this time of morning? It was barely three o'clock.

Catching sight of Guy, the *Directeur* waved. Guy nervously waved back, and turned to return to the archives.

He had to reach the *bibliotheque*. He had to get the head—his head—out of here.

As he continued down the hall, adjusting the empty backpack he'd brought to take the head home, he heard the *Directeur's* voice. Turning, terrified the old man was following him and wanted to engage in some small talk, Guy was further alarmed when he heard other voices.

Sweating, he stole his way back to the end of the corridor.

The *Directeur's* voice was raised now, boisterous: his public voice, representative of the institution. A woman responded, followed by a deep, guttural growl, like that of a mastiff, and a soft, barely audible gurgling voice.

Guy quietly lay flat on the floor, and slowly, ever so slowly stole a glance around the corner.

There were three figures standing with the *Directeur,* who seemed somewhat intimidated while checking identification papers the woman had in her hand. No wonder he was intimidated: the two men with her were strange. The one looked normal enough, but wore a hat, sunglasses, a scarf, and gloves, baring not a fraction of his skin.

The other wore a trench coat, but that was his least impressive aspect. He was gigantic, fiery red, like some sort of demon. He dwarfed the *Directeur* completely.

As Guy stole a final look, he could have sworn the red man had hooves.

They didn't see him, not even when he scraped himself away from the corner and stood on shaky legs, his hands at his face.

They were here for the head, he knew it. They were here for his treasure, with an entourage of demons to spirit it away.

As the *Directeur's* voice raised anew and their collective footsteps reverberated through the hall, nearing the labs, Guy darted away. He could hear the distinctive tap of the *Directeur's* cane as he walked, and something else:

Hooves.

He had to get to the *bibliotheque*. He had to rescue his savior, and be off, but they were between him and the library. He wasn't thinking straight; all he could think of was getting to the archival lab before they did.

He would think of something there.

"What's in the backpack, Guy?" the *Directeur* inquired. He gently prodded the pack with his cane.

"I brought some books. To read. Later," Guy stammered. The *Directeur* seemed satisfied and left the pack alone, resting there by the door.

"We like to hire readers," the *Directeur* explained. "Even our janitors are educated men, you see?"

The woman had been eyeing Guy ever since she'd set foot in the room. Guy busied himself with sorting the files, arranging the stacks from the middle sections of shelves, but he couldn't stop sweating.

The red giant eyed the shelves opposite Guy, while the man in the hat, scarf, glasses, and gloves simply stood in the doorway.

"And you say all you've found so far seems in order?" the *Directeur* asked. "Nothing unusual?"

"Well, the shark embryos gave me a start the first night," Guy chuckled. And sweated.

He furtively glanced over his shoulder at the woman, who stood her ground and held her implacable glare.

The *Directeur* seemed satisfied, but the woman touched the old man's sleeve.

"May I?" she asked, still pinning Guy with her gaze.

Ever affable, the *Directeur* said, "But, of course."

Guy looked away. Sweating. He could feel her staring as she moved behind him and took a position between himself and the far door, where the muffled man still stood.

"Guy, I'm Dr. Kate Corrigan —"

"Doctor of?" he stammered, afraid to face her, still stooping over the files he uselessly shuffled. The *Directeur's* cane tapped Guy's elbow.

"Guy, you are to fully cooperate. We have nothing to hide, have we?"

"Guy," she continued, her voice flat and dark as slate, "we are investigating some archival materials we have reason to believe found their way here over fifty years ago."

Guy finally turned and glanced at her legs. He was sweating, sweating still. The demon turned its attention from the odd collection on the shelves to him, now. The muffled man was facing him. The *Directeur* looked stern, his brow furrowed over his wire rim glasses.

"What is it, then, can you tell me?" Guy shakily asked, gathering the nerve to look her in the eye. "Can't you tell me what it is?"

The demon spoke, his bass voice causing Guy to flinch.

"We're not sure. It was a head, but made of stone or metal, and—"

"In pieces, it was in pieces, *oui?*" Guy stammered, stepping over to the shelves behind him, the shelves that led to the doorway where the muffled man stood. The muffled man was stepping into the room now. Guy had their rapt interest, all eyes were on him.

"You know of such a thing, Guy?" the *Directeur* whispered. "Why didn't you bring it to someone's attention?"

He stumbled over to the shelves, running his hand along the upper ridge of the highest shelf he could reach. The shelves by the door weren't attached to the wall, they were free standing; if he could reach them—

Kate stepped between Guy and the doorway as the muffled man moved in closer. Guy stole a glance at the red giant, who seemed less interested in Guy than what might be up on the shelves Guy seemed to be motioning to.

"I—I thought it was a puzzle, just a puzzle," Guy blurted out, finally gaining hold of the edge of the free-standing shelves. "I thought it was just a teaching tool, or a puzzle."

"Where did you put it," the woman named Corrigan said without inflection.

"Here, up here, right up here by these—"

For a moment, all eyes moved to the shelf above Guy.

Stealing his chance, he pulled with all his might on the free-standing shelving unit, and suddenly the woman, the muffled man, and the *Directeur* were lost in a shower of paper and cardboard and jars and fetuses and glass.

As the heavy shelving toppled onto them, Guy leapt over the racks. The red demon took a swipe at Guy, but he was clear of the monster's reach with the shelving taking up almost half the floor space now. Guy snatched up his empty backpack and darted out of the archives and down the corridor.

Hellboy rushed to lift the shelving unit off the trio. Free of its decades-old burdens, the shelving was light and lifted easily, but the contents had buried all but Kate's head and Abe's legs. Kate was coughing, but Abe was making a horrible sound.

"Katie! Abe—are you all right?"

"The *Directeur*," Kate managed to sputter, "help the *Directeur*—"

Abe was in trouble. All around him was broken glass, some of it jutting from oversized jar lids. A tangle of fins and fur and tentacles lay over his coat and head, and the one gloved hand Hellboy could see was twitching in agony. The smell of formaldehyde was pungent and everpresent.

"Jeez, Abe," Hellboy muttered as he lifted his friend up from the debris with one arm, and spun the other to unwrap the scarf from his throat. The formaldehyde had saturated the scarf, Abe's clothes, and his gills were making a wrenching sucking sound.

"Christ, help the *Directeur*," Kate shouted, pulling herself free of the wreckage.

"We're losing Abe," Hellboy insisted, prompting Kate to take her first look at their partner since they'd entered the *Faculte*. Hellboy had succeeded in getting the wraps and headgear off Abe's head and neck, but he was clearly in trouble.

Kate rushed to Hellboy's side. "There were some bathroom showers down the corridor," she recalled, "I'll get him to them. Help the *Directeur*, find out where that miserable little bastard lives."

With an exchange of looks and Abe's trembling self, Kate and Hellboy switched places. By the time Kate had managed to hustle Abe out of the room, Hellboy had uncovered the *Directeur*. Shards of broken glass pierced the old man's face and there was blood everywhere, but the cuts seemed superficial. The state of shock the old man was in, however, was deepening.

Hellboy didn't try to lift the old man. He swept the debris laying on and around him aside, clearing a space for the *Directeur*. Hellboy took off his trench coat and draped it over the old man. It looked huge over the frail fellow, covering him completely like a blanket.

"Try not to move, *Directeur*," Hellboy whispered. "We'll have a doctor here in no time."

"Guy—" the old man whispered back.

"I'm after him. Do you know where he lives?"

The *Directeur* swallowed once, twice, then raised his voice.

"He takes the Metro—to Boulevard *Richard'lenoir*—a second floor *appartement*—the number—"

Guy cradled the head in his lap. Thankfully, no one else was on the Metro this morning, so he could pull the edge of his backpack down and look at it now and again. Even when it was covered, it spoke to him, soothed him, comforted him.

It whispered fortune and infamy, purges and pyres, and chuckled at the threat of women and demons. They were nothing to fret over, it assured him.

It offered more predictions, and told Guy of the armies they would sire together.

But first, it was hungry.

He made his way to the door, which was partially open. He could see the backpack, empty on the rug, and heard something crooning inside.

Hellboy eased to the door of the *appartement*, hoping to get a look at whatever was inside. There was a light on, and Guy sat in an odd position in the middle of the bed at the far side of the room. He was still sweating like a pig and moaning softly, and seemed to be cradling something in his lap.

The fellow remained oblivious to Hellboy's presence as he stole further over the threshold to gain a better vantage point. Now he could make out the bandages across Guy's chest, blood-stained in the front; some of the stains were fresh, shiny wet amid broader expanses of dried rusty hues.

Guy was rocking gently and groaning like an idiot, one arm bent back and braced against the bed to support him, the other cupping something that looked like a pink-tinged bowling ball at his crotch. Coiled around his legs were more bandages, stained with blood.

"Guy?" Hellboy whispered.

The spell was broken. The emaciated young fellow cocked his head in Hellboy's direction, his eyes narrowing in fear and rage.

"Get owwwwwwwwwt!" Guy hissed, leaning protectively over the thing at his crotch, throwing both of his spindly arms over it.

His brow furrowing, Hellboy strode into the *appartement*, straining to get a look at the object Guy was so protective of. Whatever it was, it seemed to struggle against Guy's grasp, turning of its own volition to face Hellboy. Startled, Guy let it go and shuddered as the head sought a new position on his lap.

Hellboy bared his teeth at the sight of the thing.

"You sick freak," Hellboy gagged. "How dumb can you get? You fed the damned thing blood and—"

"—unborn infants," the head exulted, licking its bruised lips, "man's milk."

Guy bent over as if he'd been kicked in the groin. He began wailing like a baby and tumbled off the bed, spilling the head from its precarious perch in his lap.

Hellboy hunkered to follow its progress, and in two steps was standing over the reddish ball as it came to rest in the center of the dingy room.

"Moro?" Hellboy rasped.

The swollen lids pulled back from the glowing orbs as it gazed at Hellboy. The widening eyes flickered with recognition, then flared with renewed hunger.

"You've come to feed me!" it spat. "Demon sssssssseed—"

Suddenly all that mattered to the creature was gaining some attachment to this new, much more powerful host. This was the key to mastering stronger men, stealing souls, forging armies. It measured its need, the hook, the influence it might command.

A word, just a word, would do it . . .

The pulpy lips bared veined gums, bursting with an ivory stubble of new teeth. The purple tongue slid over the enamel white heads, licking away the froth of fresh blood and semen before curving with the word—just a word, *the* word—

"Father," it whispered. "I will tell you of your father—"

Without hesitation, Hellboy brought his hoof back and punted the thing across the floor.

As the engorged head spun across the room, the sinewy tendrils dangling from its throat seemed to congeal into extremities: knotted vestigial limbs, a threadlike weave suggesting arms and legs, hairlike fingers and toes.

For a second, it arced gracefully, its minute parody of a body seeking balance like an acrobat; then it hit the wall, and the delicate tapestry evaporated in a splash of snot and blood and bone.

Guy bolted up from his fetal position on the floor and screamed. His eyes were distended, unable to believe this fresh turn of events. For a moment Hellboy hesitated, preparing to take the emaciated boy out with one controlled blow if he tried anything. But Guy was beyond attack; he had lost everything, living like a ferret, sucked dry, and he certainly didn't dare to take on this new monster. It was so terrifying, its skin the color of flame, its right fist so huge, clad in armor that could crush him in an instant.

But the head, its promise—

Grunting with satisfaction as Guy stayed clear, Hellboy returned his attention to the head. He strode over to its resting place and stared down at it.

So monstrous an evil; so fragile a vessel.

"Professor Trevor Bruttenholm was my father. All I need to know."

The head was split from crown to the stump of its throat. A dank tar seethed from the uneven network of fissures, pooling in the broken cup of its lower jaw. Tiny arms and fingers wriggled in the stain spreading beneath.

Still, its streaming eyes drifted to Hellboy's own. Its blackened tongue arched, straining against the fragmented jaw as its torn lips vainly struggled to form the word.

"Had your say, Moro," Hellboy grunted. "Don't care to hear any more."

He brought his hoof down on the pathetic object. At the sound of it, Guy shrieked and slammed his own head against the wall.

Moro leered up at Hellboy, his eyes still brimming with hunger. Moro could feel the cheated heat of centuries-past pyres building within his skull. Even as his skin began to blister and smoke, his essence was seeping into the rug. It could not end this way, his minions and armies forever stilled here, at the threshold of their rebirth. There was still a chance, if he could only find a way to—

Hellboy brought his hoof down again, and the jigsawed sections of the head shattered apart, prompting another wail from Guy. Intent on his task, Hellboy ignored the man's cries and pulverized the damned thing, bringing his hoof down time and time again, smashing it into shards that smoked and began to spark.

Still, the pulped orbs simmered in their baking brine, the seared lips stretched like worms on a hot brick.

With every blow, Guy dashed his own skull against the wall.

Something gave inside, and he felt his face go utterly numb. He slammed his head against the mirror—Francine's mirror—until it, too, shattered.

His cries stopped after he'd broken his own jaw and his bleeding tongue had nearly swollen the back of his throat closed. He mewed like a kitten instead.

Still, the hoof pounded down.

When he could stand no longer, Guy slammed his face against the iron posts of the bed, the edge of the dresser, until he was on his knees grinding his ruined face against the chair, the bed frame, the floor. He crawled to the scattered remnants of the head and kissed them, though they were now glowering like coals.

As Hellboy's hoof dealt the decisive blow, all that remained of Moro burst into flames.

Groveling amid the shards, stuffing them in his mouth, Guy's hair and skin caught fire. Blind, he couldn't see the red demon as it turned from the detritus on the floor to seize a cistern of water and rush to Guy.

Having rammed his ears against the knob of the bedpost, he couldn't hear the demon as it implored him to stop, though he felt the cooling splash of water.

Softly banging his head against the floor still, he felt strong hands and arms slide beneath him. He felt the weight of his nights lift and drift off as he was cradled and carried by his savior, and for a moment, just a moment, he thought he heard the Sunday morning stirring of the *Boulevard Richard'lenoir* outside his window.

He imagined he heard Francine's voice, felt her touch on his lips, his eyelashes, his brow.

Francine came to call twice a week at the most unusual hours. She looked like an angel, but many feared her nonetheless.

Her nursing credentials were impeccable, so it was said, and the hospice authorities never questioned her presence, whatever the time of night or day. There seemed to be some long-standing attachment between them, and the *Monsieur le Directeur* demonstrated an uncharacteristic reverence in her company. In fact, it seemed she had her own key, given the ease of her comings and goings in the pre- and post-dawn hours, usually calculated to coincide with the shift change.

No surprise, then, that none of those who worked at the home seemed to know anything about her. One shift saw her coming, another saw her going, and she never lingered long enough for either to engage her attention, though she clearly galvanized theirs, like a phantom. She was unfailingly courteous, but she never fraternized with the staff, nor answered even the most tentative queries about herself or the center of her attention.

The rumors circled but never clung. She was a pauper, it was whispered, pouring all she earned into her loved one's care. She was wealthy, it was said, through a recent marriage, and her husband tolerated her eccentricities linked with the invalid home visitations out of Christian regard for her prior affections for one long gone.

No, no, she was widowed, others said, and she came to visit her only surviving family member (who might be either her father or brother, depending on who spoke of the matter).

He was a patient here at the home, the old man they called "Puzzle."

Puzzle's identity remained equally cloaked in mystery. His records were sealed and kept under lock and key, as more than one curious staff member had discovered. He never spoke clearly or loudly enough to ascertain any accent or origin, and bore no mark to provide any clue as to who he might have once been.

Old, withered, and emaciated, his scarred visage ruined beyond repair, he steadfastly avoided eye contact, and indeed seemed to harbor a dread of seeing anyone's face or of being seen.

Those who tended him did so reluctantly, respecting his silence and distance while unable to avoid stolen glances at his single eye, his ravaged scalp and tattered brow, his crater of a nose. He screamed at whispers overheard, and sobbed uncontrollably at times for no apparent reason. His bed was bolted to the floor without any clearance beneath, and his terror of what might lurk beneath other beds, tables, chairs, or cabinets was self-evident. He shunned books and shelves, and could not be forced to even pass the door to the hospice's meager *bibliotheque.*

Puzzle stared out at the trees in the spring as their buds swelled into leaves, enchanted by the spectacle. He was at his calmest and most childlike behavior throughout the summers, counting on his fingers as he blissfully gazed up at the leaves shimmering in all manner of weather; his daytime attendants vigilantly moved his wheelchair throughout the afternoons so he would never be looking up into the sun, a reasonable concern given the constant intensity of his lone eye's upward gaze.

He was at his absolute worst in the autumn weeks, fretting over the fall colors and weeping pitifully as the leaves that fell outside were raked into piles and burned. He sobbed as he frantically counted his fingers, as if calculating some eternal, unfathomable loss.

Rumors that he was thus because of the Great War and perhaps the last surviving member of *le Union des Gueules Cassees* seemed unlikely, though he looked nearly a century old. This lent some credence to the belief that Puzzle was father to the mystery woman, though the tale of his barely audible reply to a nurse who had once pressed him on the matter—"I had her as often as I wished, my *cherie*"—sparked gossip of incest, prompting many to give Puzzle and his female visitor an even wider berth.

So, too, did the persistent asides about her arriving with a strange man bundled up like a burn victim and wearing sunglasses in the dead of night, and an unnaturally tall, bearded "red man" who accompanied them—an Indian, perhaps? They had never seen an Indian from America, except in the movies. Could they grow to such size in America? The red giant supposedly had called him "Jigsaw," and had words with Puzzle that seemed to bring him some comfort.

Francine clearly brought him comfort, too.

His fear of faces and being looked upon evaporated only in her thrall. Like an infant, he gazed upon her as if she alone were his world—the world—and nothing else had or would ever matter.

She tended to him faithfully, and at times her singing could be heard lilting, ever so softly, from his cramped chamber.

"Guy," she whispered, so softly that none but he could hear, "*cheri.*"

And, oh, she loved to touch him, especially when he was asleep in the very early morning, and the dawn light played upon his face.

This one is to Marj. Special thanks to two excellent friends: Jean-Marc Lofficier, for considerable assistance and inspiration, and John Totleben, for sweeping up and finding the original head. I owe a great debt to the work of David Kunzle, comics' greatest historian, from which I drew all the material on Jean Leger and the Piemont atrocities. Last, but never least: *merci,* Mike, Chris, and Scott.

A MOTHER CRIES AT MIDNIGHT
PHILIP NUTMAN

He stared at me sadly over his steaming cup of coffee and I saw then how the terrible weight of his responsibility had crushed his spirit. Instead of fathering hope and life, instead of saving lives, he had given birth to the most destructive force known to mankind. There had been no irony when, as Fat Man exploded, he had said, "I am become Death, destroyer of worlds." For eight years he had had to deal with that terrible knowledge.

"How are things at the Bureau?" my friend J. Robert Oppenheimer asked, pulling his pipe from his pocket. "How's Trevor?"

"Quite well. He asked me to send his best," I replied, watching him pack the pipe bowl with a pungent tumbleweed of Balkan Sobrane tobacco.

The waitress suspiciously eyed the back booth in which we sat. Not because of the cloud of thick, sweet smoke now pluming above Robert's head, but I sensed it was my presence that made her uncomfortable. Even though we were only a few miles outside of Roswell, New Mexico, and since 1947, shortly after I moved away, the locals had grown used to strange sights, and even stranger goings-on, having a large, red creature seated in your diner was certainly unusual. Beneath my duster, I tightened my curled tail lest it slip below the hem. Some women, I had discovered, frequently found the tail to be more than they could handle.

"They've taken away my clearance. I'm persona non grata," he said into his cup. "But I can't be a party to it anymore. They're not going to stop. It's all about bigger and better bombs. And they don't want me as a conscience. My opinions are uncalled for."

His angular features were pinched. You didn't need to be a rocket scientist to see he was in pain.

"But that's not why I asked you to come . . . I'm acting as middle man. Do you remember Jamie MacDougal?"

I nodded.

I remembered him well. A spry Scottish-American research scientist, MacDougal and Trevor Bruttenholm had spent many an evening playing chess during the year we lived at Roswell. As I had come to look upon Bruttenholm as my father, at that time Jamie MacDougal had been like an uncle.

"He's here, stationed at Los Alamos. Very hush-hush. Now I'm considered a liability, I can't have any contact with him. But somehow he managed to get a note to me, requesting I contact you to see if you'd come." Robert puffed slowly, savoring the rich aroma.

"I'm here. So what's the problem?"

"His son's disappeared."

A half-crescent moon rode high in the sky like a severed quarter as I walked the arroyo running parallel to the road where young Malcolm MacDougal had last been spotted. I was five lonely miles outside of Los Alamos, heading southwest into the foot hills of the Jemez Mountains. I was searching for a stream, for there I hoped to find a woman who would lead me to the boy.

"They believe he's dead," Jamie MacDougal had said earlier that evening. "He's been gone a week. They called off the search on Monday—said it was a waste of manpower—that he must have perished because no seven year old could survive the night temperatures.

"But I know," he said, pouring himself a generous glass of single malt. "I'm his father, and I know in my bones he's still alive."

I hadn't seen Jamie in nearly eight years, and the river of human time had eroded his once-full head of red hair, and reshaped his features like a rain-washed statue. He looked closer to sixty than his fast-approaching forty-seven. It was his birthday next week. I had remembered en route to Los Alamos from Roswell. Robert had stopped the car outside Santo Domingo Pueblo so I could buy a gift. The Anasazi pot sat on Jamie's dining table, ground zero between the two of us.

"Go slow, old friend," I said. "Start at the beginning."

Jamie took a hearty swig of his malt, and sighed.

"Lucy—his mother—died a year ago. Car crash. Almost a month to the day," he added, wistfully staring into his drink. "So the base provided us with a housekeeper, a nanny of sorts who could take care of him. Dona's her name. Local woman of Zuni extraction. But of course he took it hard. We both did. And a seven year old wants his mother, not a stranger."

He was right. All boys need a mother. Even a Hellboy. I, however, had no recollection of a mother, or a father. Or of anything before I appeared in the ruins of an old church in East Bromwich, England nearly ten years ago.

"Yes," I said, "go on."

"Dona's a good sort. Takes excellent care of him—or did until she let him wander off.

"The last couple of months have been very hard, what with the anniversary coming up, and I've been working long, long hours in the lab.

"I should have been there for him," he suddenly exclaimed, slamming a hand on the table top, almost spilling his drink and knocking over my pot.

It took a while, and another drink, to calm him.

Malcolm, I learned, had taken to wandering away from the base over the last few months. There was nothing unusual in that. Boys will be boys, and with so many ruins to explore, the summer-kissed landscape surrounding the cold, uninviting barracks-style housing could be a place of endless wonders to the over-active imagination of a seven year old. Summer was gone now though, swept aside by an early, harsh fall, and the nights came cold and hard at this elevation. But Los Alamos was a safe town, perhaps the safest in the United States due to the secret nature of its inhabitants' work, and Dona had thought nothing wrong in letting the boy play outside after sunset. But that all changed when he met the woman.

There was a good reason why New Mexico was called The Land of Enchantment, for there are arcane energies here, powers present which defy rational explanation. Was it a coincidence Los Alamos became the Secret City, birthplace of the atom bomb, or that Fat Man's explosion happened at Trinity Site? Why not Nevada, or some other desert state with even more wide-open spaces? Why did a supposed extraterrestrial craft crash at Roswell? Trevor Bruttenholm believes this state forms a nexus of paranormal energies, and when the US military insisted on relocating me from England so I could be studied at Roswell, he was only too happy to accompany me. During the time we lived here, he immersed himself in the myths and legends of New Mexico and took me along on frequent investigatory trips.

One of my first memories was of our visit to the Santuario de Chimayo which was nestled in a secluded valley in the Sangre de Christo foothills. Like the pilgrims who had trekked there over the centuries, predominantly the sick and enfeebled, we went to experience the mysterious healing powers of its magical soil. Bruttenholm was convinced it cured his arthritis. All it did to me was make me itch.

I had so many other stories and experiences during that early period in my life perhaps it was no surprise I decided to follow my adoptive father's line of work. We spent nights in the ancient mission of Isleta Pueblo, hoping to see the restless corpse of Father Padilla and his cottonwood coffin rise from beneath the altar, as he had done so on numerous occasions over the past two hundred years (he didn't). We spent days camping on low mountain slopes, sitting up through the night in case a fireball-riding bruja passed by overhead (we never saw a witch, but I saw my first shooting star).

New Mexico was like the Navajo rug Bruttenholm bought as a gift for me before we left Roswell for the East coast and the BPRD headquarters in Fairfield, Connecticut. It was a simple rug, just two rows of white, rectangular clouds outlined in black against a light blue background. But the rug had a deliberate line woven through its lower border, a "spirit line" worked into the weave in case a soul became trapped during the weaving and needed a way out. New Mexico itself seemed like a spirit line, a gateway between realms, and some of what sought freedom here was of a malevolent stripe. Then there are those forces which are a reflection of the soul of the beholder, neither good nor evil, merely a mirror to our needs. She was one of them. The one known as La Llorona, The Weeping Woman.

A particular manifestation of New Mexico and its Hispanic heritage, La Llorona's story had many variations concerning her origins and nature, but I knew she was more than a myth. I knew because I met her.

Back in early '47, a few months before the Roswell crash and our departure for the lush New England green of Connecticut, Bruttenholm had taken me to Santa Fe where he was visiting Fray Angelico Chavez, the renowned historian and restorer of ancient churches. Fray Angelico had been researching the recorded appearances of Fray Padilla, and he invited Trevor to read the first draft of the paper he was preparing. Although I had only been on the earthly plane for a couple of years, I had already reached adolescence and was suffering the restlessness of youth. So, as the day waned and the magical spring twilight bathed the Sangre de Christo range ruby red, and as Bruttenholm and Fray Chavez continued their impassioned discussion, I walked out into the streets of Santa Fe.

Since I was still wary of the reactions of others to my unusual appearance, I walked away from the bustling plazas, sticking to narrow side streets lined with sleepy adobe homes squatting behind hand-carved wooden gates, half-hidden by gnarled cottonwoods or softly hued hollyhocks, and made my way down to the banks of the Santa Fe River. It was peaceful there and calmed my troubled thoughts as I followed the water eastwards.

Maybe it was the onset of adolescence and the need to understand who and what I was. Or perhaps it was the natural questioning of an orphan concerning his parentage, but for weeks I had lain awake at night tossing and turning, wondering and wanting answers to an enigma. The enigma of myself. Seeing the other children who lived on the Roswell base play ball with their fathers, go shopping with their mothers, made my heart heavy. Trevor Bruttenholm was a kind, compassionate, and thoughtful mentor, as fine a father figure as a Hellboy could have. Yet when sleep would not come, I would lie in my room wondering what it must feel like to lose one's self in a mother's embrace or rage at my inability to remember where I came from before a magical rite summoned me to this world.

Did I have a mother? Did she mourn for the loss of her son?

These thoughts vexed me daily, but that evening as I walked the river bank the preternatural calm of Santa Fe soothed my soul and my mind turned towards more intellectual ideas. Albert Einstein had visited Roswell with Oppenheimer the week before and spent hours with me explaining his theory of relativity. Trevor was intent on providing me with the best educational opportunities, and who better to help explain physics than Einstein? I savored the time we spent together, even though the deluge of knowledge he unleashed threatened to sweep me away. So it was with a head full of equations and formulae, I wandered into the dark, barely aware of the distance I had traveled or the fact that night had almost completely descended in its diamond-studded velvet glory.

At first I thought the sound was that of an animal. But as I listened more carefully I realized it was a human sound, a sorrow-filled lament. Then, maybe two hundred yards ahead, I saw a figure standing on the bank where the river curved. It was a woman clad in a long gray dress, her head and shoulders cocooned in a black woolen shawl.

The wail ripped from her lips with a terrible strength, a power born of great emotional pain, and I realized she was about to fling herself into the water.

Again she cried out: "*Ayyyy, mis hijoooosss!!*"

I didn't understand what she was screaming, but her intentions were clear.

I started to run as she threw herself into the river, shedding my long coat like a second skin as I dove after her. The chilly waters made me gasp, shocking me like an unexpected slap to the face, but I doubled my efforts as I saw her head disappear beneath the surface. It was instinct, pure and simple. I had no time to think, only moments to act. The undercurrent was surprisingly strong considering the seemingly slow momentum of the surface, and at the bend I saw sudden turbulence as the now speeding water rushed over jagged rocks. If I couldn't reach her in time, she'd surely be smashed to a pulp against their sharp peaks.

An Air Force sergeant at Roswell had taught me how to swim, and I put every ounce of strength into a fast crawl which would have made him proud. And not a moment too soon: I grabbed her hand as she went under a third time, trying to halt my forward momentum in the midst of frothy whitecaps a dozen feet or so from the bend. Somehow I managed to pull her now-limp body towards mine, but I couldn't fight the flow. Turning, cradling her against my chest, I managed to spin around so my broad back hit the first partially submerged boulder. The impact felt like a mule kick. And then we were moving again, leaves in a hurricane, tossed from one boulder to the next.

I don't remember seeing the low-lying branch or grabbing it. Suddenly we were in stasis, surrounded, pummeled by the river's wild waters, but not moving, not at its mercy. Not completely, at least. The fact the branch didn't break, and, amazingly, that I was able to pull us out and up the bank one-handed—well, I guess those Charles Atlas exercises Trevor encouraged me to do on a daily basis paid off. I saved us through dynamic tension.

Chest heaving, lungs aching, I lay on my back on the muddy bank beneath our benefactor, the tree. She lay beside me, conscious now, sobbing softly. In English this time.

"My children. My children . . . "

Placing a reassuring hand on her shoulder, I stood, swaying slightly with adrenaline-driven vertigo, my equilibrium still spinning like a gyroscope after the dervish dance of the rushing waters.

"It's okay," I mumbled. "It's going to be all right."

"I'll get my coat. Need to keep you warm."

Stumbling through the scrub, my mind still a tilt-a-whirl, I don't remember hearing the sudden silence as her sobbing stopped. Scooping up my full-length tan duster, I turned towards her and—

—She was gone.

Vanished.

Into thin air.

Later, seated around a roaring open fire in the rectory of Loretto Chapel, Fray Angelico explained I had been blessed by encountering La Llorona, and that my selfless act would bring good fortune.

"La Llorona is ancient; her true origins go back, way back before the time we have recorded. She was a part of this landscape long before the Spanish came. She even predates the indigenous Anasazi peoples."

"I've heard tell—"

Fray Angelico waved a hand to silence Trevor. "Listen. And learn. If not for your own sake, then for Hellboy's—for this special child has been blessed.

"She is not always so forgiving. Nor is she so vulnerable to the eyes of others. One might hear her sorrow. One might see her struggle with her pain. But to see her in such naked despair . . . That is highly unusual."

Felicia, Fray Angelico's housekeeper, brought me a mug of steaming hot chocolate. Its warmth revived my shivering senses, and I listened intently to the legend of La Llorona.

"There once was a girl," the priest began, "who was said to be very beautiful. Because of her looks, people didn't treat her like others. And the more beautiful she became as she blossomed into womanhood, the more people shunned her. Even her own family felt ashamed for not being able to provide for such a beauty.

"One day a stranger came to the pueblo. He was well dressed, obviously a man of wealth. Generous, too. And his largess made him very popular with the locals.

"The stranger soon grew tired of the pueblo and was preparing to move on when he laid eyes on the beautiful woman, and he was entranced. How did such a woman come to be here in a poor pueblo surrounded by nothing more than cacti and dust? He had never seen such fine elegance and decided to stay, to court this ravishing woman. When he proposed marriage, her family encouraged her to say yes, for this fine man could provide for her, give her the future they believed their beautiful daughter deserved.

"They wed, and the match seemed Heaven-made. The stranger was given the respect of a mayor, and the beauty found happiness beyond her imagining. Soon they had a child. The beauty's joy was such she could barely believe it. But as time passed the stranger grew tired of the sleepy village. Even his devoted wife bored him, and the child had eyes only for its mother. It was not what he had expected. His money was running low and he thirsted for adventure, for the temptations of the big city. And so one day he left without saying a word.

"His beautiful wife waited. Each night, after she had put the child to bed, she would light a candle by the door. Each morning she would awaken the child with a kiss then blow out the candle. Days turned into weeks. Even though her husband's disappearance worried her, she never gave up hope. Weeks became months. No one came to visit. Not even her family. They were sure she had somehow chased the stranger away with her formidable beauty. She started to go crazy not knowing what she had done to turn everyone against her."

Fray Angelico paused, as much to savor his snifter of Benedictine brandy as for effect.

"The weather changed with the seasons, and the monsoons began building. The heavy air exacerbated her already fevered imagination. At night, the winds picked up and mesquite thorns rubbed against the windows. The heavens opened up. It was as if the sky was crying a torrent of tears, soaking their adobe home. Mud seeped into the house, bringing with it the smell of the grave. The beauty could stand it no longer. She grabbed her sleeping baby and raced out the door into the storm.

"Driven mad by the desertion of her husband, her family, she raced to the river. She had lost all reason. And there, standing beside the overflowing river bank, she threw her child into the raging waters. And in that terrible instant, she regained clarity of mind—albeit for a painful second—and let out the most agonizing cry. Unable to accept the horror of her obscene sin, she threw herself into the storm-swollen waters.

"It was the worst deluge anyone in the village could remember. Few people could sleep that night, for cries too terrifying to describe were heard all over the valley.

"To this day, when rivers fill and flow fast, some say they see a beautiful woman walking the banks. Should you get too close you may hear an eerie cry, and some say an elegant hand may even touch your shoulder."

Fray Angelico set down his glass. He looked me deep in the eye. "You, dear boy, did a very noble act. You touched her. I am certain the beauty will not forget."

"But there are other variations of the legend, aren't there?" Bruttenholm interjected.

"Yes," Fray Angelico nodded.

"Often times she is seen by the side of a road. Those who stop to offer her a ride either find she disappears as they approach, or she scares them away."

"How?" I asked.

"Instead of being a beauty she is either a hideous hag or has the face of a skull." He chuckled a dry laugh. "Those who see her this way are often adulterous lovers returning from or going to an illicit rendezvous. It seems she does not appreciate unfaithfulness."

"But I've also heard she protects children," Bruttenholm added.

"Indeed. Those foolish enough to play by rivers after dark are known to encounter her."

This, apparently was what had happened to Malcolm MacDougal, I learned from Dona. But instead of scaring the boy, La Llorona had entranced him.

Dona was working in the kitchen, preparing a late dinner for Jamie. She was so absorbed by her task she lost track of time. Then, when she realized it was past nine and the boy hadn't returned home, she started to panic. She had gone but a few yards from the house when she found him wandering, dreamy and distracted. He told her he had been to the river, and there he had met a beautiful woman who told him his mother loved him and that she was well, waiting for the day they would be reunited. At this, Dona scolded Malcolm and told him to never, ever go to the river at night. Sometimes, of course, forbidding a child from doing something was the worst advice an adult can give, as the young are naturally curious about things they should not do.

The next night, Dona insisted Malcolm stay home. Surprisingly, the boy agreed and read in his room. Relieved that he calmly accepted her request, she went about her household chores not thinking anything was amiss. But when she went to call Malcolm for his supper, she discovered the bedroom empty, the window wide open.

Jamie was beside himself when he heard the news, so distraught the base commander refused to allow him to join the search party. Besides, it seemed straightforward. A technician driving in from Jemez Springs reported seeing what he thought was a young boy by the side of the main road. He had stopped to investigate, but the figure disappeared into the woods a mile from the river. However, a night-long search proved a failure. Malcolm MacDougal had vanished into thin air. There was no stopping Jamie the next morning.

Every stream and tributary was searched, and the section of river where Malcolm had told Dona he had seen La Llorona was dredged. A week later, with the hunt for the boy dissolved, I was Jamie's last hope.

Coming out of the arroyo, I headed in the direction of a lush sloping pasture and the forest beyond. Half an hour later, I located a stream and sat down to wait, hoping my instincts were right.

At midnight, my suspicions were confirmed, my patience rewarded. The sound started low, mournful at first, then rose steadily in pitch. To the unsuspecting, it could have been a coyote call, but I had heard that soul-wrenching cry before. It was impossible to forget. For a moment, the years slipped away, pulling me back to the banks of the Santa Fe river. Then, suddenly, it stopped. The silence following felt eerie, almost suffocating in its intensity.

I waited, my eyes trying to penetrate the jet-black shadows cast by the trees. Nothing moved.

When the hand touched my shoulder, I nearly leapt out of my red skin.

I turned. There, beside me, stood the Weeping Woman. My first encounter had been hectic, fraught with frantic actions; I had never got a clear look at her. Now, I saw her beauty was remarkable, almost too painful to gaze upon. To try to describe this ethereal creature would be foolish. Besides, the deep, dark olive of her haunted eyes drew me in, made me a fellow prisoner of her sorrow.

"The boy," I said softly, barely a whisper. "Please, take me to the child."

La Llorona took me by the hand, leading me away from the stream and into the stygian secrets of the forest. She remained silent. I didn't know what to say. What could I say to this spirit?

We reached a clearing. Although Old Man Moon's light was largely obscured by the towering oaks, spruce, and Douglas firs, I could make out a rocky hill ahead. She led me around it and, on the opposite side, stopped before a thick tangle of bushes. Those sad eyes stared at me a moment before she stepped forward. Since she touched me she had appeared solid. Now, she dissolved through the bushes, letting go of my hand, freeing my arms to fight through the undergrowth. Behind them was a small cave mouth, and I stooped to enter.

Instead of pitch blackness, the cave was softly illuminated, and it took me a moment to realize she was the light source. La Llorona glowed from within. The cave floor sloped down, and she took my hand to steady me as we descended. The natural rock walls narrowed, the ceiling lowering, forcing me to bend. The tunnel curved before opening into a subterranean chamber.

Malcolm MacDougal lay on a bed of leaves beside an underground pool the size of a goldfish pond. His eyes were glazed, feverishly delirious. His left leg was broken and lay at a painful angle. How had he come to be here? Had she carried him?

"Mother," he said. "Don't leave me. Stay with me. I don't feel well."

She said nothing, but a strange smile crept across his dirt-smeared features. He had his father's mouth, his mother's eyes. I sensed something pass between them.

"I'm here to take you home," I said.

The smile faded.

"Yes, Mother said it's time to go now," he mumbled.

I scooped him up as carefully as possible, and, as La Llorona led, we made our way back.

His head felt hot, his body thin and fragile. The water had kept him alive, but the boy was famished and the fever had drained him. As I navigated my way through the trees, I sensed she was no longer with us. Turning, I saw she had faded into the night like breath on a cold day. She had done her part, and now I had to finish mine. I hoped my luck would continue; perhaps we'd run across a passing motorist who wouldn't crash at the sight of a large red creature carrying the body of a small boy.

Malcolm murmured in his delirium.

"Mother . . . don't leave . . . me . . ."

His condition was worse than I first thought.

I wanted to run. I needed to get him to the Los Alamos hospital. Every step seemed to rattle his bones. Sudden movement was out of the question. I hoped for a car or truck. Otherwise, all I could do was take it one step at a time. His breath came in a short dry wheeze.

One step became another. Keeping my eyes on the ground, my mind wandered. Halfway across the meadow, I realized I had left the forest behind.

And realized Malcolm was dead.

Tears of frustration spilled from my eyes. I lowered myself to the grass, cradling the small corpse. Too late. I had failed.

"We're cursed," Oppenheimer had said as we drove to Los Alamos. "I believe those of us who made the bomb, or continue to work on the program, will never be forgiven for what we've done. Whatever your faith, whichever God you believe in . . . it doesn't matter. We're cursed. We committed the greatest sin against life. Men create to destroy. Women create. They create life. We only destroy it."

Those words echoing in my mind, I looked down on Malcolm's urchin-like face. In death, his features more resembled those of his father. Poor Jamie. What could I say to him? In helping to father weapons of destruction he had lost sight of the life he had helped create, unintentionally pushing the boy towards the arms of a delusion.

A tear fell from my face and ran across Malcolm's cheek, wiping away a smudge of dirt. It looked like he, too, was crying. A tear of joy, for I hoped he was with his mother now.

And I wondered, in that unguarded moment, who would mourn for me?

From deep in the woods, I heard La Llorona let loose her painful lament.

DELIVERED
GREG RUCKA

W ay I figure it, I'm kinda a citizen of the world, you know? Which I suppose is a healthy attitude for an individual who was summoned more than born. I've got allegiances, of course, and as far as I'm concerned I'm absolutely Red, White, and Blue, an American through and through, but if citizenship is birth, well, I'm most likely British. And let's not even talk about my mother.

Speaking as an American, I've got a fondness for New York City, for its vitality and roaring energy, for the way that it just never can slow down, even for a second, even if it's heading for a cliff—which, more often than not, it is. Liz puts it best: she says, "New York City, the place where you can get anything you want, any time, day or night. And you can get it delivered."

Says it all, really. I know the city pretty well, having hoofed it through town on more than one occasion. That's another reason I like NYC—I get marginally fewer stares wandering through the Village than elsewhere. Not like red with a tail and lumpy doesn't raise eyebrows, but down on Christopher Street, hell, it's the Halloween Parade every day.

Where I'm heading this time, though, I don't know the neighborhood all that well. Alphabet City, which from what the papers and politicos say is going through urban renewal, and to me looks maybe like Alphabet City itself never got the notice. The buildings are in sad shape, just inside of code, and it's nowhere I'd want to live.

It is, however, not unlike a lot of the places where I end up doing my work.

This isn't work, though. This is personal.

I'm a clothes-on-my-back sort of guy, don't have much that I really call my own. My friends, they're my most precious possessions—and I don't really like calling them that, but you get what I'm saying. When it comes to gifts from friends, I take those to heart. Like my pistol, the one Commander Freedom gave me.

I'm not a gun guy, but in my line of work, it's a necessary tool. And the pistol, it's as fine a piece of work as you're likely to ever come across. Wood inlaid handle, custom machined cylinder, tailored trigger tension, a custom job all the way. Freedom himself taught me how to cast the bullets for the thing, seeing as how the caliber is unique and you can't just walk into your local ammo shop and pick up a hundred rounds.

Back at the Bureau, I've got a space set up just for casting the bullets. There are plenty of folks there who'd do it for me, of course, and sometimes Dr. Manning or someone will even say that I should leave it to the support-services people.

"You've got more important things to do, Hellboy," they tell me.

Yeah, and maybe it's true. But I like taking care of the pistol, I like settling down and melting the lead and mixing the powder and filling the casings. It's a Zen thing in a way, and it's how I honor Commander Freedom.

So when I lost the gun, I was pretty damn pissed off.

What happened was this.

A week ago, Saturday, I'm in the City, going to hit Pegasus Books up on the high West Side. Just shopping, looking for collectibles and rare firsts, like that. Gorgeous day, one of those New York City days where the air is clean and clear, and the sun is just warm enough you don't even hesitate about not bringing your jacket.

Course, I'm wearing my jacket, because I use it to cover the pistol.

Cutting through Central Park, and I get a little hungry, so I grab myself a vendor's hot dog and a bottle of Dr. Brown's Cel-Ray, settle in on a bench. Sunlight is actually *dappling* through the leaves, casting hot spots on the paved path and moving pedestrians. There's enough of a breeze that I can hear the branches moving gently in the park behind me.

I'm enjoying the day.

Then I hear this snapping, the sound of a leaf breaking.

I turn, and there's this rat.

Now, a New York City rat is not to be mistaken for any other member of the *rattus norvegicus*, and if you've seen one you know what I'm talking about. I personally know what I'm talking about, because in my line of work, I've seen a mother-lode of rats. Trust me on this. I know rats.

This rat, he's a big black one, almost two feet long, and easily fifteen pounds, a little monster. Beady black eyes looking at me, and it's not quite intelligence I'm seeing, but almost impatience. Like he's waiting for me to finish eating so he can have the crumbs.

I stare at the rat, the rat stares at me, and then I hear more of that leaf snapping, and sure enough, here comes another one. This rat, he's a little smaller than the other, and he settles in beside the first one, giving me the same look.

And then comes another, and then another, and suddenly I've got fifteen-odd rats all looking at me, and it's like they're all saying, "C'mon, get on with it."

It's hard to eat when you've got fifteen rats staring at you, I tell you that much.

Fine, I figure, and I chuck what's left of the dog over my shoulder, get up, continue heading across the park. I'm halfway to the bookstore when I realize, hey, my right side is feeling a little light.

And that's when I notice the pistol is gone.

I am not, as you might imagine, pleased with this discovery. It's not something that's ever happened to me before. I've jumped out of airplanes and crashed—literally—through the roofs of buildings, and that pistol has remained in my holster. It does not just disappear. It is not an item that I forget.

I spin and head back into the park, looking at the ground, trying to figure when I last actually saw the damn thing seated in its leather. I know I had it when I bought the dog, because I keep my wallet in the pouch on my belt just left to where the holster hangs, and it was there when I paid.

I retrace and retrace and double-check and do it all again, and I don't find the pistol. I am getting pissed off.

I head back to the bench, giving it another look over, and that's when I notice the teeth marks on the wood. Like one of the rats was gnawing at the slats against which I had rested my back.

I know I had that pistol when I sat down, I know that.

And I'm now pretty damn sure I didn't have it when I got up again.

The conclusion, therefore, is that the rats took my pistol.

This is not as unlikely as it might at first seem, by the way. Like I said, I know rats.

Or at least I thought I did.

So it takes me a week of looking, and now here I am in Alphabet City, at this address that a homeless guy gave me. I've been talking to a lot of homeless guys and gals this week, because they live in close proximity to the rats, and the rats, they don't like to talk to me.

The homeless folks, they've told me some interesting things. Told me about how Chas and Denny and a couple others, they used to be on the street, but they've disappeared. And before they disappeared, they were seen in the company of a lot of rats. Like hundreds, maybe.

This address I'm now at, it's a mess. The front door to the building is just gone, plain and simple, and the mailboxes in the foyer, all of them are broken. The postal carrier didn't even try to sort the letters, just dumped them on the floor. Looks like somebody took a piss on them, too.

Inside, it's dank and pretty dark, even though it's bright daylight outside. I head for the stairs and after the second step begin to think maybe they won't hold my weight, the way they're creaking and the way I'm hearing wood snapping from inside the wall. But I keep heading up, and I make it to the fourth floor without trouble.

The hallway is even messier than the foyer. I'm looking at all sorts of crap on the ground, now, including broken needles and empty bottles and fast-food wrappers and what's left of an inflatable raft.

"Weird," I say to myself.

I knock on 4W. I knock with my left hand, because if I knock with my right, I'm pretty sure I'll just send the door to pieces.

There is a pause, and then I hear this voice saying, "Hellboy, come on in."

"Really weird," I say to myself, and open the door.

The apartment is a serious contrast to the rest of the building. It's not neat—in fact, it's so cluttered I have to turn sideways to make it through the entry hall. But it's almost clean, not filthy. And the smell is better, too, less human waste and more human life.

But when I say cluttered, I'm absolutely sincere, here. I mean, the place is wall to wall stuff, the kind of clutter where you need to step outside just to have enough room to change your mind, know what I'm saying?

I stop for a second in the hallway, just trying to take it all in, trying to find a word for this onslaught of material. I'm looking at books, a lot of books, easily thousands of books, on shelves, on the floor, open, closed, torn, sealed in plastic, you name it. Hardcovers, paperbacks, trade originals, even funny books, you know, comics. But it's not even just books, no. I see shoes—fancy running shoes and cheap tennis and some boots, mostly mismatched, one with its sole just missing. Toys, action figures and building blocks, and shiny plastic orbs and yo-yos and maybe an infinite supply of pogs. Trading cards, baseball and hockey, and even some other cards with pictures of dragons and stuff on them. Stuffed animals, one a dolphin, something like six bears, two badgers, four snakes—one's a cobra, the other three I'm not so sure about—a pony, a tiger, and something that looks like maybe Walt Disney designed it while he was channeling Azathoth. On the walls there are posters and paintings, something that looks like a Cézanne hanging next to a glossy shot of some luscious *Playboy* Playmate.

The word I find for all of this I say aloud.

"Junk," I say.

"Hey, I don't knock your shit," the voice says. It's got a Bronx edge to it. "Through here, end of the hall."

I edge towards the voice, passing an open bedroom. Lying on the bed, wearing silk pajamas, is a man in his fifties, balding, white hair. Pale, but not in a sickly way. A fedora is perched on the lamp on the bed-stand beside him.

"Ignore him," the voice says. "Denny had a late night."

"That's Denny?"

"Sure. Cleans up good, don't he?"

"Sure," I say, and keep on edging, past the kitchen now—cluttered like the hall, but again, mostly clean—and I come out into what must be like the living room.

This room, it's as cluttered as everything else, but now there's furniture to make it worse. Four televisions are stacked atop one another in a corner, and a full media center fills a wall, videotapes, laser discs, DVDs, CDs, LPs pouring off it. The thing is so over-loaded that the shelves are actually sagging from the weight put on them. Somewhere under the pile opposite the televisions, I'm pretty certain there's a couch.

In the center of this room, there's this beautiful desk, huge thing, maybe mahogany. Papers are piled high, and there's a multi-line telephone blinking away on one side. A computer is whispering to itself, too. The whole thing rests on a pile of maybe five or six Oriental rugs, the real high quality ones, I'm thinking.

And behind the desk there's this rat.

This giant frickin' rat.

Who, when he sees me, stands up, pushing back his chair, and offers me a paw.

"Hellboy, right?" the rat says. "I'm Mick."

"Huh," I say.

He's about six feet tall standing on his hind legs, black fur, splotchy, missing it in a couple places. His belly is that pink-white you get on . . . well, the underside of most rats. His fur is thick and coarse, but clean and maybe even combed, which must be a hell of a job. His tail is hairless and straight to the end, where it curls back on itself, like spelling the letter Q. His eyes are black and I can't tell if there's a pupil in there or not.

Mick the Rat coughs discreetly, glancing at his extended paw. He's extended the left, requiring me to extend my left in return.

I take his paw and he shakes firmly, like we're drinking buds, and I see that he has somehow acquired an opposable thumb. He lets go of my hand and gestures, says, "Take a seat."

I look around and realize that the mound of magazines behind me—most of them of the titty variety—conceal a chair.

"Just knock it on the floor, no problem," Mick the Rat tells me.

The magazines thump to the ground and I take a seat. We look at each other for a while, and then his eyes wander down to my right hand.

"That it?" he asks. "That's the hand?"

"My hand," I confirm.

"Can I see it?"

"Sure." I extend my hand, laying it on the desk with a thud.

Mick the Rat produces a set of half-glasses and perches them on the end of his substantial and narrow nose, then leans in. I feel his whiskers brush my knuckles. He looks up over the rims at me for confirmation, and I nod, so he touches my hand. He's got a light touch, and the way he does it, his whole manner, makes me think of some bizarre cross between a bookie and a jeweler.

He takes most of a minute before leaning back in his chair, removing the glasses. His mouth does this thing that really shows off his teeth, and I figure it must be a smile.

"That's one of a kind," Mick the Rat tells me. "That's a hell of a collectible you've got there."

"Yup."

He gestures with one paw towards the kitchen. "You want a beer or something?"

"No, thanks."

Mick the Rat nods. "On to business, then. Right."

"You're a pack rat," I say.

The thing with his teeth gets more pronounced and he starts shaking his head. "Man, do I hate that name. Pack rat. I'm *not* a pack rat, you think that's what this is? I'm an object-retrieval facilitator, that's how I see it."

"You have a pistol of mine," I say. "The one Commander Freedom gave to me. I want it back."

"Sure, sure, I got it, and yeah, it's all yours, no problems." He pats the desk, indicating one of the drawers on his side. "Safe, no problems, like I said. I won't even ask for a finder's fee for returning it."

The teeth thing again, which now I am certain is a smile, and which, since I do not find this amusing, I do not return.

After a second, Mick the Rat stops with the teeth thing.

"Hellboy," he says, leaning forward. "Look, can we talk, here, you and me?"

"Sure," I say.

"You know what I do here, right, you've figured that out?"

I nod.

"I mean, I'm not a bad guy. Denny back there, he was on the streets until three months ago, nobody would give him the time of day. Me, I take him in, clean him up, give him a job. I'm not a bad guy here, you understand that?"

"What kind of job did you give Denny?"

Mick laughs, which is this remarkably high-pitched sound compared to his voice, which so far has been pretty low, not unlike my own. "Well, take a look at me, will ya? I mean, you think you get stares on the street, what do you think I get? I walk down Broadway, I've got cops coming outta my ass. And the Rat Catchers."

"He's your people person?"

Mick the Rat gestures, indicating that I've hit the nail on the head. "That's right, yeah. He's not the only one, of course. I've got people everywhere, these days, this is a big enterprise now. Chas—you were asking about Chas, I know—he's in London right now, doing some shopping for me. You know Chas? Guy's fluent in three languages, just the kind of help I need."

"And for his help, he gets . . .?"

"Food, lodging, an expense account." Mick gestures grandly. "Just 'cause I live with my stock, don't mean I make my employees do the same. I treat them good. They even got dental."

"Dental's good," I agree.

"So, look, Hellboy, you wondering what this is all about, right? Why you, right?"

"Right."

"Thing is, this. My business, my . . . collecting, okay, we'll call it that? . . . I get all sorts of stuff that I think you and your employers might be interested in. All sorts of stuff that Bureau you work for might be happy getting their hands on."

"Like?"

Mick the Rat points a paw at me and springs from his chair. He's a quick mother, and I'm starting to get up—way too late to do anything—before I realize he's not going for me, he's headed for that pile by the couch. He bends down to dig through it, his tail waving around, books and papers flying through the air.

"Here somewhere . . . saw it this morning . . . not that . . . nope . . . nope . . . aw, come on, where the hell? . . . Ah, ah-hah!"

He springs back to the desk, triumphantly clutching a volume that, charitably, I'd call moldy. He slaps it on the desk in front of me hard enough to make the piles of paper tremble and a puff of dust spill from the pages.

"There!" he says in triumph.

"Nice book," I say.

His big eyes get bigger. "You kidding me? This isn't nice, this thing is pure rotten evil! You know what this is? This is an original copy of *Unausprechlichen Kulten* by Von Junzt! In the original German, printed 1850-something, I don't remember. But what I do know, Hellboy, my friend, is that there were only six copies of this baby published, and five of them have been destroyed. That's what I know."

He looks at me proudly.

I nod and look at the book. It's bound in rotting leather, but I expect it's the real deal. I've heard of it, before, too, the famous tome *Nameless Cults*. One of the seminal texts on modern Old Ones.

Dr. Manning would crap a brick if I brought this baby back.

Mick the Rat misreads the look on my face, which happens to me a lot, but I suppose also happens to him, what with the teeth thing. He goes on quickly, "I've got more where this came from, too, I've got books and books. I've got a *De Vermis Mysteriis* from 1542 at my place in Cologne, I've tracked down all twelve volumes of *The Revelations of Glaaki*, and if I don't got it, I can get it."

Mick leans forward, lowering his voice and winking at me. "I've even got a lead on *The Seven Books of Hsan*."

"Geez," I say.

He settles back in his chair. "What? You're not impressed?"

I shake my head. "All I wanted was my pistol."

Mick the Rat opens the drawer he whacked earlier and sets my gun on the desktop. I start to reach for it but he keeps his paw on the gun, looking at me intently.

"We got a deal?" he asks.

"What?"

"You know, you and me, we got a deal?"

"I just want—"

"Your pistol back, I know. But I went through all this trouble to get you here, to give you my pitch, and you're not even interested? You don't want to play ball here?"

"You . . ."

Mick the Rat nods. "Yes, yes, I had my posse, you know, my rats, they grabbed your pistol, brought it here. I knew you'd come to get it."

I look at him and blink.

"Geez," I say again. "You coulda just sent me a note."

"What, from a giant rat? What would I have said? 'Dear Hellboy, please come visit me in Alphabet City. I have a large collection of occult items and am interested in striking a business arrangement with the Bureau for Paranormal Research and Defense. By the way, I am a giant, over-developed, talking rat.' You think that woulda done it?"

"Yeah."

Mick the Rat raises both eyebrows in disbelief.

"Trust me," I say. "We've gotten stranger letters. What do you get out of this?"

"Me?"

"Yeah."

"In exchange for being the primary supplier of your occult and paranormal reference needs," Mick the Rat says, "I want part of the government package."

"The what?"

"The package, Hellboy. The benefits package. Insurance is killing me, here, and I got no way to protect my employees' futures. I want the full government package, disability, pension, the whole shebang."

I blink at him a couple times. "Insurance?"

"That's right."

"For your employees?"

"Exactly."

"Are you for real?"

"I'm a giant talking rat, Hellboy. Of course I'm for real."

I reach over and he moves his paw, so I pick up the pistol. It's been unloaded, but other than that looks fine. Not a scratch on it that I didn't put there myself.

I put the gun in my holster.

"Throw in that copy of *Unausprechlichen Kulten* and you've got a deal," I say.

Fifteen minutes later I manage to leave—Mick the Rat wants to show me everything, and it takes some doing to explain that I've got somewhere, anywhere, to be—gun in my holster and book under my arm. I head on out of Alphabet City and for the train, and as I'm passing a park, a bunch of kids point and stare and giggle at me. I wave and they wave and eventually I get to the subway stop, catch a ride to Grand Central.

I'm waiting for my train back to Connecticut, when the same damn rat—the huge one from that day in Central Park—climbs up on the platform beside me.

"Hey, buddy," I say to the rat.

And I swear to God, the rat winks.

Only in New York.

FOLIE Á DEUX
NANCY HOLDER

1967, Yokosuka Naval Base, Yokosuka, Japan. It was monsoon season. In Japan, the rain was like a steady stream of water escaping from an overhead boiler pipe. Vietnam, it was said, was raining blood, there was so much killing. The blood on the jungle floor made you slip and slide, and if you fell face down, you drowned in it.

Rice was coming up pink, because the paddies were saturated with blood.

As Hellboy strode through the hospital grounds, men in blue pajamas, blue-and-white-striped summer bathrobes, and rubber thongs of various colors turned to stare at him. He was used to it: His skin was crimson and cracked, as if someone had peeled the outer layers away, the new skin crosshatched with blood vessels. He had no feet; but while some of the men who stared at him, slack jawed, were double amputees, Hellboy's legs ended in hooves. From beneath his trench coat, his tail alternately curled and bobbed against the tarmac.

Hellboy was a double amputee in his own right—however, it was his thick, enormous horns that had been sheared off.

His right hand was made of stone, or of something like stone. Still, it was something to stare at in revolted fascination. Which these men did; these men who had been mutilated and deformed.

Not by design, as Hellboy had been, but by war.

It was 1967, and the conflict in Vietnam was raging. Yokosuka was one of the hospitals that received the US military war wounded.

Physically wounded, and psychically wounded; despite the best efforts of the field hospitals to maintain a workable system of triage, dozens, if not hundreds, of the men sent to Yokosuka to be put back together were beyond repair.

Some of the faces that stared at him as he walked past the hospital incinerator—a small, dark tower that reeked of cooking meat—were definitely beyond repair. Eyes missing, noses, jaws, the spark of life missing. There were men in wheelchairs and men on crutches and men walking along very slowly in the extreme humidity, shuffling in their rubber sandals like mummies from a horror film.

War, what is it good for?

Absolutely . . . nothin'.

Only, Hellboy didn't believe that. There were causes worth going to hell for, and back. And if he wasn't so goddamned indestructible, he'd have been in one of those wheelchairs—or in the incinerator, in pieces—long ago.

But that was as far as philosophy took him. He was here on assignment from the Bureau. He planned to carry out his mission and get the hell out of Japan. The humidity was miserable.

The atmosphere, worse.

The MPs were edgy today. Though alerted—warned—of Hellboy's visit, briefed and debriefed about his appearance, the guards had tightened their grips on their M-16s when he had been escorted onto the base. To make matters worse, the Japanese Communist Party was holding a demonstration later in the day; soon the streets outside the insular world of the base would be congested with men, women, and children who were being paid 360 yen—one US dollar—plus lunch, to scream, "Yankee, go home!"

As Hellboy neared the door to A-22, the lockup ward, he caught the movement of an armed Marine—an MP—the man's hand slipping toward the sidearm in his holster. Hellboy looked at him—simply looked—and the man paled and dropped his hand to his side. He gave Hellboy a nod of his head, as if to grant him permission to proceed.

Not that Hellboy needed any.

The office of the Chief of Psychiatry was just inside the door, giving the doctor immediate access to the inmates. Hellboy was surprised: in his experience, shrinks usually sealed themselves away, and it was the patients who came to them.

A corpsman looked up from a desk in the outer office and executed a shocked double take. Then he rose, sharply saluted, and said, "Mr. Boy, sir. Capt. Broderman's expecting you."

Hellboy said nothing. The corpsman—who couldn't have been older than twenty-two, and that was being generous—crossed the room and rapped on a door.

"Yes." The voice was gentle.

"Dr. Broderman, Mr. Boy is here."

There was a chuckle. "Please ask him to come in."

Hellboy crossed the office, his hooves making noise on the government-issue tile floor. The hospital had been taken over after the defeat of Japan in 1945, and he had no idea when it had been built. It felt old.

Today, Hellboy felt old.

Back at BPRD headquarters, Dr. Tom Manning had briefed Hellboy on his assignment. As a result, Dr. Broderman was precisely what he'd been expecting. Tall, rugged, with precise military bearing. Not your most compassionate psychiatrist, according to his dossier.

"Hellboy," the good doctor said, rising from behind his desk.

Hellboy inclined his head. "Capt. Broderman."

"Thanks for coming. I appreciate it." He gestured for Hellboy to be seated while he looked past his shoulder at the corpsman. "Coffee for two. Both black."

So. Broderman had been briefed on him, too.

"Yes, sir," the corpsman said, and withdrew, shutting the door behind himself.

As soon as the knob stopped turning, the mask came off. Broderman slumped and wiped his hand over his face. He seemed to age twenty years in fewer seconds.

"Christ," he said. "Do you drink?"

Hellboy shrugged. "Sure."

Broderman pulled open a drawer and pulled out a bottle of Scotch. Also, two glasses. He poured a couple of shots and passed one to Hellboy. They both slugged it back.

Broderman leaned and folded his hand over his chest. "I don't know what you read about me, but most of the information you have is obsolete."

"Your job is to weed out the nutcases," Hellboy said.

Broderman sighed. "Kids shot all to hell. Legs riddled with shrapnel. Faces that look like melted wax. A lot of them are farm kids. A lot of them are . . . kids." His voice was strained and hushed.

"And yes, it is my official duty to decide which of them is sane enough to stay in the service, get patched back together, and sent back to fight. And which of them is too crazy to trust with a weapon. Who's honestly shellshocked and traumatized, and who's trying to fake me out so he can escape back to the world."

He sounded disgusted. He raised the bottle with a question mark on his face and Hellboy nodded. Men you drank with told you more than men you embarrassed by refusing their booze.

"I've got two cases. Clancy and Grant. They don't know each other. They've never met, from what I can tell. But they're both on A-22, and they're both telling me the same story."

He opened a brown cardboard chart. "'A hideous demon burst out of the sea and killed all my buddies.'"

He closed that one, laid it aside, and opened another. "'A monster tore out of the jungle and massacred everyone except me.'"

"Do you think they fragged their own men?"

The psychiatrist shrugged. "No bodies were ever found. No trace of a struggle, or combat. Just . . . no soldiers. Except one lone survivor. Or so they both claim."

Hellboy took that in. He said, "So I'm here."

"So you're here." Broderman wiped his face. The air conditioner was rattling in the window, but the room was stifling. "It's so hot in the officers' mess that the butter melts on your plate," he said.

He closed the file. "Of course, in Vietnam, no one's eating butter."

There was a knock on the door. It was the corpsman, with the coffee. Broderman said to him, "Bring Clancy in first."

Hellboy picked up his coffee cup with his left hand. Anything that didn't need smashing or maiming, he did with his left. His right hand—the stone one—was for everything else.

Death, mostly.

In silence, the two men sat, each with his thoughts. Hellboy figured Broderman was thinking about the Scotch.

He himself was thinking that it was too hot to be drinking coffee.

After about ten minutes, there was a jingle and a shuffle in the hallway. Broderman looked up. Hellboy kept trying to read the opened medical chart upside down. It contained the records of Clancy, Paul R. There was his social security number, and there his date of birth.

He was nineteen.

"Paul," Dr. Broderman said. Hellboy was surprised by the warmth in his voice. Professional, or genuine? "This is Hellboy, Paul. Remember?"

"Y-yes," Clancy stuttered.

Hellboy turned. A kid. Pale blond hair, nearly colorless blue eyes. There was a scar running from his temple across his nose to the opposite earlobe. His legs were chained. He was cuffed.

Hellboy looked at Dr. Broderman and said, "I want to take him to get a Coke. Just him and me."

Broderman thought a moment. Hellboy gazed at him.

The doctor made his decision. "Spec-4 Clancy, do I have your word you'll cooperate with this civilian?"

"Yes, sir," Clancy said. There were tears in his eyes. His mouth trembled.

Hellboy stood.

"There's a small room off the ward," Broderman said. "My corpsman will show you."

The corpsman's name was Shiflett. Hellboy saw it on his name tag.

Got shipped out to Vietnam a few weeks later.

No one ever saw him again.

But for now, he was alive, and he escorted Hellboy and Clancy out of the office and onto the ward. What struck Hellboy was the silence. Maybe because of him being there, but maybe not.

They went into the little room. There were a couple of gray overstuffed chairs, and Clancy sank into one of them. Tears slid down his face.

Shiflett left.

As soon as they were alone, Hellboy said, "I'm one of the good guys."

"It's not you," Clancy whispered. "I was stationed in Qui Nhon. It's a port city. On the South China Sea. Supply ships come in. The stuff gets unloaded, and then we convoy the supplies to the troops inland. There are only two roads into and out of town. Easy for the bad guys to attack our convoys. Impossible for us to sneak past them. Like a turkey shoot."

"They've got Fanta in this machine," Hellboy said. "Grape or orange. Root beer. That's it."

"Fanta grape, please," Clancy said. He let out a harsh sob, which he immediately stifled. "On the ward, we get soda if we're quiet."

Hellboy put in some coins and pressed the buttons with his left hand. The first bottle clattered down the chute. He pulled it out and used the built-in bottle opener. Got the same for himself.

Guys you drank the same stuff with usually told you more than guys you didn't.

Hellboy handed the soda to the inmate. Clancy took a swig. He leaned his head on the back of the chair and the tears flowed like a river.

"It's not a big city," he said. "The tallest building's probably eight stories. The people smell weird. Not bad. It's all the fish they eat. The hookers tell all the guys that we smell different. It's our diet. They wear baggy black pants, even the hookers."

"What happened?" Hellboy asked him.

"People make houses out of crushed beer cans. It smells bad. The sewers are open. There's this beach—"

"What happened?"

Clancy wrapped both hands around the bottle of Fanta. "Do you know," he asked shrilly, "that in the incinerator they burn up all the pieces they cut off us?"

Hellboy remained silent.

"It came up out of the sea!" Clancy shouted. "It came up and it ate them! It ate them!"

He threw his bottle against the wall. It shattered. Grape soda flew everywhere.

Two corpsmen rushed in with a strait jacket and a hypo. Clancy shrieked and struggled. Nothing he screamed made any sense.

But the screaming made sense.

Hellboy had to give him that.

Hellboy was escorted back to Broderman's office. The doctor wasn't there, and Hellboy spent the time reading both the patients' accounts in their charts. Which may or may not have been Broderman's intention.

When the man came back in, he said, "We had to sedate Clancy. Grant too. He became uncontrollable when he realized we wanted him to tell you about what happened. If you want to wait a while, he'll come around. I'll sit in." He looked tired and frustrated. "I should have done that with Clancy."

Hellboy shook his head. "I've got a plane to catch."

Two weeks later:

The jungle reeked of death.

Layers of rotting foliage covered decomposition far more repellent, like an American flag on a coffin at Arlington. The government was shipping home boxes of teeth, because that was all the jungle left behind.

It ate the dead.

So maybe those guys weren't so crazy after all.

Maybe they were fit for duty.

Hellboy grunted at the gross stupidity of his mission—two weeks and counting, with nothing to show for it, not even jungle rot—and slogged through the soaking wet undergrowth. The trees dripped with moisture. Insects by the hundreds tried to penetrate his skin, to no avail.

There were some advantages to being inhuman.

He crushed vines and other things as his hooves struggled for purchase in the slimy, congealed earth. He couldn't imagine a worse arena for battle. The heat and the mud, the insects, and the terror of men who can't see the forest for the destruction.

About an hour later, he came to a clearing.

A man-made clearing.

It had been a village. Now it was a patch of charred ruins and bodies. A woman in traditional dress had obviously been shot in the back. Another, half-clothed, in the head. Men. Children.

Violent death was everywhere.

It had been a massacre.

Not the first he had seen in two weeks, and he was certain it wasn't the last.

In a perimeter around the village, Hellboy found American weapons on the burn site. That didn't signify much; the South Vietnamese troops— the ARVNs—were supplied by the US, and with better stuff than the

Americans carried—M-16s to the Army's Brownings. The North Vietnamese were also well equipped, also with American material, lifted from convoys and on the black market.

But here, there were no bodies. No sign of soldiers.

That was new.

Maybe this whole deal wasn't so stupid after all.

Hellboy continued to survey the area as the sun set. It was as hot at dusk as it had been at noon.

He barely noticed.

He didn't care.

In the dark, he sat, listening to the creeping through the bushes. It was human, of that he was certain. Also, alone.

It was sneaking toward the village ruins. All he had to do was wait, and it would come to him.

Someone began whispering. In Vietnamese.

Hellboy waited.

Five minutes later, the moon glowed down on an old man in a white shirt and black trousers. He was stooped with age, and he was weeping. Hellboy remained in the thick, moist shadows, observing. The man fell to his knees and covered his face. Hellboy thought of Spec-4 Paul R. Clancy, back in Japan.

Then suddenly, as if he had fallen asleep, Hellboy became aware of advancing footfalls from dozens of pairs of boots. Rifles clacked. A radio crackled.

"Stay where you are! *Arrete!*" shouted an American voice. Hellboy assumed it was the platoon's sergeant—unless these troops actually took orders from their Officer in Charge.

The old man looked stricken. He raised his arms and murmured, "*S'il vous plaites, messieurs.*" The French had occupied Vietnam before the Americans had come in. French was still the language of choice among the older educated locals.

"Let's shoot 'im, Sarge," one of the soldiers said. "We'll have to drag him all the way back to base to interrogate him."

"Everything's burned," another voice said. "Look. The people were burned."

"Where are our guys?"

"Napalm?"

"That would still leave something. You know that."

A few of the soldiers chuckled.

"The old guy's got nice ears," someone drawled. "If we kill him, I got dibs."

The old man continued to plead. No one was listening to him.

No one but Hellboy, who caught it the moment the old man switched from French to some other language, something that was not Vietnamese, was not Asian, was not anything spoken anywhere.

Once a Baptist preacher had tried to kill him, because he claimed Hellboy could hear "the voice of evil." It was true that on occasion, Hellboy understood languages no one else could decipher.

This was one of those occasions.

While the soldiers theorized about what had happened to the village and the troops, Hellboy heard every word the old man uttered as if it were in heavily accented English:

"I call you, Xin Loi.
Xin Loi, which is what they say when they kill our women.
When they rape our school girls.
When they dismember our sons and grandfathers.
I call you, avenging demon!"

A hot, wet wind rolled through the forest undergrowth. It was like being slapped with a boiled towel. The soldiers felt it through their cammies. They turned on their heels, spooked, startled. A few aimed into the darkness.

"Hold your fire!" the sergeant shouted. "Damn it, what if there's Cong out there?"

"Xin Loi!" the old man keened. "Xin Loi!"

"What's he going on about?" someone demanded.

"Nothing. Let's shoot him and move out." There was fear in the voice.

The forest shook.

The earth trembled.

Hellboy watched the old man, who was sobbing. He cried, "Xin Loi! *Allez-y!*"

And the sky turned red.

From one side of the horizon to the other, it blazed scarlet. It was searingly hot; the winds blew; the old man covered his face as the crimson glow made his skin translucent and lit up his bones.

Hellboy remained hidden.

Remained silent.

"What the hell?" one of the soldiers cried. "Look at the sky!"

Above the horizon, where there should have been stars and black night sky, an immense shape rose up. It was vaguely humanoid, but its features were hideously contorted. Horns sprouted from its head. Its eyes were glowing red slits, and its mouth a cavernous bad dream of fangs and flame.

It threw its long, taloned arms over its head and raised its face to the sky.

The soldiers were shouting, scrambling, tumbling over one another to get the hell out of there. A small, dark man went down; a heavier man ran right over him in his haste to escape.

The demon shrieked. Lightning crashed around it. Clouds gathered.

It began to rain.

To rain blood.

Heavy, thick droplets of pungent blood, which sizzled and burned where they landed. As Hellboy watched, three soldiers burst into flame. Staggering, the living columns of fire collided, fell, tried to pick themselves up.

The demon lowered one hand, and picked the fiery bundle up. As the men burned and died, it popped them into its mouth.

It wasn't raining after all. Far from it.

The demon was crying.

The blood was its teardrops.

It kept sobbing; the soldiers kept burning and dying.

The old man chanted, urging the demon to kill all their enemies, to destroy them utterly.

Then Hellboy stepped from the shadows.

"*Bon soir*," he said. Good evening.

The old man stared at him. He fell to his knees and said in French—which Hellboy understood—"We are lost. The Americans have a demon, too."

Hellboy raised a hand and said in French, "Stop this, grandfather. Now."

"*I?*" The old man looked shocked. "Why should I?"

Hellboy had no answer.

"We destroy both sides," he informed Hellboy. "All we want is peace, my avenging angel and I. That is all. We kill the killers. That is all."

"And these villagers?" Hellboy asked.

He shook his head. "Your people did that. We came after."

"Stop," Hellboy said again.

But the old man shouted to the demon, and the demon opened its mouth to rain fire down on Hellboy.

Hellboy successfully dodged the gout of flame. Then, as the demon grabbed for him, Hellboy swung his right, stone fist like a pile driver into the demon's forearm. The creature howled in fury and pain. Hellboy was relieved. He'd thought the thing was more like a ghost, something he might not be able to fight.

But now, knowing he could harm it, he lunged for its hands and arms, smashing both fists into its strangely pliant flesh. While it reared back up into the sky, he felt in all the pouches of his belt. There were talismans and wards against evil in all of Hellboy's pockets, but he couldn't fathom how to use them against this thing. A grenade? Possibly.

Browning? Not hardly.

Then it was grabbing at him, tears flowing freely. As the droplets hit the earth, they sizzled and burned, exactly like napalm.

Through his own tears, the old man smiled fiercely.

"Xin Loi will kill all of you!" he shouted. "And our country will rise from the ashes without soldiers!"

"Wrong, old man," Hellboy said. "Your guy's going down."

The demon came in for another round, grabbing at Hellboy as if to hold him still and burn him to cinders, like a hot dog on a coat hanger at a campfire. The fire flared across Hellboy's back, but he arched, hard, and spared himself.

Then he doubled into a ball, yanking the demon's arms with him, and threw an uppercut beneath his left forearm with his huge stone hand.

The demon wailed again. But although it was in pain, it appeared to be unhurt.

"You see?" the old man exulted. "You cannot kill Xin Loi. And I will create more. An army of them! My country will be free of you all! There will be no more fighting."

"And very few people," Hellboy drawled.

The sorcerer's eyes gleamed as tears slid down his cheeks. "Our women are fertile."

And it was the way he said it—as if individual lives didn't matter; and all that mattered was ending the war—that chilled Hellboy to the bone.

He thought of American generals, and admirals, and shrinks, and guys walking around like zombies.

He darted forward before the old man realized what was happening, and broke his neck. For a second, the man registered shock. Then rage. And finally, the most intense grief Hellboy had ever seen.

With a shriek, the demon blew fire over the jungle. Within seconds, the dense foliage was fully ablaze. Hidden inside it, men began to scream. Some in Vietnamese, some in French, and some in English. The forest was crawling with dying men from both sides. All sides.

Then the demon soared straight up into the burning sky, screaming like a bomb, shooting as fast as a grenade launcher, shrieking and babbling and sobbing.

Amid the crackling, Hellboy stood, a lone survivor.

The night blackened.

Ash mixed with blood and earth, and covered the body of the dead old sorcerer.

Dawn finally came.

The jungle was hotter than the firestorm.

It was hot as hell.

Two weeks later, Hellboy sat in Broderman's office. Only, Broderman was gone. He had resigned his commission and gone back to the States.

Larousse—a French name—the new Chief of Psychiatry, was an officious little man. He folded his hands on top of his spotless desk and said, "I really don't understand what this is about."

"Clancy and Grant," Hellboy said. "On the lockup ward."

"Oh." The man sat back. "Clancy returned to duty last week."

"In Vietnam," Hellboy said flatly.

"In Vietnam," the doctor confirmed.

"Grant."

"Grant." He sighed. "He told Dr. Broderman he massacred his entire platoon. Then he found a way to commit suicide."

Or was helped, Hellboy thought. They did it with guys like that.

He stood.

He went out onto the ward. In a bed against the wall, a young man—a very young man—was rocking and sobbing.

"Somebody's gotta stop this madness," he said.

Hellboy grunted. "Yeah."

Then he left.

DEMON POLITICS
CRAIG SHAW GARDNER

C igar smoke hung in the room like a slightly sour-smelling fog, draining the color from the floor-to-ceiling bookcases and deep mahogany furnishings, making the whole place look a bit like an old-fashioned, tinted photograph. Hellboy studied Senator Lipton, so small against the dark green, overstuffed chair in which he sat. Well into his eighties, the once vigorous Lipton had seemed to shrink back into himself. The senator had stopped mid-sentence to stare off in the distance, perhaps at some pattern in the hanging smoke, or maybe at something in his past.

Hellboy had known Lipton for over half a century, since the senator, under another name, had—with a group of others, including Hellboy's pseudo-adoptive "father," Professor Trevor Bruttenholm—taken in the small, strangely formed youngster during the height of World War II. More than fifty years, and every year seemed to have added an extra line to the senator's face.

Hellboy glanced down at his own well-muscled hand, the deep-red skin halfway between the color of clay and blood. He didn't age in the same way as others. He didn't know if he would ever grow old. Now, though, he got to see those who had raised him, those who had been his childhood heroes, fade and shrivel and die one after another.

"Hope," Lipton said suddenly, the word harsh, as if torn from his throat. He looked back to Hellboy. "I had hoped it would never come to this. But it always does, doesn't it? Always."

"Senator," Hellboy replied, doing his best to get the old man to focus. "I need to know why you asked me here."

"You're the only one. I've known since the beginning. It was always you." He laughed, a brittle sound from deep in his throat. "We always surmised that your arrival among us had to do with those desperate Nazi experiments near the end of the war. They were looking for the damnation of the world. Instead, I'm hoping they gave us our salvation."

Salvation? It was Hellboy's purpose. He had a talent for rooting out evil wherever it might hide. Before he had seen Lipton's distracted manner, he had assumed that was the reason the senator had called him to his office. Now he wondered if even the senator knew why Hellboy was here.

"Excuse me, senator? Hellboy? They're waiting for you."

The senator's young assistant, Crowley, was at Hellboy's side. Hellboy had been so intent on the old man's words, he had not even noticed the younger man's arrival. Crowley smiled as he helped Lipton from his chair. His smile held a real warmth, unlike so much in this place.

Hellboy realized he had become preoccupied. He was looking for what he couldn't quite see.

Ever since he had entered these historic corridors, Hellboy had sensed— something. And he would find it. He always did.

This was why the senator had asked him here, after all. Whether Lipton remembered it or not.

Hellboy held secrets of his own. Secrets he drew on to defeat the dark forces he was compelled to face. Secrets even Hellboy did not want to examine too closely.

Before he had walked the earth, Hellboy had had another existence. He did not know if he could call it a life.

He remembered fire and pain, as constant as sunlight and star-filled skies. He carried the memories—always.

Fire lived behind his eyes. The images were sharp, burned into his brain, always there even though he couldn't understand them, like pictures from some family album full of strangers.

The fire was in his past, his future, some part of him that existed elsewhere.

But it was only when he fought the demons that he remembered more.

Pain was everywhere. It lived within his muscles, whispered to his thoughts. He expected to hear new cries of pain at every waking moment, and wondered if those cries might come, not from his memories, but from inside himself.

Too many secrets.

Every time he faced the unknown, he learned more about what had made him, and what he would meet again. These small confrontations, someday, would lead him to a larger battle, a battle with whoever, or whatever, was lord of the fire.

The senator walked slowly, but he moved with only the assistance of a stout cane with a knob shaped like a lion. Hellboy remembered when Lipton had been given that cane, before he ever became a senator, and everyone had known him by another name.

"I see you recognize my walking stick," the senator called over his shoulder as he moved diligently ahead. "Another time, Hellboy. It was another time."

And another country, Hellboy thought: France, toward the end of the war. They had saved a village from German mortar fire. The villagers wanted to give them something in return. Lipton had laughed and said the walking stick made him look distinguished. Maybe he would amount to something after all.

Everyone had laughed at that one.

Crowley smiled apologetically. "The meeting is just down this hallway."

Hellboy walked half a step behind Lipton, letting the old man lead the way. The senator moved with a singleness of purpose, as if he refused to give in to infirmity. His feet shuffled along the floor, barely rising above the polished hardwood, but he walked forward with a steady, stubborn rhythm.

Crowley stepped ahead of the others to open one of a pair of large, mahogany doors. "Gentlemen!" he announced. "Senator Lipton and Hellboy!"

Hellboy had to duck slightly to pass through the doorway. The new room looked much like Lipton's office, save that it was somewhat larger and dominated by a long conference table, around which close to a dozen people were already seated.

A white-haired man at the far end of the table, almost Lipton's equal in years, glared at Hellboy's entrance.

Hellboy's sense of unease grew greater with every step he took into the room. Whatever he had felt before was much stronger here. It was quiet, but far from peaceful. The room felt as though everything was hushed and waiting.

Waiting for what?

Hellboy sensed the forces gathering, getting ready to strike with all their unknown strength. He felt the muscles tense along his arms and back. When things moved quickly, Hellboy had learned to save understanding for later.

He looked back to the conference table. He realized everyone was staring at him.

"What is that creature doing here?" the other elder demanded.

"Senator Shorter!" Crowley spoke quickly. "Surely you received my memo—"

"Of course he did!" Lipton called from the doorway. "It's just that people aren't always as—prepared for Hellboy as they might think. Seven feet tall, three hundred pounds, bright red, one normal hand, one shaped like a sledgehammer—well, some people end up looking twice."

Hellboy was all those things. But he was surprised by the change in Lipton's voice. Now that he was among his fellow senators, he sounded far more like the Lipton of old.

"Senator, this creature isn't even human!" Shorter shot back. "How can we possibly—"

"Enough!" Lipton rapped his lion's-head cane on the end of the table. "I would trust Hellboy as I would my own son! He and I have worked together for years. Besides, he is a specialist in—certain areas I would like to discuss."

Shorter snorted as if Lipton's words were the stuff of farce. "How dare you bring this sort in here. If I had my way—"

"Unfortunately, you don't," a woman spoke sharply from midway down the table. "This is still a democracy. And a free country, last time I looked."

"Of course." Her words seemed to deflate Shorter. He smiled, his tone suddenly affable. "As I must remind my more extreme constituents from time to time. Very well. Excuse me if I was overly harsh. We have all been under a certain strain. Why doesn't Mr. Hellboy give us whatever information he might find pertinent. Then, after he is gone—"

"Hellboy isn't going anywhere," Lipton snapped. "We need him right here if we are going to—"

The smile fell from Shorter's lips. "Who gave you the authority to dictate—?"

"Senators," the woman interjected. "We are aware of your differences. But we are meeting to find a solution. If Hellboy would care to take a seat?"

She indicated an oak chair considerably larger than the others in the room. So someone—Crowley most likely—had made special arrangements for him. Hellboy sat. Even with the chair's greater size, he barely fit. Crowley sat to his left. The woman introduced the others in the room: representatives of the armed services, the FBI and CIA, the House of Representatives, even the Supreme Court. Her name was Celia Gibbons. She was an aide to the president.

Once they were both settled, Lipton spoke again. "If I may, I will outline the situation."

This time, no one objected. The senator looked straight at Hellboy and spoke again.

"There is a cancer within our government. There have always been arguments between the political parties, and quiet power struggles between the different parts of government. But our current situation goes far beyond that."

A couple of the others in the room shifted uncomfortably as the senator continued.

"The situation has become so extreme, it is apparent that none of us can contain it. And *everyone* knows." Lipton laughed derisively. "You have seen it on the evening news. House members, senators, special prosecutors, even the president himself, all battling over anything and everything from politics to personal lives. The Capitol looks more like a street brawl with every passing day!"

"We are beside ourselves," Ms. Gibbons added. "So much so that we are attempting to put aside our differences long enough to seek outside help. Senator Lipton suggested that there might be some solution beyond our expertise."

Hellboy nodded. Explaining what he did was not his strongest suit, but he would make an attempt for Lipton's sake.

"I already know I'm up against something out of the ordinary. I could—feel it—as soon as I entered the building. I'm sorry I can't be more specific. Sometimes I don't understand what I sense, until it confronts me directly."

"Then I was right to bring you here," Lipton's voice rose above the grumbles of a couple of the others in attendance. Hellboy nodded to his old friend as he asked those around the table to give him specifics. One after another they spoke, slowly warming to the topic.

Senator Lipton had brought him here. Hellboy imagined it was Lipton's reputation that brought the others and made them cooperate.

Hellboy glanced over at his old friend as he heard the stories of irrational anger, forbidden sex, and eruptions of violence. Lipton appeared to hang on every word, a fire deep in his eyes, a final spark, perhaps, of his energy from long ago.

He had called himself Commander Freedom.

Hellboy remembered how, as a child, he had looked up to the man in the blue costume with the silver shield.

He was very fast, very strong, and very smart. How he had gotten these more-than-human powers was never well explained. It was the war. Loose lips sink ships.

When Hellboy had been afraid, Freedom was there. That had been enough for a child.

Hellboy had been very lucky when he came into this world. He had been found by a team of soldiers and scientists, working for the Free French, but composed mostly of Brits and Yanks, men and women, researchers, scientists, soldiers, heroes. Though Trevor Bruttenholm had been primary among them, Hellboy had had the equivalent of a dozen parents. Much like the villages of old, he had been able to gain insight and experience from a dozen different perspectives.

Lipton had been the trusted, much-admired "uncle" whom he had looked up to with a little bit of awe. Commander Freedom never got angry, never seemed tired, and always had a moment to listen. Oh, he wasn't always there—they were fighting a war after all—but every time he returned, Hellboy found he could talk to him about almost anything.

In those early days, Hellboy had been a large child, as powerful as many adults. Hellboy's strength would often destroy, usually through awkwardness, occasionally through anger. Some seemed cautious around the boy, a few even afraid, but never Commander Freedom. He spent long hours teaching the child to know his own strength and when to use it, and an equal time talking, finding the reasons for the youngster's anger, and exploring other ways to express his feelings.

After Hellboy's arrival, other things came from the unknown, creatures of darkness, creatures without Hellboy's innocence. Whether they came seeking Hellboy, or they simply followed the same path that the small red child had taken to earth was unknown. Commander Freedom was among those who turned them away. As he grew older, Hellboy learned to help. The war ended, but Freedom fought on, against foes both natural and supernatural. Eventually, Freedom retired, but Hellboy, as part of the Bureau for Paranormal Research and Defense, went on.

Lipton might have hung up the mask and the shield, but he wasn't done. He still wanted to make a difference, so, like generals and astronauts before him, he'd gone into politics.

Another thirty years had passed. Thirty very hard years. Hellboy's memory didn't fit the senator before him.

Commander Freedom had been nothing but muscle when he had fought the war. It was hard to see those strong lines now in Lipton's fallen face.

Hellboy had visited the senator once before, maybe a dozen years back. He had seen the first faint signs of age even then, the graying hair, the worry lines. That time, they had talked about how the world had changed. And Lipton had spoken about how he had succeeded in the world of politics.

"You learn to bend, or you will get nothing done," he said at the time. "So different from the war."

But now Lipton—the former Commander Freedom—had a new war on his hands. And Hellboy would be his soldier.

Hellboy listened as one after another of those at the table recalled the incidents— always disquieting, sometimes violent—that had been occurring with increasing frequency in these halls. Name calling, screaming matches, fist fights, even a bomb scare and a hostage situation. All unfortunate, each one seemingly an isolated incident, until you looked at them together, with those events already reported in the media, and saw the rising level of strife.

"I think you do have reason to be concerned," Hellboy replied when the others were done, "but nothing you've said so far has given me a clue as to what it is." Actually, he had some idea of what was happening here, but he wasn't sure if the others at the table, Lipton included, would be ready to hear about it. He had to learn more. He needed a delaying tactic to allow him time to further explore the problem.

"Maybe," he suggested, "if we evacuated the government buildings, one after another—"

"What?" Senator Shorter would have none of that. "You are talking about the US government here! You want us to stop running the country while you chase your fool notions?"

Hellboy smiled. "Only a suggestion."

"And if that is the level of suggestion we're going to receive, I'd say you've already wasted far too much of the government's time!" Shorter rose from his chair, a sure sign that, for him, the meeting was over.

"If *I* might make a suggestion?" Ms. Gibbons asked. "We could arrange for Hellboy to take a tour of the other sites. I'd look forward to whatever else he might discover."

"The meeting is over!" Shorter insisted. "I have other business!"

"As our distinguished colleague said," Ms. Gibbons agreed with a sigh. She rose from her chair as well.

Hellboy frowned down at his old friend. All of Lipton's energy seemed to desert him the moment the meeting adjourned. He stared at the table with half-closed eyes, as if only waiting for death.

Hellboy realized that that was why it was so important to be here now. He and Lipton, fighting together one last time, with words rather than fists, but it was a good fight nonetheless.

Commander Freedom wasn't dead yet.

Lipton shook his head slowly. "Sorry, Hellboy. I thought I could get them to understand."

"Some of them did," Hellboy replied softly. "Maybe the others will come around."

Lipton nodded and rose with a groan. "Back to the office. We need to discuss strategy."

No, Hellboy thought. If what he guessed were true, this had passed the discussion stage.

"If you'll excuse me, senator, I think I might be able help." Hellboy walked over to stand next to the departing Shorter. "Wait."

The senator looked both surprised and uncomfortable.

"You're going to hound us, aren't you?" Shorter demanded.

"But Senator—," Hellboy objected mildly.

"How blind can you be?" Shorter demanded. "All of you!"

Hellboy decided that Shorter was almost in the proper mood. He stepped forward. "Senator? There's one thing we need to clear up. If I might have a moment of your time?"

"What?" Shorter glared at him, his hands shaking with rage. "I thought I made it quite clear in the meeting—" He stopped abruptly, pushing past Hellboy and heading for the exit.

Hellboy followed at his heels until both of them were out in the hall. He stepped nimbly to Shorter's side.

"But it's because of the meeting that I need to talk to you. Well, not the meeting exactly. It has more to do with what I felt in the meeting, and what I felt as you were leaving."

Shorter stopped mid-stride to turn his anger back at his pursuer. Some of the others from the meeting room had gathered around, drawn by the conflict. Hellboy would have to be careful that no one got hurt.

Shorter's eyes were wide, his whole body shaking now. "Leave me alone! I will have you thrown from the building!"

Hellboy smiled. "Or should I say, 'What I *didn't* feel'?"

Shorter's head jerked to one side. "Is that an accusation?"

Hellboy took a step closer. "I would say it is more a statement of fact."

"I resent—I—" His head jerked left, then right again. "I—I will not have you meddling—I—I—" He started to jerk so severely that he appeared to lose the power of speech.

Hellboy lifted his more-human hand toward Shorter. "Senator, I've seen this kind of possession before. You're not in control of your own actions."

"In control?" His voice was much higher pitched than before, and didn't seem to come from his mouth. "I'll show you who's in—control."

Hellboy lifted the hand that looked like a hammer. "C'mere, you."

"Control!" The old man shook so rapidly, he seemed to blur. Smoke rose above the senator, like a cloud appearing in midair. "Control!"

The cloud gained eyes, then a face, then shoulders and arms and hands and talons. Demons had no practice with direct confrontation. Detecting the creatures was sometimes difficult, but Hellboy never had a problem calling them out.

"Attack him!" the cloud screamed.

Hellboy was ready.

"Attack!" the cloud demon wailed again.

Hellboy realized then the cloud was calling to others. He took a step away from the smoke ghost to survey the hallway.

Others around them were shaking in much the same manner as the senator. The man from the CIA, the representative from the Navy, even the clerk from the

Supreme Court. The possession was quite widespread. Lipton was right to have involved him. Only Hellboy could save them now.

"Hellboy," one of the new smoke ghosts screamed. "You have meddled with our kind long enough!"

The others added to the high-pitched chatter:

"We have found a home!"

"We will not be displaced!"

"We will destroy you first!"

Hellboy heard shouting down the hall. A pair of armed policemen ran towards them down the corridor.

Hellboy had dealt with these kinds of creatures before. All the cops could do was get themselves hurt or killed.

"Back!" he called to the pair. "Bullets won't do a damn thing."

The cops hesitated. Hellboy would have to act quickly. He studied the smoke ghosts, trying to determine their nature, and how best to destroy them. Under their cries he heard another noise—their life energy perhaps—not so much a heartbeat, more like the sighing of the wind.

The ghost from within the senator floated closer.

If one attacked, Hellboy knew, it would be a signal for all.

"We are everywhere," the ghost moaned.

Hellboy glanced away for an instant and saw another half-dozen of those at the meeting blurring as clouds formed over them. It was more than simple possession, it was an infestation.

Very well. Hellboy would fight them all. He would defeat them with something they understood—the strength of Hell.

"We will take Hellboy!" The first ghost swept toward him. Hellboy jumped away. The thing's talons felt like ice where they brushed against his chest. He grabbed the ghost as it passed, its substance like cotton in his hands, and pulled the head from its shoulders.

Its shriek of fury was cut short. The cloud dispersed like water vapor in the sun.

But all the other smoke demons cried in anguish.

"Not the American way!"

"Hellboy is an interloper!"

"The will of the people!"

"Hellboy must die!"

"Not the right demographic!"

"Destroy! Destroy!"

They swarmed towards him, close to a dozen strong. His hammer hand punched a hole in the first to arrive. The ghost staggered back, its talons frantically scraping the ragged cloud-stuff back into place. Hellboy calmly pulled its head from its body before it could finish repairs.

The remaining creatures grew even more frantic.

"Noooooo!"

"We need life!"

Ten of the creatures surrounded him now.

"Strife gives us energy!"

They pressed in on every side. They joined together as the ring tightened. He was surrounded by a circle of fog.

"We will take you!"

They would all attack at once. He pushed at the cloud stuff, tightening like a noose. The smoke spread through his fingers. He could not grasp it properly.

"He is a most perfect specimen," the ghosts cried.

"He has so much energy to drain."

He struck out again. His fists felt like they were moving in slow motion.

"We cannot enter!" one cried.

"We will find a way!" another retorted.

"What are you made of, Hellboy?" a third asked. "Snips and snails and puppy dogs' tails?"

Its laughter was muffled as the cloud stuff closed around Hellboy's head. He would drown in the stuff. He had to find some way to break free.

He had trouble even grabbing them, and they seemed to have a similar problem with him. If he just moved quickly enough . . .

Hellboy launched himself with his powerful legs, whirling about as quickly as he could, once, twice, three times!

"Noooooo!" The smoke things spun away, breaking apart to their individual forms.

Hellboy moved quickly then, shredding the rest of the insubstantial forms with a combination of speed and brute strength. In less than a minute, the cloud things were gone.

He looked around, expecting some further attack. But the corridor was quiet. The two cops still stood some distance away. Both of them stared open-mouthed. Everyone else seemed to have fallen, unconscious, to the floor, as the demons inhabiting them had risen to the attack.

Everyone.

Hellboy realized that Senator Lipton was one of the fallen.

Hellboy heard a series of groans from the floor. A couple of the younger victims sat up.

Hellboy rushed over to Lipton, and knelt by his side.

"Hellboy," the senator whispered. "Lift me up a bit—so I can see you."

Hellboy gently placed a hand behind Lipton's head and lifted his head and shoulders off the floor.

Lipton tried to smile. "We sure had some battles, didn't we?" He drew a ragged breath.

Hellboy struggled to understand. "What happened, Senator?

Lipton closed his eyes for a moment. "I could not admit it to myself—not consciously." Lipton's voice grew even more hoarse. "I let them inside. One compromise too many. I think they were all that was keeping me alive. A deal with the devil, hey?"

His eyes fluttered again.

"Senator?" Hellboy called. "We'll get help."

Lipton smiled again. "I feel a peace I had forgotten."

He was quiet for a moment after that.

"Senator?" Hellboy called again.

"Call me Freedom," the senator whispered.

His breathing stopped, his eyes staring somewhere beyond this world.

Hellboy lowered him gently to the floor.

Commander Freedom had won his final battle.

Hellboy looked around the hallway.

The others were pushing themselves back to their feet. Most of them looked confused, but no one seemed to be in pain. The younger and stronger would easily revive. Even Senator Shorter, still spread out on the floor, only seemed to be sleeping peacefully, his chest rising and falling, a slight smile on his lips.

Hellboy didn't feel like smiling.

He was drawn to confront these things day after day. As close as they had come, the creatures had not been able to overwhelm him. Perhaps he was immune. Or perhaps such things lived in him already, only waiting for the proper moment to appear.

The others were not so lucky. Every person in that meeting, all movers and shakers in the government, had harbored these secret creatures within. If this was any indication, the demons were everywhere in this place.

"I think I might have to do some further investigation," Hellboy called to the others.

This time, he got no arguments.

"Ms. Gibbons? What say we start with the oval office?"

Hellboy had some work to do.

A GRIM FAIRY TALE

NANCY A. COLLINS

He was nursing his second cup of coffee when Liz Sherman walked into the conference room with the early edition tucked under her arm.

"Have you looked at the morning paper?" she asked.

"No. Should I?" he grunted, arching an eyebrow.

"See for yourself," she replied, tossing the newspaper so it slid half the length of the table.

Even if he didn't have eyesight many times keener than average, he still could have made out the headlines from across the room:

Who's Hizzoner Gonna Call?

Mayor Taps BPRD For Missing Tots Case!

"Great," he growled, flashing a fang in disgust. "Who let the cat out of the bag?"

Liz shrugged. "It's the Big Apple—I'd rather fight poltergeists with Attention Deficit Disorder than get involved with the press in this town."

He sighed and, despite his better judgment, reached out to draw the tabloid closer for further inspection, setting aside his coffee in order to use his left hand. Using his right hand was not an option, as that particular appendage was only good for pile-driving or crushing cinderblocks, since it was made of living stone and disproportionately large for his body. The overall visual effect was not unlike that of a gibbon wearing a solitary boxing glove.

Then again, when it came to the rest of his body, none of it was exactly what anyone would mistake for "normal," at least not outside of Dante's *Inferno*. Standing over seven feet, weighing in at close to five hundred pounds, with bright scarlet skin, cloven hooves, and a long, prehensile tail that looked like a cross between a lizard's and a monkey's, he certainly fit the only name he had ever known—the only name he had, to his memory, ever been called:

Hellboy.

He scanned the newspaper article, which was long on hysteria but short on real news, typical for the tabloids. The only thing of real interest was the side bar, which featured pictures of the missing children—twelve total, so far.

It was clear, despite the overheated prose, that New Yorkers were genuinely worked up over the disappearances. While such concern might seem odd for a city that prided itself on its history of indifference, there were several factors that made it an emotionally volatile situation: First, the age of the missing children—none older than six years; second, they had all been taken from Central Park, the city's most sacred reprieve from the concrete and glass that surrounds it; third, the abductions all happened in broad daylight, within feet of the children's parents or guardians; fourth, all the children were from good, upper-income families and were well cared for, even pampered; fifth, no ransom note had been received by any of the families in the six weeks since the disappearances began, giving the distinct impression that the motivation for the kidnappings was depraved, not financial. Someone was stealing the children of Midtown Manhattan, and now, four days after the twelfth child was plucked by unseen hands from one of the gaily painted horses on the Carousel, there was finally some evidence that pointed to a paranormal force behind it all.

Which was why Hellboy and the others from the Bureau for Paranormal Research and Defense had choppered in at the crack of dawn from their headquarters in nearby Fairfield, Connecticut to meet with the mayor at Gracie Mansion. Who had yet to show.

Typical. Hurry up and wait. Hellboy grunted.

Suddenly the doors to the conference room flew open and the Mayor entered, flanked by several of his aides and a personal secretary, and Professor Bruttenholm at his elbow. The mayor looked like a man trying to eat breakfast, finish dressing, and call his office for messages all at the same time. It was occasions like these that Hellboy was glad his job only required him to fight monsters.

"Look, Mitch—I don't care what you think, the Sanitation Workers' Union has our nuts in a vise and they know it!" The mayor barked into the cordless phone while giving his tie a final adjustment. "Life in this city is a big enough pain in the ass as it is without commuters crawling over trash bags to and from work. And let's not get into the tourist thing! Let the Budgetary Committee squawk! I refuse to have a garbage strike on my watch, and that's final! You don't make it to the Governor's mansion on a mountain of disposable diapers. Look—I got other things to worry about right now. I'll get back to you on this later." Rolling his eyes in frustration, the mayor closed his phone and handed it back to one of his aides. "I'm so sorry to keep you waiting."

Hellboy rose from his seat, extending his left hand to the Mayor. "That's perfectly understandable, Mr. Mayor. . ."

A true politician, Hizzoner didn't even blink as he shook the hand offered him.

"I'm honored to make your acquaintance, Mr. Hellboy."

"Just Hellboy, sir," he explained, returning to his seat, which groaned uneasily under his immense weight.

Professor Bruttenholm coughed dryly into his fist. The old man was physically quite frail—after all, he was well into his nineties—but the fire in his eyes belied whatever physical shortcomings his age had brought him. As the Bureau's founder and Hellboy's foster father, Trevor Bruttenholm was still a force to be reckoned with.

"I had my men sweep the area where the last abduction is reported to have taken place. The spectrogram results indicate without a doubt that occult energy was expended at the sight. Whatever is stealing these children is of a paranormal nature."

The mayor frowned. "You think it's Satanists?"

Bruttenholm shook his head. "Not of the nature you are suggesting, no. But demon worship as a motive for the abductions is not out of the question."

"So how soon do you think Hellboy can find these kids and get them back safe and sound?"

There was an uncomfortable silence and exchange of glances amongst the BPRD members. After a long moment, Hellboy spoke up.

"Mister Mayor . . . sir . . . I don't like to make this situation any more distressing for the families than it already is, but there is less than a one percent chance any of those kids are still alive. Whatever is stealing them is doing it for one thing and one thing *only*— consumption."

The mayor visibly blanched and his personal secretary looked like she was going to be sick.

"My God. You mean—a cannibal?"

"I don't know about the cannibal part—but we're certainly dealing with an anthropophagus entity," Bruttenholm explained.

The mayor's brow creased. "A *what*?"

"Something that eats humans," Liz said helpfully.

"What kind of thing would do that?'

Bruttenholm rubbed his chin thoughtfully. "There are *numerous* creatures with a taste for human flesh—but given the types of victims and the circumstances of their disappearances, I'd hazard that we're dealing with an ogre—possibly a minor demon of some sort. Both are known for their fondness for child-flesh. Then again. . . it also shows signs of classic fairy abduction."

"I *beg* your pardon?" said one of the aides, who wore a pink triangle button on his lapel.

"All legends and folklore have their basis in fact, young man," Bruttenholm replied sharply. "There are numerous accounts of children being charmed by the fairy folk and carried off to The Land Under The Hill—Never-Never Land, if you will."

"Are you saying Peter Pan stole these children?"

"Not Peter Pan per se, because he was a work of fiction—but the reality on which such fanciful characters have been based."

The Mayor shook his head in disbelief. "I thought I'd seen and heard it all after a lifetime of living on Manhattan, but this *really* takes the cake! Are you *sure* it's not Satanists?"

"Pretty sure."

"Damn." He stared at the ground for a few moments, then he began to smile, as if something had suddenly occurred to him. "If the children were abducted by leprechauns or whatever the hell they are—at least they're *okay,* right? I mean, fairies aren't *dangerous*— they're just little women with butterfly wings, right?"

Hellboy glanced at the Professor, who shook his head. The old man was probably right. The less said the better in some cases, especially when it came to political types. The Mayor was desperate to find some kind of happy face to put on the situation should it go balls up. Telling grieving parents that their kids had been spirited away to Rock Candy Mountain by the Pied Piper certainly sounded better than saying they'd been eaten alive by an ogre.

It was decided that, given the size of Central Park, it would be better if the Bureau operatives placed themselves in strategic locations. Liz was stationed at the Children's Zoo, the Professor was keeping watch by the Carousel, while Hellboy found himself assigned to the Heckscher Playground.

With two jungle gyms, a sandpit, several sets of swings, and a Punch-and-Judy-style puppet house, Heckscher was the largest of the park's twenty different children's play areas; and given its easy access from Columbus Circle, it was considered the most likely target should whatever was preying on the park's young visitors strike again.

Dressed in his brown leather duster, his collar turned up, and with a wide-brimmed hat pulled low over his brow to hide the stumps of his amputated horns, Hellboy sat on a wooden bench not far from the swings and did his best not to look suspicious.

Thank goodness he was in New York City, or else he would have been failing miserably.

As he watched the hordes of children race back and forth amongst the swings and slides, it occurred to Hellboy that he had never before been exposed to such a large number of human children all in one place at one time. He was amazed by the energy and intensity they put into their play-time activities, as if the fate of the world hinged on how high they could ride the swings, or who went down the slide first.

Hellboy wasn't very comfortable around kids. His had been a solitary childhood—if it could be called that at all. However, Hellboy's uneasiness around children was not merely the result of his being raised apart from them. His biggest problem with rugrats was they tended to break real easy. Given his bull-in-a-china-shop reputation, Hellboy was terrified of even touching them.

Since he had been raised in laboratory-like conditions, where his every development, both physical and mental, was measured, weighed, and documented, Hellboy had never been exposed to other children his own age, much less his own species. He had known of their existence, of course. He could still clearly remember when the Professor handed him that first copy of *Fun With Dick and Jane*, and how baffled and dismayed he had been to discover that not all little boys had bright red skin and cloven hooves.

Still, Hellboy did not consider his an unhappy childhood. The Professor had tried his best to raise him as he would a human child, given the unique conditions they found themselves in. And whenever Hellboy thought about how he might have turned out had his upbringing been left to the Nazis responsible for his deliverance upon this mortal plane, he shuddered. Still, these things did not keep him from experiencing a twinge of loss as he watched the children romp and play.

As the day wore on, Hellboy was surprised how many children were out enjoying the park, despite the dire events of the last few weeks. However, if the children were oblivious to the sinister cloud hanging over their favorite playground, the same could not be said for the adults accompanying them.

As he scanned the neighboring benches, Hellboy couldn't help but notice how intently the parents, nannies, and other care providers were watching their individual charges, eschewing the usual idle chitchat in favor of stony vigil. He understood their concern, but it would do little good, given the nature of the enemy they were up against. Mere human eyesight was of little use against forces more ancient than the standing stones of the Druids.

He sniffed the air, casting for the tell-tale stink of the paranormal, but all he caught was the odor of horse manure from the nearby Bridle Path and, when the wind blew from the east, the reek of far more exotic beasts that made their home at the zoo.

"Hellboy—come in, Hellboy. Do you copy?" Liz's voice buzzed in his pointed ear, thanks to the tiny headset he was wearing.

"Yeah, I hear you loud and clear, " he growled into his lapel mike. "'Sup?"

"Nothing much. I thought I might have spotted our target, but it turned out just to be a garden-variety pedophile."

"*That's* a cheery thought."

"Do you think the newspaper coverage might have scared it off?"

Hellboy shrugged, even though she was not there to see it. "That's assuming it has the brains necessary to read the papers, much less the pocket change to buy them. You know the drill, Liz. We stay put until Bruttenholm says otherwise. There's too much at stake here."

"You're right, Hellboy. Still, I can't help feeling we're spinning our wheels here."

"We'll see. The day's not through yet. Over and out." After another hour, however, Hellboy was beginning to agree with Liz about the stakeout being a total bust.

There was a sudden throbbing just above his brow. Hellboy sat up straight, every sense razor sharp. He always got phantom pain from his horns when there was a paranormal being in the area.

At first he mistook it for one of the parents, but there was something about the way it moved that caught his attention. It walked with a swift dedication to purpose, like an underwater welder who knows he only has a certain amount of time before his air runs out, stranding him in a hostile environment. It was dressed in loose-fitting, flowing garments, with a scarf over its head, obscuring its features from the casual observer. It was too willowy to be a man, but too tall to be a woman. It ignored the other children crawling over the playground equipment like ants on a piece of candy and headed towards a pair of towheaded children who were off by themselves, playing with a toy ball.

The stranger called out to the children, who stopped what they were doing to look up at its hidden face. The little boy, the older of the two, immediately smiled and dropped the ball.

Hellboy spoke hurriedly into the transmitter as he got to his feet, his left hand going instinctively to where he kept his gun.

"*Professor! Liz! Come in! I see it! It's here!*"

"*Hellboy!*" Bruttenholm's ancient voice crackled in his ear. "What is it?!? What are we dealing with?"

"Tell Cartier he wins the office pool," Hellboy growled back. "We got ourselves a fairy."

"What sub-species?"

"I can't tell from here. It's zeroed in on a couple of kids."

"Can you shoot it?"

His dislike of supernatural creatures was so strong, he was tempted to go ahead and fire, but at the last minute his Bureau training took over. "I can't—there are too many civilians in the area—mostly kids."

The mother of one, if not both, of the children, left her seat on a nearby bench and hurried forward, grabbing the stranger's sleeve. The creature turned towards the woman, removing its veil to momentarily reveal an androgynous face with high cheekbones, almond-shaped eyes, and smooth skin. Its radiant, sexless beauty was so pure it transfixed and disarmed instantly, like the face of a saint. However, the feral hunger burning in its golden eyes was far from beatific.

The woman's face went blank and her hand fell away from the stranger's sleeve and hung at her side as if dead. Without saying a word, she turned around and resumed her seat on the bench, staring off into space, caught deep within the same glamour that had once ensnared Merlin, long centuries before.

As the creature moved to replace its veil, Hellboy glimpsed gossamer-fine hair the color of a robin's egg. His eyes widened. The fairy turned its hypnotic gaze back on the kids and took their tiny hands in its own and began to walk from the playground, back in the direction of Columbus Circle. The children obediently followed their abductor without a cry or whimper.

"Crap," he groaned.

"What? What's going on?" Bruttenholm demanded testily. "Hellboy—talk to me!"

"It's a Cailleach Bheur."

"That's what I was afraid of," the old man replied. "Try to keep it there. We're on our way."

"Too late, Prof. It's made the grab and it's impossible for me to engage it—not under these circumstances. I'm going to try and follow it."

"Follow it—?!?" Bruttenholm blustered.

"It's going to ground, Prof—if I track it, maybe I can find the others."

There was a moment of silence on the Professor's end, then the old man's voice came back over the receiver, sounding far older than even Hellboy knew him to be. "Very well, son—go ahead and follow it. Don't forget to turn on your homing beacon."

"Thanks for the reminder, Prof," he replied. "I'm already halfway across Columbus Circle."

Hellboy's big worry was that the fairy would hail a cab and disappear into the city. That concern disappeared when the creature led its prey down into the subway, only to be replaced by a new fear of losing them on the crush of the platform. Hellboy clattered after it, cursing under his breath as he wedged his sizable bulk through the turnstiles. He spotted his quarry standing on the downtown side and was secretly relieved to see that the little boy and girl, outside of being extremely quiet and docile, seemed otherwise unharmed.

Hellboy carefully jockeyed himself in the crowd so the creature would not accidentally catch his scent. The last thing he needed was it getting wind of him and hurting the kids. However, the fairy seemed to be too preoccupied with keeping both children under its control while maintaining its own semblance of humanity to pay much attention to anything else.

As Hellboy surreptitiously followed the fairy onto the train, he couldn't help but marvel at how well its race had adapted to the modern world. He wondered how many of the faces on milk cartons were the direct responsibility of creatures like the one he was following. After all, fairies had been abducting mortal children for centuries—long before the gray UFOnauts ever thought of making the scene. Why should they stop now?

The problem with fairy infestations was that modern humans didn't believe in them anymore, which gave the more vicious variants room to run wild. As far as the average human was concerned, fairies were thumb-sized little girls in tutus with butterfly wings, quaint little figments of the imagination best suited for children's books and animated films and nothing else.

Of course, "fairy" was something of a misnomer. There were numerous species and subspecies, just as there were with such catch-all descriptions as "bird," "primate," and "fish." All were, at best, tricky and unpredictable, and many were genuinely baleful creatures. They came in various shapes and sizes, and had apparently existed alongside mankind since the most ancient of days, thanks largely to their gift of "hiding in plain sight" via a supernatural ability to cloud the minds of humans.

The fairy race ranged from such creatures as the strikingly beautiful Seelies to the gnarled Kobolds, to the shapeless horror of the Brollachan. In this case, he was faced with a Cailleach Bheur, one of the most dangerous and unpleasant members of the whole damned family.

In ancient Scotland, before the Christian religion took hold, they were one of the most feared breeds of fairy folk. Back then, they had been known as Blue Hags, infamous for their cruelty and their rapaciousness. They were especially dangerous to travelers and children sent to collect firewood or fetch water from the highland streams. As time passed, and civilization grew, it became harder and harder for them to rely on such direct methods of predation. They were forced to become more daring and inventive if they wished to remain fed. So they used their power to cloud the minds of men—to cast glamours, or spells—to make themselves more attractive to their prey. And so the fearsome Blue Hags were replaced, in time, by the beautiful Blue Fairies.

And humans, being what they are, romanticized this history of systematic predation by writing ballads and lays and all manner of fanciful crap about fairylands and fairy brides and changelings. All of which was complete and utter bullshit. *Tam Lin, La Belle Dame Sans Merci, Le Morte d'Arthur, The Faerie Queene, Peter Pan, The Pied Piper of Hamlin* . . . all of it a total crock. Those lured away by the fairies didn't go to a world under the hill where it was always summer and no one aged and they danced and fiddled all night long. They went directly into the fairy's belly, if they were lucky. If they were unlucky, they were used as incubators. Hellboy hated dealing with fairies. They were invariably tricky bastards, and deceptively hard to kill, given their build.

The Cailleach got off the train at the last stop before Brooklyn. Hellboy wasn't surprised it had chosen to make its lair in the East Village. Walking amongst the sullen, black-garbed, heavily pierced and tattooed denizens of Avenue A, the Cailleach and its victims were the picture of normalcy. Even Hellboy didn't rate a raised eyebrow past Avenue B.

The fairy was headed toward the deepest reaches of Alphabet City, where the real-estate developers had yet to lay claim to the dilapidated tenements and chase the remaining crack-heads and junkies from the shadows. In this blighted neighborhood, isolated from the financial rejuvenation that brought sushi bars and trendy boutiques to the northern end of Houston Avenue, there were still shooting galleries and rats the size of small dogs brazenly feeding from overflowing garbage pails. Here, the streets were still mean, the shadows still dark. It was a perfect location for the likes of the Cailleach Bheur to tend to its grisly business unmolested.

Hellboy hung back by a half block, watching the Cailleach as it entered a dilapidated tenement with boarded-over windows and a crumbling facade heavily marked with graffiti tags and human urine. He increased his pace, hooves clattering loudly on the pavement. He couldn't wait for the others to join him. He had to move in now, or it would have all been for nothing.

The interior of the building was gutted, resembling a squalid four-story atrium, with criss-crossing wooden beams overhead. What was left of the first floor groaned under his weight as Hellboy tested it with his hooves. Even with his keen, dark-adapted eyesight, the gloom inside the abandoned building was too heavy for him to see what might be lurking in its shadows.

Grumbling under his breath, he removed his Bureau-issue flashlight from one of his duster's inner pockets and played the beam along one of the rafters directly overhead. They were swaddled in some kind of blue-white webbing, below which was a pendulous nest, similar to those created by weaver birds, made from the same substance. Hellboy cast the beam farther and was rewarded by the sight of a large cluster of silken sacs plastered to the far wall. He didn't have to count to know there were twelve of them.

A movement caught the corner of his eye. Instinctively, he moved the beam towards it. There was a man splayed across the wall, his arms and legs spread akimbo, as if making snow angels in mid-air, his wrists and ankles held in place by the webbing that composed the Cailleach's nest and pantry sacs. Judging from the tattered remains of the suit hanging from his wasted frame, he was some hapless commuter the Cailleach had seduced from the trodden path—a modern-day Tam Lin lured into Never-Never Land by la Belle Dame Sans Merci.

The man twitched convulsively a second time. Hellboy moved closer.

"Hey, buddy—hold on—the cavalry's arrived," he whispered gruffly.

The commuter's head rolled back on his shoulders. His flesh was gray and covered in sores, his eyes sunken into their orbits. Save for a grotesquely distended belly, he looked more like a scarecrow than a human being. A pained, gargling sound was all that came from the dying man's throat. Whatever had turned him from commuter to incubator had taken his tongue.

With a roar of anger and disgust, Hellboy reached into his coat and withdrew one of the flares he kept for emergencies and struck it against the crumbling brick wall. A flame as red and baleful as those of the lakes of his birthplace leapt forth, giving light to the darkness, while at the same time creating contorted shadows.

"That's it! I'm through pussyfooting around, you bargain-basement maleficent!" he bellowed, his throat sacs bulging like those of a bull ape. "*I* know you're here and *you* know I'm here! So show yourself!"

There was a hiss like a basket of angry cobras from high overhead and Hellboy looked up and saw the Cailleach standing on one of the exposed beams, flanked on either side by the stolen children.

"The mortals are *mine,* demon! Go find your *own* child-flesh to fill your gut!" growled the Cailleach.

"No thanks—I prefer Chef Boyardee, if it's all the same to you," he snarled in return. "By the way—how the hell did you get up there?"

In reply, the Cailleach launched itself at Hellboy, revealing a pair of semi-opaque membranous wings, like those of a wasp, growing from its back. The fairy struck Hellboy with surprising force, knocking him onto his back and snuffing the flare.

The Cailleach straddled Hellboy's broad chest, raking the rhino-like hide that covered his face and upper body with long, sharp talons. Now that it no longer had to worry about keeping up appearances, the fairy was showing a face that no mortal had ever lived to tell about.

Gone was the ephemeral beauty that was so important in luring its human prey away from the herd, and in its place was something straight out of an exterminator's nightmare. Within seconds the fairy metamorphosed from a delicate, sylph-like creature of fancy into a hideous humanoid insect.

In place of a mouth were ferocious, segmented, pincer-like appendages capped by fangs dripping venom. Its golden eyes ballooned into bulbous, compound orbs. The long, silken robin's-egg-blue hair quickly sprouted all over the rest of its body, like the fur of a tarantula. Long, whip-like antennae flailed atop its head.

Hissing in frustration, the Cailleach arched its lower body, and Hellboy quickly rolled out of the way just as a foot-long stinger stabbed where he had been less than a moment before.

"You'll have to do better than that, sister. I'm not some clueless commuter from Long Island," Hellboy growled, getting back onto his hooves, his tail lashing back and forth like that of a stalking tiger.

The Cailleach made an agitated, chattering sound, as if sounding an alarm, then sprayed viscous streams of silk from its mouth glands, catching Hellboy across the eyes.

"Damn it!" he snarled, staggering backward, clawing at the sticky mess covering his eyes. Caught off-balance, he staggered backward, colliding with the ensnared commuter.

The tongueless man made one last choked cry and spasmed as the obscene swelling in his belly trembled violently. A multitude of tiny winged creatures, none bigger than the tip of a baby's finger, swarmed forth, exiting from the dead man's mouth, nose, and ears in a great, stinging cloud.

"Oh—great! Just what I needed ! Pixies!" Hellboy growled. Without thinking, he used his right hand to swat the nymph-stage fairies, squashing the majority of the bothersome hoard against the wall with the massive stone gauntlet. The impact shook the gutted building to its crumbling foundations like a bomb blast, knocking the hypnotized children from their deep trances.

Hellboy froze, unable to take his eyes off the children overhead. He cursed himself under his breath for his rashness. To come so far, only to nearly kill them with a single, thoughtless action!

The little girl was the first to stir. She blinked, as if wakened from a dream and began to tremble and whimper. The boy rubbed his eyes, like a sleepwalker wakened in mid-step, and looked around, disoriented.

"Kids! Whatever you do—don't move! Just stay put!" Hellboy called out.

The little boy looked down, following the sound of his voice, and promptly lost his balance, slipping from the beam.

Hellboy took a flying leap, hoping against hope he would make it in time. The Cailleach snarled and moved to block him, but Hellboy was too fast for it. He caught the child in his outstretched arms a split-second before he struck the ground—and then fell through the rotted floorboards into the darkened basement below.

Hellboy pulled the child close to his breast and curled himself around the boy, doing his best to protect him from the impact. He hit hard, sending up a small atom-cloud of dust, but was completely unscathed.

They landed in the basement, not far from the disused furnace, the door of which hung open like the mouth of a hungry god. He glanced up at the hole he'd made as he regained his footing and saw the Cailleach's compound eyes peering down at him, dripping venom from its fangs just before it leapt onto him.

Hellboy instinctively turned his back to the creature, cradling his tiny charge as tightly as he dared. As the fairy's stinger plunged into his flesh, he grimaced and looked down into the upturned face of the child in his arms. The little boy's thumb was in his mouth and his eyes were so wide with terror they seemed blank. For the first time, Hellboy felt fear—not for himself, but for the tiny mortal held in the crook of his arm.

The Cailleach's sting was painful, but did not have the same paralyzing effect it would have on a human. Instead of shutting down his autonomic nerve center, it burned like someone had injected prussic acid into his spine.

"Get off my back!" he growled.

With surprising speed for his size, he reached behind himself with his right hand and grabbed the Cailleach's stinger as the creature struggled to plunge it home yet again. The Cailleach's shrill, insectile laughter quickly turned into shrieks of pain.

Hellboy spun around, using his tail to knock his opponent off its feet, then grabbed the wounded fairy's wings in his rocky grasp, crushing them as easily as he would a balsa-wood airplane. Ignoring the pain in the base of his spine, he then hurled the Cailleach into the open maw of the disused furnace.

Carefully switching his precious burden to the crook of his right arm in order to free up his left hand, Hellboy reached into one of the leather pouches on his belt and removed a small metal sphere.

"Heads up, girlfriend!" he barked, lobbing the activated thermite bomb into the furnace as the Cailleach struggled to free itself, then promptly turned his back and hunkered down tight, wrapping his tail completely around himself. There was a bright flash, followed by intense, searing heat, and a last, dreadful scream from the Cailleach Bheuh, then the stink of burning hair and roasting flesh.

A second later Hellboy opened his eyes and stood up, frowning at the small inferno that surrounded himself and his young charge. He'd forgotten about the trash that filled the basement, which had instantly caught fire. For the first time since awakening from his trance, the child in Hellboy's arms began to move, whimpering like a frightened baby animal.

"Hold on, kid," he said, trying his best to sound calm. "Hold on—I'll get us out of this—somehow."

The flames surrounding Hellboy suddenly lowered, then snuffed themselves out as abruptly as the gas ring on a range.

"Your friendly neighborhood pyrokinetic, at your service," Liz Sherman said, poking her head through the hole in the basement roof. The attractive young fire-manipulator was kneeling on the ragged edge of the hole, shaking her head in mock dismay. "What would you do without me to save your big red tail, Hellboy?"

"Roast like a chicken on a spit, I guess," Hellboy replied with a wry smile. "I was beginning to wonder when you guys would get here."

"We'd have been here sooner, but you try and get a surveillance van out of mid-town this time of day," Liz said, snorting in disgust. A look of concern crossed her face as she noticed the child clutched in his arms for the first time. "Oh, Jesus—the kid? Is he—?"

"Alive? Yeah. But he's in shock."

Liz quickly motioned for a paramedic team which was hovering behind her to move forward. Hellboy held the child over his head, handing him off to the emergency rescue workers, who quickly whisked the boy out of sight.

"You need help getting out of there, big guy?" Liz asked.

"Naw—I'll be out of here in a jiffy—there are some stairs down here that look like they lead to the street. They're padlocked—but that's not a problem."

Less than a minute and a strong shoulder later, Hellboy was standing on the sidewalk. There were several NYPD cruisers and ambulances lined up along the street, their red-and-blue emergency lights throwing garish-colored shadows in the gathering dark. The look on those well-seasoned professionals' faces as they saw the horrors that lay within was one Hellboy was all too familiar with.

"*Hellboy!*"

The Professor was standing on the curb by the BPRD's tracking van, an oversized thermos of espresso coffee in hand.

"I thought you might appreciate this," Bruttenholm said.

"You know me all too well, old man," Hellboy smiled. As he sipped the steaming, bitter brew, a paramedic emerged from the building, carrying the little girl wrapped in a shiny thermal blanket.

Despite her ordeal, the child seemed remarkably self-possessed. To Hellboy's surprise, the little girl smiled and waved at him as if he was a purple dinosaur.

"*Mr. Beast!*" she shouted excitedly. "Thank you for saving us!"

Hellboy frowned. "What did she call me?"

"She thinks you're The Beast," Liz explained matter-of-factly as she joined Hellboy and the Professor.

"*What?*"

"You know—from Beauty and the Beast. The monster that's really a handsome, heroic prince on the inside."

Hellboy grunted and returned the little girl's wave.

But he was smiling.

SCARED CROWS
RICK HAUTALA AND JIM CONNOLLY

Just after dark, the rainstorm swept across the mountains to the west and blew eastward, heading toward the cold, gray Atlantic Ocean. The small town of West Buxton, Maine, was just one of many small New England towns in its path.

It was late October and already past peak foliage season this far north. The storm's powerful winds blew sheets of cold rain that shined like silver strings in the few streetlights that lined the all-but-deserted Main Street. Fast-running water, dead leaves, and blown-down branches choked the rapidly overflowing gutters. Nearly every resident of the town, at some point or another that evening, muttered some variation of: "Good thing this ain't snow, or else we'd be buried alive."

Moving perhaps a little too fast, a battered Chevy pulled into the rutted dirt parking lot outside a bar called the Crossing, which was located on the outskirts of town, just past the railroad crossing. Water and gravel from the muddy puddles splashed against the underside of the car, which sagged noticeably to the left because of the massive weight of the driver. Dark, wet leaves, looking like bloated leeches, stuck to the mud-splattered sides of the car as it lurched to a stop in the far corner of the parking lot where the red neon light of a beer sign didn't quite reach.

There were only two other vehicles in the parking lot that night—a black, late model Ford pickup that was pitted with rust and holes, and a mud-splattered Nissan Maxima sporting New York plates.

The driver of the Chevy killed the engine but didn't get out right away. For a minute or two, he sat there behind the steering wheel, listening to the sudden gusts of wind that punched against the side of the car like powerful, invisible fists. He focused on the rain that was pouring out of the rusted gutter above the bar door. Finally, with a belly-deep grunt, he grabbed the travel cooler that rested on the seat beside him, took the key from the ignition and pocketed it, and opened the car door.

His long, tattered trench coat was soaked through the instant he stepped out into the storm. Rain ran in glistening streams down his face, making the deep red tone of his skin look like flayed meat. Taking long strides, with the travel cooler banging against his leg, he made his way to the front door of the bar and entered. A gust of wind slammed the door shut behind him, but even with the door closed, he could hear the high-pitched whistle of the wind and the splash and splatter of the rain outside.

The bartender, a man named Kyle Kelly who owned the Crossing Bar and lived in the small apartment upstairs, glanced up. His eyes widened ever so slightly when he saw his new customer, but Kyle had been a bartender pretty near his whole life, so he knew not to show too much surprise.

"'Evenin', Hellboy," he said with a quick nod.

He was about to follow this up with something on the order of *Kinda surprised to see you 'round these parts again*, but thought better of it.

"Damn good thing this ain't snow," he said as he watched Hellboy stride over to the booth at the back of the bar and sit down heavily, not bothering to remove his sodden trench coat.

There were only three other customers in the Crossing tonight. Two regulars— brothers named Jed and Tommy Farrow who did odd jobs around town whenever their welfare checks ran out—were seated at the far end of the bar, close to the jukebox, which was playing a sad-sounding song by Emmylou Harris. Also seated at the bar, closer to the door, was an attractive, dark-skinned woman. She'd already told Kyle that her name was Lorraine, even though Kyle wasn't one to pry. After ordering a beer, she'd gone on to inform him that she was on her way to North Conway to attend her sister's baby shower. Not finding any fast-food restaurants handy, she'd stopped in here for a quick bite to eat and a cold one. That "cold one" had turned into a few more beers, and by the time Hellboy arrived, Lorraine was looking just a wee-bit tipsy.

Unlike Kyle, all three patrons—if a place like the Crossing can actually honor its customers by calling them "patrons"—watched Hellboy with varying degrees of thinly veiled interest. Tommy, the younger of the Farrow brothers, couldn't help but hoot with laughter at the sight of the new customer.

"Whoo-ee," he said, slapping his brother on the back and smirking with a wide grin that made him look like even more of an idiot than he generally did. "Just when you think you've seen it all, huh, Jed?"

Jed, the older and slightly more level headed of the two brothers, simply sighed and shook his head before turning around and silently hoisting the beer he had in hand.

"How 'bout that, Big Bro?" Tommy went on, jabbing his brother's arm again, almost making him spill his beer. "The things you see when you don't have a gun, huh?"

Jed snorted and kept drinking, his Adam's apple working rapidly up and down in his thin throat as he drained his glass.

"And—Christ on a cross—was that really a freakin' *tail* I saw sticking out from under his coat?"

"Just shuddap and drink," Jed said as he slammed his empty glass down on the counter and signaled to Kyle for another one.

But Kyle, ignoring Jed for the moment, called out, "What can I get for you, Hellboy?"

Resting his left hand lightly on top of the cooler, which he had placed on the table in front of him, Hellboy glanced over at Kyle with a deepening scowl, then said softly, "How 'bout a pitcher of beer . . . and two glasses."

Lorraine's eyes were a bit unfocused as she leaned forward and whispered to Kyle, "Do you *know* him?"

Kyle glanced over at Hellboy again, then nodded slightly but said nothing before drawing a pitcher of draught. He was happy for the business. With the storm and all, it wasn't looking like tonight was exactly going to bust the bank. He grabbed a couple of clean glasses and walked over to the table without answering her.

Lorraine couldn't help herself. She spun around on her chair and stared at the man—if this was, indeed, a man—seated in the shadowy corner. She had never seen anything like him—especially his huge right hand that looked like it was made out of stone or something.

"Who the hell is he?" she whispered out of the corner of her mouth to Kyle once he was back behind the bar, drawing another glass of beer for Jed.

When Kyle didn't answer her right away, she leaned across the bar so far her ample breasts flattened against the smooth, water-stained surface.

"Does he live around here?"

Kyle ran his teeth over his lower lip, his eyes darting nervously back and forth between Lorraine and Hellboy.

"No," he finally said, his voice dropping to a whisper. "He's not from around here . . . and neither are you, so it's just as well you don't ask. 'Kay?"

"Come on," Lorraine said, snagging Kyle's shirt sleeve and giving it a quick tug.

Kyle licked his lips, and when he spoke again, his voice was so low she could barely hear him above the sound of the storm outside and the jukebox, which was now playing an old Roy Orbison song.

"We had some . . . ah, some trouble out this way 'bout a year ago, and he . . . sorta helped fix it."

"It was *exactly* a year ago tonight."

Hellboy spoke so suddenly that Lorraine couldn't help but squeal as she wheeled around to look at him.

"He's got good hearin', too," Kyle added.

Now that she had her opening, Lorraine—never one to be shy—got up from the barstool and started toward Hellboy's table. He looked like an illusion to her—a figment from some terrible nightmare made real. His red skin was slick and still gleaming from the rain. On his forehead two huge circular bumps shadowed his eyes, which glowed dull orange with what seemed like their own internal light. His jutting lower jaw kept his thin lips in a straight, unsmiling line.

Halfway to the table, Lorraine's foot caught on something, and she almost fell, but she caught herself and quickly regained her composure. Tommy, who was still intently watching all of this, let out a sharp bray of laughter that cut off quickly when his brother elbowed him in the ribs.

"Mind if I join you?" Lorraine asked.

Before he could answer, she collapsed into the seat opposite him and leaned forward on the table.

"My name's Lorraine Martin, from New York City," she said, slurring her words slightly as she held her right hand out for him to shake.

She cringed when he took her hand into his huge right hand and lightly shook it. His touch was stone cold, and she could feel the terrible power trembling in his grasp. She knew he could easily crush her hand to a pulp without even thinking, but he shook her hand gently and then let it drop.

"I'm Hellboy," he said, his voice making a deep rumble that reminded her of distant thunder.

"Are you gonna drink that beer," Lorraine asked, "or did you bring your own in that cooler?"

"I'm waiting for someone," Hellboy said simply.

There was a finality in his voice that told her not to pursue it any further, but Lorraine had had enough to drink so she didn't care. She was burning with curiosity to find out who this guy was and what he was doing here.

"A friend of yours?" she asked.

"Sort of. Someone I work with," Hellboy replied with a quick nod.

He looked past her. When Lorraine turned to see what he was staring at, she noticed the small clock above the array of liquor bottles behind the bar.

It was a quarter to eight.

"Well, until this friend of yours shows up, what say you buy me a drink?" Lorraine said.

When she leaned forward and rested her hand lightly on his arm, she couldn't help but notice that Hellboy turned his body ever so slightly, as though shielding the travel cooler from her.

"What've you got in there that's so important?" she asked, but he didn't answer her. He simply stared at her with a glowering scowl that made it all too clear that he wasn't going to talk about it.

"So . . . are you gonna buy me a drink or not?" Lorraine asked.

Hellboy looked over at Kyle and said, "Get her a glass of whatever she's drinking."

Kyle nodded and, without a word, drew a beer and walked over to the table. His face was expressionless as he placed the glass down in front of Lorraine.

"I have to tell you one thing," Lorraine said once Kyle had retreated back behind the bar. "I don't like drinking alone."

She clinked her glass against the untouched pitcher in front of Hellboy. "What say you join me?"

When she reached across the table for the pitcher, making as if to pour him a beer, Hellboy snatched it from her and poured into one of the glasses. Holding it out to her, he said, "Here's looking at you." With that, he tipped his head back and drained the glass in several huge gulps.

Lorraine took a long, slow sip from her beer, all the while watching him in amazement over the rim of her glass.

Once the glass was empty, Hellboy wiped his mouth with the back of his hand and placed the glass on the table. After filling it again from the pitcher, he sat back and drained it a second time.

"Well, you certainly don't mess around, do you?" Lorraine asked, unable to conceal her amazement.

"I probably should have something to eat first," Hellboy said. "I haven't eaten all day."

"So tell me," Lorraine said after a moment of silence. "Who're you meeting? I can tell, just by looking at you, that you're an interesting guy who must do a lot of interesting stuff."

"I already told you," Hellboy said, his scowl deepening. "It's someone I work with."

"Well then, will you tell me what kind of work you do?"

"It's . . . kind of complicated," Hellboy said with a dark scowl.

"Does it have anything to do with what you've got in that cooler? C'mon. Tell me. Whatddaya have in there?"

"Cold stuff," Hellboy replied, and for a brief instant, the glow in his eyes seemed to intensify.

Lorraine nodded and sat in silence for another moment. Then she said, "Does this have anything to do with what happened a year ago tonight?"

Hellboy's scowl deepened. The two beers seemed to have gone straight to his head, and he shook it to clear it, then looked at Lorraine and nodded.

"Matter of fact, it does," he said. "I'm waiting to meet up with my friend. A guy called 'The Finn.' Our friend, Red Shirt, died a year ago tonight. We're meeting here to raise a glass to his memory."

"Or a pitcher," Lorraine said with a slight laugh.

"Yeah. Maybe a pitcher," Hellboy said as he grasped the near-empty pitcher and raised it above his head to let Kyle know that he wanted a refill.

While they waited for the fresh pitcher to arrive, Hellboy refilled his own and Lorraine's glasses. Lorraine settled back in her seat and took a deep breath, taking it all in. One thing she couldn't help but notice was the sour stench that emanated from either whatever Hellboy had in the cooler, or else from Hellboy himself. Maybe he didn't smell so good after being out in the rain, she thought.

Kyle arrived with the full pitcher, placed it on the table in front of Hellboy, and walked away. He had caught only a few snatches of their conversation but, knowing what he knew about the events that had transpired this time last year, he didn't want to know any more.

"So," Lorraine finally said, unable to hide her interest, "are you gonna tell me how your friend Red Shirt died? Or am I gonna have to get you drunk first, and pry it out of you?"

Hellboy shook his head and then belched loudly. This got a reaction from the Farrow brothers, both of whom turned in their seats and glared over at the table.

Once again, it was Tommy who spoke.

"Hey, you wanna keep it down over there?" he shouted. "This isn't a fucking barn, you know."

Lorraine saw the orange glow in Hellboy's eyes flare up as he stared back at the two brothers.

"You might want to watch your language with a lady present," Hellboy said. Then he sucked in a deep breath and belched again, louder.

"Lady?" Tommy said, gawking back and forth like a chicken, looking for grain. Then he crossed his arms and puffed out his chest. "I don't see no *lady* here. All's I see is a drunk slut Flatlander and some kinda freak that looks like he escaped from the circus."

Sensing trouble, Kyle quickly stepped over to Tommy and got his attention.

"Chill out," he said under his breath, "or I'll have to ask you to leave. Trust me. You don't want to mess with him."

After catching the scathing look from his older brother, Tommy turned back and continued drinking in silence.

"Ahh, forget about them," Lorraine said with a dismissive flick of her hand. "They're just a couple of dumb-shit rednecks. Tell me about your friend Red Shirt. How'd he die?"

Covering his mouth with his huge right fist, Hellboy belched again, softly this time, as he settled back in the seat. The cushion groaned beneath his weight.

"It's kind of complicated," he said.

When he spoke, Lorraine noticed a faraway look in his eye. She glanced at the rain washing down the window beside them and said softly, "I ain't going anyplace in a hurry."

"Well," Hellboy said, "The Finn will be here pretty soon, but I guess I can tell you about it. You see, about a year and a half ago, this town had a problem with a serial killer, a man named Moses McCrory. He'd killed something like nine women—some of 'em young girls, really, before the cops finally ran him down."

"So he's in jail?"

One corner of Hellboy's mouth twitched. "No," he said. "The police shot and killed him." He paused to take a single gulp of beer. "That's when the real trouble started."

Lorraine squinted at him and shook her head. It crossed her mind that this whole episode was beyond strange. Here she was, sitting in a bar in a town she'd never been to and never intended to visit again, talking about a serial killer with a big red guy with a stone fist and bumps that looked like sawed-off horns on his forehead. For all she knew, *he* could be the dangerous killer, and he was setting her up as his next victim. But she couldn't deny that she was fascinated. She had to find out more.

"I don't get it," she said. "If they killed him, then that should have ended it unless—Oh, wait a second. I get it. He wasn't the real killer, right?"

"Oh, he was the real killer all right. He strangled his victims with a piece of piano wire that pretty much took their heads off. But shortly after they killed him, more people started dying, only this time in much more gruesome ways."

"I know what it was," Lorraine said, snapping her fingers and jumping excitedly in her seat. "I saw a show about this once on A&E. They had what they call a 'copycat' killer, right? Someone who started imitating the first killer."

Hellboy shook his head, then reached for the pitcher of beer and refilled his glass. "Not exactly. You see, I only get called into things when they get *really* weird."

"And this got really weird?" Lorraine said. Feeling suddenly uncomfortable, she shifted in her seat and glanced over at Kyle, slightly reassured by his presence.

Hellboy nodded and then, with a what-the-hell shrug, finished off his beer.

"Once the killings started again, the local police couldn't handle it," he said, "so they called in the State CID"

"CID?"

"The Criminal Investigative Division. They pieced together a few things, like how the victims were killed, and that the killings only happened on rainy nights, but the staties couldn't handle it, either. These recent killings were *really* bad."

"How so?"

"The victims were all beheaded. That's how they died. Only this time, the killer strangled them with a length of barbed wire, and he pulled it so tight their heads came right off."

"Oh my God," Lorraine said, shuddering and hugging herself as a slow chill ran through her. She suddenly felt alone and very vulnerable.

"Yeah," Hellboy said, "and then he'd stuff their open necks with straw. Also, all of the victims were missing body parts . . . arms, legs, internal organs . . . different parts from each victim. That's when they called me, and I brought along my friends, The Finn and Red Shirt."

"Well then," Lorraine said, taking a deep breath and slumping back in her seat. For a while, she'd forgotten all about her glass of beer but now her throat was parched, and she picked it up and took a quick sip. "If you're waiting for The Finn, like you said, then it must've been Red Shirt who died, right?"

"Kind of a no-brainer," Hellboy said. "Yeah. It was Red Shirt who died."

"Was he an Indian? His name sounds like it's Indian."

Hellboy sniffed with laughter as he raised the pitcher above his head, signaling for Kyle that he was ready for a refill.

"You know, you're a regular Sherlock Holmes," Hellboy said. "Yeah, Red Shirt was a Native American and, as it turned out, I needed him to help me figure out what had happened to Moses."

"Wait a second," Lorraine said. "I thought you said Moses was shot and killed by the police."

"He was," Hellboy said, barely acknowledging Kyle when he came over to the table and replaced the empty pitcher with a full one. "It took us a while to piece it all together, but you see, the cops found Moses in a corn field when they tracked him down. When they shot and killed him, he was right beside an old scarecrow the farmer had left in the field."

Hellboy paused, and in that brief moment of silence, he eyed the full pitcher of beer. His head was spinning from what he had already had to drink, but he refilled his glass again from the pitcher and took a few gulps. He was just replacing his half-empty glass on the table when Tommy spoke up.

"Christ, you see that, Jed? He drinks like a fuckin' animal!"

Hellboy shifted forward in his seat, as if to get up, but before he did, Kyle stepped over to the two Farrow brothers.

"I'm gonna have to ask you fellas to leave," he said in a low, controlled voice. "I don't want no trouble here tonight."

"I ain't causin' any trouble," Tommy said, his voice winding up higher. "He's the one who's causin' trouble. Why do you even serve a goddamned freak like that?"

"All right. That's it," Kyle said, scooping away Tommy's and Jed's glasses and pointing at the door. "You fellas will be welcome here tomorrow night provided you learn yourselves some manners 'tween now and then."

"What the fuck?" Jed said. "I didn't do nothin'. I was just sittin' here drinkin' and mindin' my own business."

"Go on! Get out!" Kyle said, his voice stern and cold. "The both of yah get home before you get into more trouble that you can handle."

"I can handle anything that freak's got to dish out," Tommy said, his body stiffening as he cast a challenging glance at Hellboy. But Jed prodded his brother to silence with a sharp jab to the ribs.

Lorraine couldn't help but smile as she watched the two rednecks make their way to the door, looking like a couple of schoolboys who had been scolded.

"Have a nice night," she called out as Jed swung the door open, and both of them stepped out into the storm.

"Pardon me a minute," Hellboy said as he shifted out of the booth and stood up. "I have some business to attend to. I'll be right back."

Lorraine was amazed by the size of him when he stood up, but she tried not to let it show. Smiling, she said, "Well, considering how much beer you've put away, it's no wonder."

She didn't bother to turn and watch him walk away. Instead, her eyes shifted to the cooler he'd left behind on the table. She was dying to know what was inside it. This Hellboy, whoever he was, sure was a strange one, so whatever was in that cooler was probably something just as strange as him.

Lorraine chuckled to herself when she thought how surprised and disappointed she'd be if she opened up the cooler and found a picnic lunch with sandwich, soda, and chips.

But—no. Hellboy had said he hadn't eaten all day, so it probably wasn't food in there.

So what could it be?

Leaning across the table, Lorraine sniffed the air. The thick, rotting aroma still lingered and almost made her gag.

Was there a fish in there? she wondered. Maybe Hellboy had been up north fishing, and this was his prized catch.

After a quick glance behind her to make sure Hellboy wasn't on his way back from the rest room yet, she reached out for the cooler with one hand. She noticed that her hand was trembling as she touched the cool, still-damp plastic. The barroom seemed suddenly dense with quiet anticipation as she ran her fingers down to the latch and slowly began to apply pressure to release it.

"I wouldn't do that if I was you."

The voice, speaking so suddenly behind her, made her jump. She jerked back and dropped both hands below the table as she spun around and saw Kyle, watching her from behind the bar.

"Trust me. Hellboy's not the kind of guy you want to mess around with," Kyle added.

As if on cue, the front door of the bar opened, and Hellboy strode back inside. His trench coat was drenched through, and his muddy hooves made loud, wet sounds as he walked back over to the table.

"Why'd you go outside? I thought you had to go to the bathroom?" Lorraine asked; her heart fluttering in her chest.

"Just had to check on something," Hellboy said simply as he wiped the water from his face. He sat down and took a healthy swallow of beer. He indicated Lorraine's all-but-forgotten glass of beer and added, "Come on. Drink up."

Lorraine's throat was so constricted she could barely swallow as she took a tiny sip of her beer. It had just about gone flat, but she didn't care. After taking a moment to collect herself, she said, "So you were saying . . . "

"Where was I?" Hellboy said.

"You were telling me how, when they killed Moses McCrory, he was in a corn field, next to a scarecrow."

"Yeah—right," Hellboy said. "Well, you see, in some primitive beliefs, it's birds—usually crows, but sometimes other birds—that usher the spirit of the recently deceased into the afterlife. If that's true, then—"

Lorraine interrupted him with a snap of her fingers.

"—Then Moses' spirit wouldn't have been taken because the scarecrow would have scared away the crows."

Hellboy nodded slowly. "You got it. It took me a bit longer to piece it all together, but you have to remember, we were in the middle of it."

"So where did Moses' spirit go?" Lorraine asked, feeling a terrible chill creep up her back.

"Into the scarecrow, of course," Hellboy said simply.

Before he could say more, and before Lorraine could ask him to explain that, the bar door suddenly flung open so hard it slammed against the wall with a resounding bang. Lorraine's first thought was that the Farrow brothers had returned, maybe with guns or knives to settle their score with Hellboy. She turned around quickly, surprised to see a tall, thin man framed by the doorway.

He was hatless, and the rain had plastered his thinning, blond hair in dark squiggles against his skull. His face was pale, almost bone white. The dim light in the barroom glanced off his high forehead and the angular planes of his cheekbones, but the rest of his face—especially his eyes and mouth—seemed to be in shadow, no matter how the lighting shifted as he looked around. Then he started over to the table where Lorraine and Hellboy sat. Without saying a word, he hooked a chair with his foot, swung it around, and sat down with his elbows resting against the back of the chair.

"I wasn't sure I had the right place," the man said in a low, gruff voice, "until I saw those two guys stretched out unconscious in the parking lot."

"What—?" Lorraine said, and then cut herself off when she realized what Hellboy had done.

Hellboy's face remained expressionless as he leaned forward and said, "Lorraine, I'd like you to meet The Finn. Finn . . . This is Lorraine."

"Pleased to meet you," The Finn said, but Lorraine couldn't be sure if he was sincere or not because the light from the bar was behind him, and she still couldn't see his face clearly as they briefly shook hands.

"I was just telling Lorraine, here, about what happened last year," Hellboy said.

The Finn made a soft chuffing sound that might have passed for a laugh before saying, "Christ, Hellboy, look at you. You're drunk on your ass."

Hellboy slouched back in his seat and seemed for a moment unable to focus his eyes as he shook his head in adamant denial and said, "No. No. I just had a little something to drink with Lorraine while I was waiting for you to show."

The Finn leaned forward and ran his hands down the sides of his face.

"What kind of lies has he been telling you?" he asked Lorraine, and she caught the trace of a smile on his thin lips.

"Oh, he'd just gotten to the part where Moses McCrory was shot and killed . . . when he was close to the scarecrow," Lorraine said, "and that the murders kept happening after he was dead, only they were worse."

"I see," The Finn said, "and did he tell you about the straw?"

"The straw?" Lorraine asked, looking quizzically at Hellboy.

"Right," The Finn said. "Once the killings started again, there was always straw around the victims . . . straw and rope fiber. It was that, and the fact that the killings only happened on rainy nights, that I was able to piece it all together."

"*You?*" Hellboy said with a dry sniff of laughter. "You didn't put *anything* together. It was me and Red Shirt who figured out about the pond."

"Wait a minute, you two," Lorraine said. "You're confusing me. What's this about a pond?"

"Okay, I'll give credit where credit's due," Hellboy said, his voice slurring noticeably now. "It was Red Shirt who figured it out. I told you that this new round of killings only happened on rainy nights, right?"

Lorraine nodded. She was still more than a little tipsy herself, and she was having a bit of trouble following the conversation now.

"Rainy nights," Hellboy repeated, nodding to himself. "Only on rainy nights. There had been a killing two nights before, but the weather had cleared, so that afternoon, the three of us went out to the corn field where Moses had been killed. We hadn't put it all together yet, and one reason was because the scarecrow we'd seen in the police crime scene photos was still standing there. But when we got there, I noticed that the scarecrow wasn't the same one from the photos they'd showed us at the police station. So I thought we'd better investigate."

"*Investigate?*" The Finn said, barking with laughter. "What the hell are you talking about, investigate? You took that cannon of yours, and you blasted the thing to pieces!"

Hellboy looked at Lorraine with a sheepish shrug. "Maybe sometimes I act before I think things all the way through," he said. "But that doesn't really matter because of what we found. See, the scarecrow wasn't stuffed with straw, the way scarecrows are supposed to be. It was packed full of body parts."

"Body parts?" Lorraine said, wincing as her stomach did a sour little flip.

"Yeah," said Hellboy. "Moses was collecting body parts from his victims and storing them inside the scarecrow."

"But I thought you said *he* was the scarecrow, that his soul had entered it the night he was killed."

"It did. He was," Hellboy replied, shaking his head as though desperate to clear it so she'd understand him. "But he had started making a new one. See, it hadn't snowed yet that year, but there had been a frost the night before. It was getting late when we got out to the cornfield. The corn was dead, but the farmer hadn't cut it back yet, so the stalks were more than head-high. They blocked our view, but I—"

Hellboy glanced quickly over at The Finn.

"I mean, *Red Shirt* noticed footprints leading down to the pond."

"Actually," The Finn said, "the footprints led up from the pond and then back down to it. Hellboy and I thought someone—Moses in the shape of the scarecrow, maybe, had walked down to the pond, for some reason, before leaving."

"But it was Red Shirt—" Hellboy said emphatically as he nailed The Finn with a hard look. "See?" he muttered. "I can give credit where credit's due. It was Red Shirt who read the tracks correctly and determined that the prints coming out of the pond were the oldest, and that the ones going back into it were the freshest."

"I—I still don't get it," Lorraine said, shaking her head.

"Okay, think of it this way," Hellboy said, slurring his words. "If you were a scarecrow, what would be your biggest fear?"

Lorraine considered the question for a moment, then said, "Probably falling apart . . . unless it was that I didn't have a brain."

"Very funny, Dorothy, but—no. That's not the problem," Hellboy said impatiently. "You can always stuff more straw into yourself if you're falling apart. Think about what would be your most dangerous enemy. What can destroy you if you're made of straw?"

"Well . . . fire, of course."

"Bingo," Hellboy said, clapping his hands together. Leaning back in his seat, he folded his arms across his chest and nodded with satisfaction. "And, if you were made of straw, you wouldn't need to breathe, either. Would you?"

Lorraine shrugged, still more than a little perplexed. The more Hellboy talked, the less sense he seemed to be making.

"No," she said softly. "I guess you wouldn't need to breathe."

"So if you didn't need to breathe, and you didn't want to burn, where's the safest place in the world to be when you weren't out killing people?"

"In the pond, I guess," Lorraine said.

"Absolutely," Hellboy said.

"And the safest time to be out and about would be on rainy nights," The Finn added in a measured, controlled voice as Hellboy nodded solemnly.

Lorraine thought Hellboy looked totally plastered and was about to pass out. His voice dragged terribly when he spoke.

"So we were down there by the pond," he said, "The Finn, Red Shirt, and me. It was getting dark, and it looked like there might be a rainstorm brewing in the west."

Lorraine shivered as she cast a wary glance at rainwater streaming down the window beside her.

"Look," said Hellboy, "I gotta take a leak." He heaved himself up and stood beside the table for a moment, weaving unsteadily, trying to keep his balance. "You tell her the rest of it."

With that, he started toward the restroom, taking short, halting steps.

"Okay," The Finn said, hunkering down and leaning forward, his arms hooked over the chair back. "You have to try to picture it. We're out there in the middle of this cornfield. It's getting on toward night. There's a steady wind rustling through the dead leaves of the corn, but the first thing I notice, the creepiest thing about the whole thing is, there's no wildlife around."

"What do you mean?" Lorraine said as a strong shiver ran like teasing fingers up her back.

"I mean nothing. No birds singing. No late-season crickets buzzing. No dogs barking. *Nothing!* Total silence except for the wind, blowing through the dried corn. Red Shirt tells us he's gonna follow the tracks around the pond. It wasn't very big."

"What about the farmer . . . the person who owned the field?" Lorraine asked.

The Finn lowered his eyes and shook his head grimly. "He was already dead. Him and his whole family. They were the first of Moses' new victims, once he'd come back as the scarecrow. I went back to the car to get some things—some flashlights, guns, and a cigarette lighter and some road flares."

"Road flares?"

"We thought of making some torches, using the corn stalks, but they were too damp and brittle. I figured road flares would burn better, even if it started to rain."

"Hey, *I* was the one who suggested that road flares would work," Hellboy said, coming up to the table so suddenly even The Finn jumped when he spoke. "If you're gonna tell the story, tell it the way it really happened."

"Yeah, okay. It was your idea," The Finn said with a half-smile on his thin lips. "Are you going to let me finish the story or not?"

"No, I'll take it from here," Hellboy said as he sat back down in the booth. Before going on with the story, though, he took the second, untouched glass, filled it with beer, and slid it over to The Finn. Then he refilled his own glass and slammed the empty pitcher onto the table.

"Glad you made some room for that," The Finn said.

Hellboy nodded. "So where were we?"

"Down by the pond," Lorraine said. "The Finn had just gone back to get guns and road flares."

"Oh, yeah," Hellboy said, and for a moment, his eyes fluttered as he leaned back in his seat. "I went down to the water, where the tracks led, and was leaning over it, trying to see to the bottom. I heard someone coming up behind me, but I figured it was The Finn, returning with the equipment, so I didn't look until it was too late."

"But it was Moses, right?" Lorraine said, anticipating the story.

Hellboy nodded. "Yup," he said, the word sounding more like a burp than a word. "And he's got this garrote he's made with barbed wire that he wraps around my neck and starts pulling. Fortunately, I had just enough of a warning, and as I turned around, I got my right hand up between my throat and the wire."

"Your *right* hand," Lorraine said, glancing at the huge stone hand resting on the table, next to the cooler.

Hellboy nodded. "Yeah, 'n' lucky for me, too, 'cause once he started twisting that garrote tighter, I'd have been a goner if I hadn't reacted so fast."

"The problem was," The Finn said, "with his hand up so close to his face, ol' Hellboy here lost his balance and fell headfirst into the pond."

"I didn't fall. I slipped," Hellboy said, glaring at The Finn. Lorraine saw the dull orange of his eyes intensify. "The edge of the pond was all muddy, and I slipped and fell."

"Either way, you ended up headfirst in the water," The Finn said. "And with that big stone hand of yours weighing down, you were helpless as a baby."

"How do you know?" Hellboy said, leaning forward and pounding the table with his stone fist. The impact made the pitcher, beer glasses, and cooler all jump. "You weren't even there!"

"That's just when I returned," The Finn said softly, looking directly at Lorraine and ignoring Hellboy. "I saw him hit the water, and then he—the scarecrow, that is—saw Red Shirt coming back, and he attacked him. I shot at Moses twice with the shotgun, but if I hit him at all, it didn't have any effect. He was charging at Red Shirt, but I knew I had to react quickly and help Hellboy before he drowned."

"I wasn't all *that* helpless," Hellboy said.

"What do you mean?" The Finn shouted. "You were stuck headfirst in the mud at the bottom of the pond, and you were drowning!"

Hellboy looked intently at Lorraine, his eyes flaring as he said, "I *wasn't* all that helpless. Honest. I'd already started to loosen the wire."

The Finn sniffed derisively. "Sure. Whatever. The way I remember it, though, I had a choice to make in a split second. I could either light a flare and help Red Shirt fight the scarecrow, or I could drop everything and keep Hellboy from drowning."

"I *wasn't* drowning," Hellboy said, slurring the words horribly and wavering in his seat.

"If you say so," The Finn said. "Anyway, it doesn't matter, because I reacted without thinking and dove into the water and got him up to the surface before he died." He nailed Hellboy with an angry stare. "I saved your goddamned life, and believe me, it wasn't easy. The least you could do is show a little gratitude."

"I didn't need your help," Hellboy said. "I was just about free of the wire by the time you got me."

The Finn scowled angrily. "Well, given the choice to do it over again, I'd sure as hell try to help Red Shirt instead, believe me."

Hellboy shook his head, letting his gaze go unfocused for a moment. "Look," he said, "either way, I got out, but it was already too late to help Red Shirt. Moses—the scarecrow—had another piece of barbed wire with him because he strangled Red Shirt so hard, his head came off. I saw that happen just as I broke the surface with The Finn clinging to me so he wouldn't drown."

The Finn leaned back and shook his head with disgust. "That's not exactly how I remember it, but go on. Get to the end of the story."

"Well, like I said, it was already too late to save Red Shirt. He was dead, and Moses had taken off, running across the field toward the woods. He was moving pretty fast, and I wasn't sure I could catch him, so I took one of the flares The Finn had brought and lit it. Then I tied it to the wire Moses had tried to strangle me with and, swinging it around my head like one of them South American bolos, I chased after Moses until I was close enough to throw it."

"That was quick thinking," Lorraine said, hoping by her praise to assuage any hurt feelings Hellboy might have.

"Yeah, and I guess I got lucky, too," Hellboy said. "'cause the bolo caught him around the neck, and after it spun around a few times, the flare landed on his back, right where he couldn't reach it."

"It was an amazing sight," The Finn added, smiling now and nodding with satisfaction.

"So Moses is running across the corn field, stumbling as flames spread across his back," Hellboy said. He leaned forward in his seat, fully enjoying the climax of his story. "There's pieces of burning straw and smoke streaming out behind him. He looked like a comet, streaking across that field. But he never made the woods."

"You mean he burned up?" Lorraine asked.

Hellboy nodded solemnly. "All the straw did, yeah, but before it was all gone, something else happened. It wasn't just fire and smoke that was coming out of him. As he was running, I—we saw this thick, black cloud shoot out of his body and up into the sky. It was his spirit—his soul, departing."

Lorraine gulped audibly and looked back and forth between Hellboy and The Finn.

"You both saw it?" she asked, her voice hushed with awe.

"Well, we saw . . . something," The Finn said. "I'm not exactly sure what it was."

"It was his soul," Hellboy said emphatically. "It was getting dark, and I'll hold open the possibility that it could have been an illusion, but I'm sure I saw something—a dark, almost human-shaped thing streak out of the scarecrow as its body was consumed with flames. And then, as soon as the scarecrow's body was gone, a huge flock of crows cawing real loud flew out of the trees, like they'd been waiting there. They swooped over . . . whatever it was, and carried it away."

"My God," Lorraine whispered, covering her mouth with both hands and staring at Hellboy with wide eyes.

For a moment or two, everyone at the table was silent. Finally, Lorraine cleared her throat and said, "But there was nothing you could do . . . for Red Shirt, I mean. He really was dead."

"Yes, damnit!" Hellboy said.

When he clenched his fist and pounded the table in anger, his hand grazed the cooler and knocked it over. The impact snapped the latch, and it opened up, spilling its contents onto the table. Lorraine let out a piercing scream when she saw a large, wrinkled object that looked like a gigantic dried prune until she realized that she was looking at a face. The lips were dried and cracked, pulled back into a terrible grimace that exposed the top row of yellowed, rotting teeth. The nose had caved in, leaving a dark V-shaped divot, and the eyes were closed and sunken in, the lids looking like thin layers of moldy onionskin.

Lorraine pushed herself violently away from the table and tried to stand up, but her legs felt unstrung and nowhere near strong enough to support her. She sagged back in her chair, gasping for breath, but she was afraid to breathe the sour, sickening smell that exuded from the severed head.

"Jesus! . . . Is that him . . . ? Is that Red Shirt . . . ?" she managed to say between gasps for breath. Her stomach clenched furiously, and a thick, sour taste flooded the back of her throat.

"Oh, no . . . no," Hellboy said, scrambling awkwardly to get the severed head back into the cooler and close it. "That's something else entirely."

"Jesus God!" Lorraine said. "It . . . that didn't even look human."

"Oh, it was," Hellboy said as he placed the closed travel cooler on the seat beside him and patted it gently. "About two thousand years ago, anyway."

"Well, then," Lorraine said, struggling to regain her composure now that the terrible object was out of sight. "It's getting way late. I . . . my sister must be wondering where I am. I'd best be getting along."

She got up shakily from the table. Her first and strongest impulse was to turn and run out of there, but she stood there for a moment, making sure her legs weren't going to give out on her when she started walking.

"Hey, wait a minute," Hellboy said. "Where you going?"

He was looking at her, sort of, but his gaze was shifting and unfocused.

"Now that The Finn's here, and you know the whole story, aren't you going to toast to Red Shirt's memory with us?" he asked.

Lorraine licked her lips, all too aware of the sour churning deep down in her stomach. She didn't know if she wanted to run away or pass out or what, but now that the head was, mercifully, out of sight, she didn't feel quite so bad.

Finally, she shrugged and said, "Ahh . . . oh, sure. What the hell?" and slid back into her seat.

For the first time that evening, Hellboy smiled as he raised the empty pitcher above his head to signal Kyle that they were ready for another round. Outside, the cold, autumn rain lashed against the window as the late October storm blew toward the distant Maine coast.

WHERE THEIR FIRE IS NOT QUENCHED

CHET WILLIAMSON

shes lay like a comforter of gray down over the hard ground. Through their soft surface timbers rose, charred black, standing like trees swept by destroying fire. Hellboy watched as one of the standing timbers swayed, held, swayed again, and with a cracking sound no louder than that of a twig being trod upon, broke near its base and fell, softly, gently, into the thick ashes, which sent up a gray cloud, incense to welcome the new offering.

The beams of the rising sun split the clouds on the eastern horizon into wispy tendrils, and tinted golden the flakes of ash that hung and sparkled in the cool morning air. Hellboy walked slowly around the ruins of piety, recognizing shapes that pushed randomly out of the ashy coverlet: the broken spines of long pews, a blackened, square hulk that might have been an organ, and less identifiable shapes, all reduced to carbon.

In the middle of the destruction was a cross that, Hellboy theorized, had plummeted from the peak of the steeple when that topmost portion of the edifice had tumbled down into the flames that had dissolved its base. Flakes of gold still adhered to the metal surface, but most had been burned away, revealing gray steel beneath. The cross had landed upside-down, and its head had dug deeply into the rubble, so that the crossbeam was flush with the ashes. It was Saint Peter, wasn't it, Hellboy thought, who had been crucified upside-down.

He got back into his car and finished his journey, driving into the town of Linden, North Carolina, thirty miles from the ashes of what had once been a Golgotha Tabernacle of Our Lord. There were a total of fifteen Golgotha Tabernacles in North and South Carolina, and it was the founder of this small but growing denomination that Hellboy was on his way to visit. He had no doubt that the call would be unpleasant, even though his way had been made straight by the Bureau. He also doubted that Donald Withers, Golgotha Tabernacle's bishop, would feel a widow's mite's worth of compassion for anyone from an organization with the word "paranormal" in it.

Hellboy was hardly relieved to be proven right. When he arrived at the large but seedy southern gothic mansion that housed the offices of Golgotha Tabernacles, the secretary, a thin, middle-aged woman sitting behind a large wooden desk in the foyer, immediately fell to her knees, buried her face in her hands, and started praying feverishly and nearly incomprehensibly, though Hellboy was able to make out, "fires of Hell," and " . . . from the demons," before they were joined by the bishop.

Donald Withers was as devoid of meat upon his bones as his secretary, and when he saw Hellboy, his eyebrows arched in alarm. Hellboy tried to smile, but felt as though he were looking into the hollows of a skull. "I didn't mean to startle her," he told Withers in a voice as soft as he could produce. "I'm from the Bureau for—"

"Yes," said Withers in a soft drawl, "I know where you're from, and I know who you are—and *what* you are. I know that you are the son of Satan."

"Through no fault of my own," Hellboy said gently. "We can't help who our parents are. I do everything I can to *fight* evil, not abet it. I believe the Bureau sent you my dossier?"

"They did," Withers said. His secretary was on her feet now, but she would not look at Hellboy. "And it's only because of that, that I'm talking to you at all. Come on in." Withers turned and went through the door, and Hellboy followed, feeling larger and far redder than he had in a long time.

There was another man inside Withers's large office, and Hellboy scarcely had time to take in the holy ambience of the room, so seething was the hatred that came washing over him from the man in the chair. The man was even thinner than Withers (Hellboy wondered if fervent religion might be an undiscovered fat burner), and his knuckles gripped the arms of his chair so tightly that his hands appeared skeletal. "Hellspawn," the man murmured.

"Hell*boy*," Hellboy corrected. "And you are?"

"This is Pastor Isaac Chambers," Withers answered for the man. "He's the preacher in two of our churches. The church that just burned down was one of his."

"*Is* one of mine, you mean," Chambers said. "We'll rebuild, though the fires of hell itself burn us down time and time again." Hellboy considered asking if this had happened to Chambers' church before, then decided the man was simply offering a rhetorical flourish.

"You think that's what it was?" asked Hellboy. "The fires of hell?"

"We don't know what it was," Withers replied. He remained standing, and Hellboy suspected it was because he didn't want to have to ask Hellboy to sit in one of his chairs. Chambers was not as polite.

"Let me tell you what little I know," said Hellboy, "and you can correct me if I'm wrong: There have been a number of church burnings in the area served by your Golgotha Tabernacles. Four of those were African-American churches, and it was obvious that arson was the cause, since gasoline residue was found. But the most recent burnings—of two of *your* churches—have no simple explanation. The fires seem to have no central source, and there's no residue of gasoline or any other incendiaries. I believe a witness who was driving by your church, Pastor Chambers, claimed that—"

"Yes, I know," Chambers said impatiently. "He said the whole thing just went up like *that!*" The finger snap was as loud as a firecracker. "But you can't believe those people! They'd tell you it was the hand of God hisself come down and smote us just because of what we preach!"

"And that is?" asked Hellboy.

"Purity." Withers answered for Chambers again. "It might not be 'politically correct,' but it's biblically grounded."

"By purity, you mean racial purity?"

"Of course. We have nothing against the other races—after all, we're all the children of God—but we were not intended to mix and intermingle. That's a law of nature as well as a law of God."

Hellboy bit back what he wanted to say, and tried to smile. "So do you suspect anyone of these burnings?"

"Of course we do," Chambers said, his hands still clinging to the arms of his chair like two white spiders. "It's technology, that's all—nothing 'paranormal.' It's the government!" The word came out *gumment.* "They're the only ones got the know-how to burn down a church and not leave any clues as to how they done it!"

"Why would the government want to burn down churches?" Hellboy asked, ready for the next round of paranoia.

"'Cause they think we burnin' down the *colored* churches, whatta you think?"

"And are you?"

Withers stiffened, and took command of the conversation. "Surely not. We don't preach violence in the Golgotha Tabernacles, Mr. . . . uh, sir. Now I'm afraid that I'm going to have to ask you to leave. I agreed to see you only in the hopes that you might have some ideas as to who's been burning our churches, but you don't know any more than we do—less, even."

"That could change if I had your cooperation," Hellboy said.

"Fat chance!" Chambers got to his feet at last. "You're lucky we don't tie you to a tree and burn *you*, Hellspawn! Send you back to the devil, your daddy!"

"I've renounced the devil and his ways," Hellboy said calmly. "The material you received from the Bureau told you that."

"Ha! 'Can the Ethiopian change his skin, or the leopard his spots?' Jeremiah 13:23!"

Hellboy shrugged and walked to the door. "'I'll be seeing you.' Sammy Fain, music, Irving Kahal, lyrics." He walked out.

It was a stupid gesture, he thought. He should have tried to get more out of them. But maybe there wasn't anything more to get. He gave a diabolical grin to the secretary as he walked by her. If she was going to have nightmares about him, might as well make them worth having.

Linden's chief of police eyed him as strangely as most people did, but at least he didn't start quoting scripture. What he did do was tell Hellboy that these fancy government (again, *gumment*) bureaus didn't mean a damn thing to him, and you'd have to be from the FBI or state police to get any cooperation. "And I hope you don't mind my adding, son," said the chief as he showed Hellboy the door, "that you'd get along a lot easier around here if you didn't dress up like some goddamn wrestler, or whoever you're supposed to be."

Well, Hellboy thought as he climbed back into his car, that took care of both church and state. The only other lead he had was the witness who had supposedly seen Pastor Chambers's church burst into flame. The man's name was Nathaniel Watson, and Hellboy found his house easily enough. It was located on the main road three miles from the burned church, and when he pulled into the dirt drive, he saw a man sitting on the crude porch of a one-story house badly in need of paint.

The man looked up as Hellboy got out of the car. Watson straightened his shoulders, and his eyes widened for a moment, but then he set his jaw and watched, unmoving, as Hellboy came toward him. "Who *you* s'posed to be?" he asked in a surprisingly smooth and mellifluous voice. "You come for my soul, I hate to disappoint you, but you had it a long time ago."

Hellboy held his hands out in front of him in a gesture of peace. "I haven't come for anybody's soul. I've just come to ask you a few questions, if you don't mind."

"You sellin' *in*surance? You look like you'd be one helluva *in*surance salesman." The man's dark mouth split in a little grin, and Hellboy couldn't help but chuckle.

He explained who he was, and the man shrugged. "Seen enough devils dressed up like angels 'round here—might as well see a good guy dressed up like a devil. What can I do for ya?"

"I'd like to know exactly what it was you saw that night the Golgotha Tabernacle burned down."

"Already tol' the police. Whole thing jes' went ka-*voom*, right all at once."

"An explosion?"

"Nope. Didn't say ka-*boom*, said ka-*voom*. Wasn't no sound of an explosion, just fire. Filled up the whole place smack bang, see it in all the windows at the same time. One second it was dark, the next like somebody jes' filled that place up with fire, glowin' behind every window."

"You were driving by at the time?"

"Yeah. Stopped at a house down the road and called the fire department, then went back to the church to watch. Next thing I know the cops're talkin' to me like *I* done it, and Ike Chambers is howlin' at them to arrest me for settin' fire to his church. Well, they look in my car and my trunk, and there's nothin' nobody could set a fire with, no gasoline, kerosene, nothin' like that, and I don't smell of it neither. Damn ol' Chief Hanson smelled all 'round my hands too. Finally let me go."

"Didn't they think it would be odd for the person who set the fire to call it in and then come back?" Hellboy asked.

"Took 'em a while to come around to that line of reasonin'."

"Did you tell them anything else besides the . . . strange nature of the fire?"

"Nope."

"Was anybody else around when you saw it go up? Any other cars?"

Nathaniel Watson paused just a second too long. "Nope."

"You sure about that?"

Watson thought for a moment. "You gonna tell the cops about this?"

"No."

"Then yeah. I saw somebody's car. When the fire started, I was watching it for about a minute, and just as I started to pull away, I saw Jack Mooney's minivan pullin' out from the trees, goin' the other way."

"Jack Mooney?"

"Yeah. Wild-ass guy. Used to be a priest, you can dig that. Live over in Shipoke."

"You didn't tell the police this yourself?"

"Don't *like* the police. And I especially don't like Ike Chambers and his church. They ain't very Christian for church folks. If Jack Mooney burned down that Golgotha church, then I say God bless Jack Mooney."

"What about the other church burnings in the area? The black churches? You as cavalier about those?"

"What kinda folks you think burning down our churches? Not folks like Jack Mooney, however he mighta done Golgotha. No, it's folks who drive pickup trucks with gun racks and Confederate-flag decals and 'Impeach Who-the-hell-ever' bumper stickers, and *go* to churches like Golgotha who burn down the black churches—with plenty of gasoline slopped all over, like the redneck dumbasses they are. Golgotha's a hate church, my man, not a love church.

"But I'll tell you somethin' else—I don't think Jack Mooney had a damn thing to do with that burnin', 'cause I don't know how nothin' human coulda made happen what I saw happen."

"So what was it then?" Hellboy asked.

"Hand of God, my man. Nothin' less than the hand of God."

Jack Mooney lived eight miles from the church that had just burned down. His house was a big two-story with pillars in front, but that didn't mean, Hellboy thought, that the man had money. The once-white paint had nearly peeled off the wood, so that the house appeared as gray as the gathering clouds. There was no minivan in the stone driveway, and no garage in sight, so Hellboy parked among some trees, out of sight of the road, and walked around to the back of the house.

There was a small shed there, and Hellboy searched that first. If people stored incendiaries, they tended to do so in a place separate from where they slept and ate. There was nothing in the shed, however, but some rusted tools and a hand mower.

Hellboy went up to the house, and was surprised to find the door open. He listened, but heard only the ticking of a clock and the low whir of the refrigerator. The boards creaked under his weight, but no one called out, and a quick sweep of the house told him that he was alone.

In nearly every room there was a crucifix on the wall, and at least one bookcase. Most of the books dealt with religion, although there were a few best-selling novels from past years. But Hellboy noticed that some of the books stuck out farther in the case than others, and when he pulled them away, he found other books behind them, uncovering nearly two dozen. Most were in very old bindings. Several were in Latin, and others were in French and German. Only two were in English.

Hellboy recognized nearly all of them by their titles. Some he had read, others he had never seen, but only heard whispers of. Even if the titles had meant nothing to him, the illustrations and diagrams would have given their subject matter away. There were several editions of the *Key of Solomon*, a *Grimoire of Honorius*, the original 1575 Basle edition of *Arbatel of Magic*, and even a German translation of the *Al Azif*. It seemed that Jack Mooney wasn't as doctrinaire as the crucifixes suggested.

Hellboy had begun to more closely examine the pages of the books in which bookmarks had been placed, when the sound of an approaching engine made him quickly replace the volume he was holding and run to the window. A battered minivan was pulling into the stone driveway at the side of the house, and Hellboy ran out the back door, around the opposite side of the house from the drive, and into the sheltering woods. He had seen enough, however, to convince him that it might be worth his time to shadow Jack Mooney.

He returned to Mooney's place an hour after dusk, and parked his car on the shoulder of the road two hundred yards from Mooney's drive. He listened to a book on tape, the earphone in one ear, the other ear free so that he could hear approaching traffic. He had listened to four cassettes of the unabridged novel before Mooney's minivan pulled onto the road and started driving away from Hellboy and the town of Linden. Hellboy followed, lights off, able to see well enough by the light of the moon.

He followed Mooney for twenty-five miles over wandering roads. Whatever route the man was taking to his goal was circuitous, as though he suspected that someone might be following, and when the minivan finally stopped, Hellboy thought they might be only five or six miles from where they had started. Mooney pulled his minivan onto the shoulder and Hellboy could see him walking away from the road. Hellboy got out of his car and followed on foot.

When he saw where Mooney was heading, Hellboy was sure he had guessed right. It was a church, a small, white, one-story edifice with a modest peaked steeple. A wooden sign had been driven into the ground near the road, and black metal letters proclaimed that it was the "Third Golgotha Tabernacle of Our Lord—Blossom, N.C."

In the bright moonlight, Hellboy could see Jack Mooney clearly. The man seemed to be in his mid-fifties, and was of medium height and stocky. The top of his head was bald but for a halo of hair, red in the moonlight. He was wearing khakis and a light jacket, and his hands were empty. If he was planning on burning the church, it wasn't going to be with gasoline.

As Hellboy watched from the shadows of the lowering trees, Jack Mooney started to walk around the church. Three times he circled it, counter-clockwise, widdershins, as Hellboy had thought he would. Then he stood before the front door, raised his left arm, and began to make a series of arcane gestures in the air, as though he were drawing pictures with his hand. After a few minutes of this, he started to speak in a language Hellboy didn't understand, but which he thought might be ancient Aramaic. Whatever it was, it was time to stop things.

"Is it a final word or a final gesture that starts it?" Hellboy said, just over Jack Mooney's shoulder. The big investigator could move very softly when he needed to.

Mooney stiffened, and his gestures ceased. But then his shoulders slowly relaxed, and he looked behind him. "Well by golly, will you look at that?" he said. "I knew it was only a matter of time before they'd be sending demons after me." There was an ironic smile on his face.

"I'm not a demon," said Hellboy.

"I know who you are," Mooney said. "You don't think I've come to this point in my studies without knowing all about your organization and the people who are in it. Do you . . . Hellboy?"

"A fire spell?" Hellboy asked. "That's how you burned the other churches?"

"The other Golgotha Tabernacles," Mooney corrected. "I don't burn African-American churches, my friend. I only burn the devil's churches. It took me a long time to figure out how to do it, but I've got it down pat now."

"What do you mean, the devil's churches?" asked Hellboy, honestly curious. "The Golgotha Tabernacles aren't Satanist churches."

"Aren't they?" Mooney snorted a laugh. "Do you want to see what goes on in the Golgotha Tabernacles? Would you like me to help you envision what goes on in the twisted hearts and narrow minds and lost souls of this sect? Because I'll be very happy to show you."

"How can you show me?"

"I learned a lot of things both before and since I left the priesthood, Hellboy. I learned that those who seem the most pious are often the most evil, and I learned, most importantly, that there were other ways to fight evil besides being one of Christ's priests. I could do more for Him by becoming one of His warriors. "

The phrase revolted Hellboy. He had heard it used too many times to rationalize violence. "You mean like the ones who bomb abortion clinics?"

"No. Those fools use a mask of religion to do evil. I use the old secrets to battle them and their kind. You want to see what goes on in this building, Hellboy?" Mooney stepped up to the front door of the tabernacle and put his hand on the painted wood. Then he held his hand out to Hellboy. "Another secret I've learned in the old books. Take my hand. Hear the walls cry out against the evil that has been perpetrated within them. Take a look into the lives and deaths of those foolish enough to 'worship' here. Come on," he went on, more softly. "How can the devil's son be afraid to look within the heart of a church, especially a *reformed* devil's son?"

Hellboy took a deep breath and stepped next to Mooney, taking his hand. He felt nothing at first except the ex-priest's warm fingers gripping his own. Then the white, moonlit walls of the church and the form of the man next to him began to shimmer and fade. He started to see the secrets that the modest building held, as in a phantasmagoria . . .

. . . There, floating before him, was the gaunt face of Isaac Chambers, his mouth twisting as he shouted that it was a sin against God to seek the help of men over the Lord . . . that a wife should obey her husband in all things . . . that with God anything was possible, even to the point of handling serpents and drinking poison . . . that sodomites were doomed to hell . . . that the black sons of Shem were an inferior race . . . that the Jews still had to pay for killing Jesus, the Christ . . .

. . . And then there swam into his view the results of those words . . . a husband and wife standing by the bedside of their dying daughter, their hands raised over their heads, their eyes closed, trying to pray away ravenous death rather than call a doctor . . .

. . . A woman sitting inside a car in a garage, breathing carbon monoxide, bold enough to finally leave the husband who beat her, but not bold enough to live with the condemnation of her spiritual brothers and sisters for that God-mocking act . . .

. . . A woman writhing on the floor of her house, other worshippers gathered around her, not knowing what to do, watching the woman and the copperhead as it sinuously glided toward the door, its venom drained, having done what it was intended to do . . .

And then they began to come more quickly. Both younger and older men, fathers and sons together, taunting, yelling at, threatening, and finally beating black men, gay men, anyone different, with non-white flesh or non-Christian beliefs.

No, not non-Christian, but non-*their* beliefs.

Through it all, all the visions, all the pain, all the hatred, Hellboy could hear the powerful voice of Pastor Isaac Chambers, damning, blessing, ordering his flock to their dismal fates. Then his vision cleared, and he was once more standing in the night, with Mooney no longer holding his hand.

"Is this," Mooney asked softly, "or is this not, a place of evil?"

Hellboy could not speak for a moment. Then he cleared his throat. "It may be. But your way isn't the way to stop them."

"You're wrong. It's the best way. It's the only way to eradicate the source, short of killing the monsters who preach such evil, and that I won't do."

"Not yet, anyway," Hellboy said. He was about to say more, but Mooney interrupted him.

"Don't preach to me. I've heard a lot of preaching in my time—done enough too."

"Then I'll just have to *stop* you—with or without explaining why."

"I know why. Because violence never solved anything, because fighting evil can make a person evil, because 'When you stare too long into the abyss . . . ' You know the rest." It was true. Hellboy did.

"If you know all of that, then you know why I can't let you burn down that church."

"You can't stop me," Mooney said. "All I have to do is make a gesture, and you'll stop dead in your tracks. I make another, and the church goes up in flames—you see, I was almost finished when you interrupted me. So now—"

"You don't have to stop him, Hell-thing," came a rasping voice from the darkness. It seemed familiar to Hellboy, but there was something different about it. And when the man stepped from around the side of the church, Hellboy felt certain he knew what the difference was. "*I* can stop him easily enough . . . "

It was Pastor Isaac Chambers, but his voice had changed to a predator's growl, and his appearance had changed as well. He was wearing the black suit that Hellboy had seen him in earlier, but it seemed too small for him now, as though he were growing inside it. His face was different too. Before it had been strained and angry and furtive; now it was only cruel and diabolical, as though what it had been hiding in the light of day was delighted at being able to come out at night. Hellboy saw the demon under the skin, and knew that Jack Mooney had been absolutely right.

"Need any more proof. Hellboy?" Mooney seemed nonplussed in Chambers' presence, and looked ready neither to fight nor flee. "I was wondering when you were going to show your true face, Chambers. He's a demon in human form, Hellboy, a servant of Satan, whose assignment is to lead people into mortal sin. Some of his ilk do that through vice or temptation or promises of worldly success. Chambers—or whatever his name is—has been doing it through the guise of salvation, leading people's souls into hell while promising them heaven. A sweet little scam, and, considering the way a lot of churches operate today, scarcely worthy of notice, unless, like me, you know what to look for."

"Nice speech," Chambers rattled. "You can give it again to the angels—you'll be seeing them soon enough." He turned toward Hellboy, who could see Chambers' forehead twitching, as though something beneath the bone was struggling to be released. The creature's eyes looked red in the moonlight. "And as for you . . . " Chambers glanced at the discs where Hellboy's horns had been cut off. " . . . *Stumpy* . . . you might get to see your daddy tonight. The Ike Chambers part of me may have wanted you burned, but that wasn't because you're the devil's spawn—it's because you betrayed your blood and denied your heritage. The genetics of hell bubble within you, boy. No matter how hard you deny it."

"Why don't you wait till the cock crows three times," Hellboy said with a bravura he did not feel. "Then I'll feel *really* guilty."

"No more jokes," Chambers said. "It's time . . . " He continued to grow then, and Hellboy saw his shirt and suit coat rip open as thick, wiry muscles burst through the fabric. In a few seconds Chambers was Hellboy's size, and continuing to grow. Horns sprouted from his forehead, and a long, pointed tail jutted priapically from between his legs. The clothes, now merely rags, fell away, and the face of hellish fury looked full into Hellboy's.

He nearly fell back before the power of it, but knew that he would have to strike first, and did. It was like hitting stone. The blow from his mighty right hand had no effect on the Chambers-thing other than to make it blink. Instead of its head rocking back on its neck, it had responded as if someone had blown a puff of air in its face.

Then he felt Mooney grab his arm and haul him backwards, away from the demon. He followed blindly, and together they ran through the open door of the church and down the aisle between the pews, toward the pulpit and a round window of stained glass dimly lit by the moon outside. Behind them, Hellboy heard the sound of cracking boards, and when he glanced back, he saw what had been Isaac Chambers forcing his bulk through the doorway, breaking the doorframe as he came.

"Through the window," Mooney said, and slapped Hellboy on the back as if to speed him. "Just go—straight through it!"

It was the only plan offered, so Hellboy figured he might as well take it. He ran faster, getting up as much speed as he could, straight toward the softly colored circle of glass. Just before he reached it, he sprang, curling up his massive body like a ball. He felt the impact before he heard the crash, and then, a split second later, another impact, as though he had been blown out of the mouth of a cannon.

Fire surrounded him like a hot, yellow-white tube, and the feel of the heat was more painful than the cutting shards of glass that fell away from him as he soared through the air, held aloft not by his leap, but by a great rush of scalding air and bright flame. Then the heat receded, and he fell onto soft grass and hard ground, and rolled until he stopped, panting, his face toward the sky, which seemed to be lit up by a blazing sun.

But it wasn't the sun, it was the Golgotha Tabernacle. It had become an instant inferno, with only the sound of a mighty flame lifting up, the same burst of flame that had helped to propel Hellboy through the now-shattered window. Already the flames were licking through the frame of that stained-glass window like a brilliant, hungry tongue, and the roof was glowing where the fire ate through the boards. The whole church was being devoured by the ravenous flames.

From the way the flames brightened the sky, Hellboy knew it would only be minutes before the cars and fire trucks started to arrive. He ran to his car, looking for Mooney, but there was no sign of him. What had the man done? Hellboy wondered as he drove away, turning down the first side road he could find, and then crisscrossing the meandering back roads. He had to have been in the church when that fireball erupted, and the only way it could have happened so quickly was if he had made that last gesture that he had bragged about.

Had he done so in order to kill the demon at the cost of his own life? Hellboy could imagine no other scenario, no possibility of escape for the man who had made certain that Hellboy escaped before he played his last trump card.

Last trump. He hoped that was what Jack Mooney, ex-priest and very successful mage, was hearing now from a front-row seat among the elect. He deserved it, after making the big sacrifice. Hellboy hoped the sacrifice wouldn't be in vain, but he knew that there were always those, demonic or otherwise, who would leap into the gap that Chambers had left . . . *if* he was truly gone.

The next morning, Hellboy made it a point to drive past the ruined Golgotha Tabernacle. The fire was out, after having burned the building to the ground. There were a few police cars and an ambulance, as well as a new black Chrysler New Yorker. Donald Withers, wearing a topcoat against the morning chill, stood looking on. When Hellboy got out of his car and started to walk toward Withers, one of the deputies put his hand on his gun, but Police Chief Hanson, to whom Hellboy had spoken the day before, said something to the deputy, who relaxed and turned back to searching the ashes.

"Another one," Hellboy said flatly to Withers. The man's face soured at the sight of Hellboy, but he didn't respond. "Who was the pastor here?"

"Ike Chambers," Withers finally said, keeping his eyes on the searching policemen.

"Does he know about it yet?"

"We can't find him," Withers said. "That's what they're looking for now."

Before Withers had even finished his sentence, one of the deputies cried out, brushing at something with his shovel. Withers ran toward him, and Hellboy followed. "Stand back," Withers said, and knelt in the ashes, oblivious to the way they clung to his dark trousers and leather shoes. Hellboy could see the charred bones of an arm and hand. Withers lifted it, and something glittered in the sunshine. A bracelet. "'Property of the Lord,'" Withers read. "It's Ike. Get a stretcher, you boys."

The chief led the deputies to the ambulance, where they alerted the two EMS men who had been taking a break in the back. While they did, Hellboy saw Withers quickly brush away the ashes from over the skull. Though the fire or some fatal magic had diminished the bones to human size, Hellboy could still see the protrusions in the skull from which the horns had grown.

Donald Withers saw them too. He reached out with his left hand, and with a strength beyond that of an old man, he pressed inward on the skull, so that it crumbled into irreparable shards of charred bone and ash. Then he looked up at Hellboy with a little smile.

"You knew," Hellboy said.

"As do you," Withers replied. "But who would ever believe you? In *my* country."

Hellboy looked at the bed of ashes that had been the Golgotha Tabernacle. The men had gone over it fairly well with rake and shovel, but there was no sign of any other body. Chambers' bones had been in the last area they had searched, having started at the edges and worked their way to the center. Jack Mooney's corpse was nowhere to be seen.

"I'm not the only one who knows," Hellboy whispered. "I'd strongly suggest that you give up the ministry. Maybe you could enter the mission field." He walked away, across the ashes, without looking back.

Reports came to him later. They never found any other body in the ashes, and Donald Withers had not left the Carolinas. He was planning to open up three more Golgotha Tabernacles when he was found in his car at the side of a country road. The Chrysler was a burned-out hulk, as was Donald Withers. There was no explanation as to how the fire started. Some people said it was spontaneous human combustion, but others, people who were former, disgruntled members of Golgotha Tabernacles, said that it was the hand of God smiting a man who had been perverting His word.

Hellboy figured Nathaniel Watson had been right after all. The hand of God. Nothing less than the hand of God.

I HAD BIGFOOT'S BABY!
MAX ALLAN COLLINS

I t started with the *National Inquisitor*, not exactly the normal course for a case to arrive at the BPRD. I was halfway through a sausage-and-pepperoni pizza when I saw the story. The newspaper, and I use the term loosely, featured another in a series of fuzzy photos of a purported Bigfoot roaming the woods of Iowa. Any other Bigfoot article wouldn't have caused a ripple around the offices of the Bureau for Paranormal Research and Defense—after all, Bigfoot's not really our bag—but this story was different. Written by a photographer, a guy named Louis Walker, the piece chronicled the year-long search for the reporter who'd been with him when he took his blurry pictures of the beast. Allegedly the female reporter had been carried off by the Bigfoot in question.

No matter what you've heard, a Bigfoot carrying off a lady reporter will always grab my interest, whether it's paranormal or not.

Accompanying the story and the blurry Bigfoot pix was a photo of the missing reporter. Cute, brunette, mid to late twenties, but her face, something about the eyes pulled my thoughts to Anastasia Bransfield. No matter how I tried to forget her she always seemed to pop back at the least likely moments.

"Hellboy, what're you doin'?"

I turned to see Abe Sapien approaching my desk.

"I found Bigfoot," I crowed. "The missing link is living in Iowa."

Sapien grabbed a piece of pizza and smirked. "Funny, I always figured that's where he'd turn up."

He took a bite of his slice. The missing link held little fascination for Abe, who was the next link—an icthyo-sapien. A gill man to those of us in the subspecies of nose-breathers. A science experiment gone wrong, Abe has been at the BPRD nearly as long as I. He was the world's oldest test-tube baby, having been conceived on April 14, 1865, the day Abraham Lincoln was assassinated. His long incubation had left Abe with skin the color of wet newspaper, piercing blue, pupiless eyes, and absolutely no body hair. At this moment he wasn't wearing the false beard, fedora, shades, and trench coat that allowed him to enter the so-called normal world and not create a stir.

Abe and I share a bond about looks. The fact that my skin is crimson—I have horns, a tail, and one hand made of stone, and am bigger than the average bear—seems to put some people off in the same way that Abe's gills make them uneasy. Go figure.

"I think we should look into this," I said.

"Bigfoot?" he scoffed. "What's next, the Loch Ness monster?"

"A woman disappeared."

That slowed him down. "When?"

"Almost a year ago."

"And you want to go look for her now?"

"First I've heard of it," I said.

Abe shook his head. "What's Liz say?"

"Haven't asked her yet."

The click of high heels on the office floor announced the entry of the third member of our team, Liz Sherman. She'd been with the BPRD ever since her pyrokinetic gift got out of control and torched her whole neighborhood back when she was twelve. Tall, raven-haired, with deep-set brown eyes, Liz had ceased looking like a child a long time ago.

"Haven't asked me what?" she said as she strode up to the desk.

Abe cocked a thumb toward me. "Hellboy wants to go tromping through the woods to find Bigfoot."

One of Liz's dark, rich eyebrows arched. "Really?"

"There's more to it than that."

"Isn't that enough?"

"Probably, but there's more, anyway."

"You gonna tell me what?"

She studied me as I laid out the story for her. When I finished she asked, "That's not really our area, is it?"

Standing just behind her, Abe grinned but said nothing.

"Probably not, but . . . "

As Liz turned to face Abe, his grin disappeared.

"And what about you?" she asked.

"I . . . I'm on your side."

Liz shook her head. "I'm not sure we should even get involved in something like this."

I kept my eyes steady on hers.

"Tell you what, Hellboy. You go and if you need us we'll come."

I nodded.

"But try and wrap this up quick, willya?"

My plane landed in Chicago just after noon. From there a cab dropped me at the *Inquisitor* office and after sweet-talking the secretary, I found myself chatting with the cigar-chomping managing editor, a fiftyish bald man named Goorwitz.

"We'll help you out on one condition," he said.

"I thought I was helping *you* out."

"Either way, it's gonna cost you."

"Cost me what?"

"Sitting still for a photo and an interview. Boy, you're *Inquisitor* material if I ever saw it!"

He hooked me up with photographer Louis Walker and a reporter named Stephanie Keenan. The three of us jumped into a rental car with the rail-thin, rawboned Walker driving, and were on our way to Iowa before sunset.

Stephanie occupied the seat next to her partner while I stretched out in the back. She wore jeans and a green Dartmouth sweatshirt over a white polo shirt with just the collar peeking out. Her blond hair, pulled into a loose ponytail, lay between her shoulders. Turning to face me, she folded one leg under her.

"Why 'Hellboy'?" she asked.

I stared at her for a moment. "Did you really go to Dartmouth?"

She laughed at that. It was an easy, free laugh that sounded like water bubbling. "I meant why not something a little less . . . obvious?"

"Like Bob maybe?"

She just looked at me, but her smile remained in place.

"Bob Hellboy," I said. "Doesn't really roll off the tongue, does it?"

"Kinda like it," Walker said without turning.

"My father, or the man I called my father, gave me my name." My eyes caught hers and held. "I like it."

"I . . . I'm sorry," she blurted. "I didn't mean—"

I waved her off. "No harm, no foul." I changed the subject. "Lou, what can you tell me about the missing reporter?"

"Her name was Pam Cervantes. She'd been with the paper for about six months when we caught the story about the Bigfoot. I thought it was probably just another asshole in a gorilla suit until I saw him carry Pam into the woods."

"So, you're a believer now?"

Walker shrugged as he passed a semi. "Sure as hell wasn't like anything I've ever seen before."

"Anything else about Pam?"

"Nice kid, right out of journalism school, went to Iowa State."

"Married?"

Walker shook his head.

"Anybody special in her life?"

Again the head shake. "She kept her personal column pretty much to herself."

Stephanie piped in, "Do you think there's a Bigfoot running loose in a state park in Iowa?"

I shrugged as noncommittally as possible and saw Walker watching me in the rearview.

"You think I'm nuts?" His voice was steady but the eyes were hard.

"No."

"Then you think I made up the whole thing," he said, his voice rising in anger.

Shaking my head, I said, "I don't know if you made it up; you don't seem to be nuts, but I don't know what the hell is going on, so that's why I'm here—to find out."

Then he fell into a sulky silence, his eyes darting between the road and the glares he threw my way in the mirror. We pretty much observed those rules for the rest of the drive to Palisades State Park, just east of Cedar Rapids, Iowa.

With the late afternoon sun sprinting for the horizon, Walker pulled our rental car through the gate and eased to a stop in front of the ranger's cabin next to a brown Ford Bronco with the words "Park Ranger" emblazoned on the door in gold. The ranger, a tall, broad man whose gut had long since turned to Jell-O, stepped out onto the porch as we climbed out of our car.

Adjusting a dirt-brown-colored campaign hat low on his brow, he puffed out his chest. "What the hell are you?" he asked, looking in my direction. Even at this distance, he smelled like he'd been dipped in Brut cologne.

"I'm an investigator for the Bureau for Paranormal Research and Defense."

That did not seem to be the answer he sought. He continued to stare at me. I stared back and noticed a pin over his shirt pocket with the name Holliman engraved on it.

"Name's Hellboy."

He nodded slightly. "Seems about right."

I told myself that I was not going to let this backwoods yahoo piss me off.

He glanced at the stubs on my head. "Them horns?"

I ignored the question. "I'm here because . . ."

"Bigfoot and this . . . photojournalist over here," Holliman said jerking a thumb toward Walker.

I nodded.

Placing his hands on his hips, curiously close to the pistol he wore on his left hip I noted, the ranger studied each of us in turn. "Ain't no Bigfoot around here. Never has been, never will."

"You're sure," I said.

"Look . . . " Walker began tightly, but I caught his eye with a cold look, and he clammed up.

"You've never seen a Bigfoot, or footprints, or—"

"I ain't seen shit," the ranger said impatiently. "Bigfoot shit or otherwise."

"Doesn't surprise me," I said evenly.

His eyes narrowed as he tried to figure out if I had insulted him. Finally, he said, "Park's gonna close. You oughta be on your way 'bout now."

"Yes, sir," I said. "Thanks for your time."

Walker took a step forward. "Are you just going to. . . ?"

"Yes, I am," I said, stepping between him and Ranger Holliman. "Come on, we're going."

The ranger's eyes stayed on us as we piled back into the car and left the park, turning east on Highway 30.

"Walker, can you find the place where Pam disappeared?"

"Sure, we were there for almost a week before she got abducted."

"Can you find it on foot? In the dark?"

At the first gravel road past the edge of the wooded park, Walker turned right and drove nearly a mile before pulling the car as close to the edge of the road as he could. Stephanie and I looked at him.

"This feels about right," he said. "I think we were just about a mile deep in the park when Pam disappeared."

Walker jumped out of the car and we followed. He opened the trunk and began rummaging through the bags of camera equipment looking for the correct night-shooting stuff. I checked the clip in my .45 and Stephanie's eyes widened even more than when she'd first seen me.

"You're not going to shoot him are you?"

"Which him?" I asked as I turned to glance at Walker.

"Bigfoot."

I jammed the pistol back in its holster. "I just like to be ready. I'm not gonna gun down any missing links unless absolutely necessary."

As night descended around us, Walker adjusted the last of three bags over his shoulder. "Ready," he said.

Stephanie said, "Geez, Walker, how many cameras do you need?"

He just grunted.

"Which way?" I asked.

Walker looked into the darkened recesses of the woods. "Mile, maybe two. There's a rise. I'll know it when I see it, even in the dark."

I nodded. "Better get goin' then."

We fell into a single-file line, Walker in the lead, Stephanie in the middle, me bringing up the rear. The uneven terrain and unrelenting darkness made for slow going. Walker convinced us flashlights would just drive our quarry deeper into the woods, so we picked our way over fallen branches, exposed roots, and the dense underbrush by only the light of the moon that barely filtered through the branches and leaves of the tall trees.

"How far have we gone?" Stephanie asked breathlessly.

Walker shushed her, then dropped to one knee and gazed through the night vision lens of his Nikon. After a moment, he faced her in the blackness. "Keep your voice down. It carries at night and we don't want to spook him."

Stephanie whispered, "How far?"

"Maybe a half-mile, maybe a little less," I said.

"Shit, this is going to take forever!"

Walker shushed her again and she waved him off.

"It's not much further," Walker said as he turned back and moved ahead.

"Fuck this," she said. "Even a Pulitzer wouldn't make up for crawling around in these godforsaken hills in the middle of the night."

"Maybe you'd like to head back," I suggested. "By yourself."

I waited till she dropped into line behind Walker.

The summer heat, which had turned the ground hard, caused beads of sweat to pop out on my forehead, back, and arms as we made our way uphill. I had fallen maybe twenty yards behind Walker, Stephanie a few steps in front of me, when I heard his scream. Actually, it was more like a yelp, and for a moment I thought perhaps Walker had tripped and fallen.

I grabbed Stephanie by the arm and barked, "Don't move," as I moved past her and up the trail toward Walker.

Halfway to him I heard an animal snarl that seemed to be coming from all around me.

Stephanie whimpered, "Hellboy, Walker—don't just leave me . . . "

I popped up to the top of the hill and looked over the crest mesmerized by the nearly seven-foot-tall giant looming on the path before me—Bigfoot!

Though the darkness remained almost complete, I could make out the height and shape of the beast that towered over the fallen Walker. In one of its massive hands it held a football-sized stone that reflected black against the moonlight.

Blood.

The photographer's blood probably, from where the stone had landed against Walker's skull.

Hearing my footsteps, the monster turned to face me, raising the stone to bash my brains in, should I stray within bashing distance. An aroma, something animal yet unrecognizable, filtered to me from the direction of Bigfoot.

"Remind me to get you some Right Guard for Christmas, big guy."

The beast grunted, its red eyes wide in the moonlight. He waved the stone like he meant to throw it, but I made no move to duck for cover. That threw the animal off a little—I don't think it knew quite what to make of my bravado.

I wasn't being that brave—I was trying to see if Walker was still breathing.

I felt Stephanie behind me, her hands coming to rest against my back as she practically ran into me in the dark.

Bigfoot's yowling grew louder, more agitated, and this time it raised the rock as if it were about to crash it down on Walker's skull again. Pressing back, I knocked Stephanie to the ground as I planted my feet and leapt forward. Bigfoot swung the stone in a long, flowing, almost artistic arc. My right hand, the stone one grafted on to my right arm, extended before me as I pushed to get to Walker before Bigfoot's rock could inflict more damage. A split second before the rock would hit Walker, it collided with my stone hand and glanced off.

Bigfoot screamed in anger and rage, his voice almost human, as he leapt out of the way of my second lunge.

I groaned as I smacked into a tree and fell to the ground. I rose to my knees and prepared for Bigfoot's counterattack, but it never came. Instead, a metallic roar erupted, lights flashed over our heads, blinding us, and dust swirled all around. I blinked furiously to clear my vision, but to no avail. I rubbed my flesh-and-blood hand across my face to clear the dust and then the lights and roar were gone. I blinked my eyes until I could see again, but gone along with the lights and noise was Bigfoot.

"What the hell was that?" Stephanie asked as we moved next to Walker.

I checked Walker's neck for a pulse—weak, but there.

"We gotta get him to a hospital."

Stephanie's voice was small. "How?"

I grabbed Walker and tossed him over my shoulder. "You lead the way," I said. "And use the flashlight. It's all right now."

"You don't think that . . . thing . . . will attack again if it gets the chance."

"No, I don't," I said, nudging her to get started. "I'll explain when we've got more time. For now, trust me. Turn on the flashlight and let's get moving. Walker's time is running out."

She did as she was told without further argument. With the flashlight we traveled only slightly faster than before. By the time we got to the car, even I was wondering whether we'd get to the hospital in time.

We sat in the waiting room while the doctors fought to save Walker. The only news I'd gleaned before we were unceremoniously kicked out of the ER was that Walker's skull had been fractured.

"Is he going to make it?" Stephanie asked.

I tried to look truthful. "Yeah, he's tough."

She didn't buy that and shook her head. "I've never seen anybody so white before. It was like he didn't have any blood left in him . . . " Her voiced trailed off.

I put my flesh-and-blood hand on her shoulder. "I told you, he'll make it."

She sat down in a waiting-room chair, picked up a plastic cup filled with coffee, and absently took a swig. Her face screwed up as she realized the coffee was cold, then she swallowed it. "What the hell *was* that creature, Hellboy?"

My eyes met hers and held. "Bigfoot."

Again, Stephanie shook her head. "I thought Bigfoot was supposed to be friendly, scared of people. This thing seemed . . . homicidal."

I shrugged but said nothing.

"What is it? You know something."

I continued to just look at her.

"Come on, spill. What was it?" Her face creased in thought, then she practically jumped out of her chair. "That noise before Bigfoot disappeared. That's it, isn't it?"

"There's nothing I can prove yet."

"But there's something, tell me."

I explained my theory. We discussed it, looked at it from every angle, examined it thoroughly trying to find holes. We were just deciding our next course of action when the doctor came into the waiting room. She was a tall, thin woman with wispy blond hair peeking out from under her shower cap. Her greens were sweaty, but she smelled surprisingly good.

"Are you the . . . people with Mr. Walker?" she asked. I guess it took her a moment to classify me as more or less human.

Stephanie stepped forward. "We work together."

"Well, you got him here just in time. He's going to be all right. It'll take some time, but barring any surprises, he should be as good as new."

"Can we see him?"

The doctor shook his head. "He's resting. Probably be the day after tomorrow before he's up to visitors."

Stephanie nodded.

The doctor answered a couple more questions for Stephanie, then left us alone.

After we got some sleep, Stephanie dropped me off near where we'd entered the park the night before, then she hit the road to interview some of the neighboring farmers to see if any of them had seen Bigfoot or signs of the monster in the fields that bordered the state park.

Though traveling through the dense forest was easier during the day, it wasn't a lot easier. The tangled undergrowth still pulled at my feet while the trail remained obscured in the shadows cast by the leaves and trees that seemed to go on forever, though I felt sure now that somewhere in this forest the trees stopped at least for a small space. Finally, I reached the foot of the hill where Walker had met Bigfoot the night before.

I made my way to the crest, then standing there I looked down at the drying puddle of blood in the grass. Bugs hovered near, and in the bright sunshine the fluid appeared more crimson than it had in last night's moonlight. Other than the pool of blood, though, there seemed to be little sign that we had been here. Even the rock Bigfoot clubbed Walker with had disappeared; all that remained were a few footprints.

Bending to examine the footprints, I smelled something on the breeze. Not the animal smell from last night, something different. I caught another whiff and willed myself to relax. I had the feeling something had been following me, and now I knew what.

I looked down into the wide, surprisingly deep footprint and watched as a faint shadow crossed over it from right to left. Moving slowly, without any apparent rush, I leaned more forward, so that my weight now rested on my hands. Then, suddenly, I extended my right leg and swung to my left using my hands as the fulcrum. My leg caught Ranger Holliman at the ankles and swept him off his feet, dropping him on his ample keester. He fumbled for his holster, but before he had the strap undone I had a hoof on his chest and my own pistol pointed at his kisser.

"You've got to stop wearing so much Brut, Ranger Holliman."

He snarled, "I should have you arrested for assault, you fucking geek."

"That's not nice," I said pressing my hoof down a little harder on his chest. "Do you really want to call me a geek?" I could hear him gasping for air but he said nothing. Tough guy. I liked that. I pressed down harder yet.

"I'm . . . , " he huffed, " . . . sorry . . . , " he puffed, " . . . I called you a geek."

I released the pressure on his chest but didn't let him up. His breaths came in short ragged gulps as he struggled to replenish the air in his lungs.

"Why don't you move your hand away from that holster so I can let you up?"

Holliman's hand remained frozen for a moment, then eased away from the pistol. Reaching down, I plucked the gun from its holster, then offered Holliman a hand and jerked him to his feet. He brushed himself off, tried to recover what little dignity he might have left and held his hand out for the gun. I ignored him.

Instead, I nodded toward the footprint on the ground. "Still think there's no Bigfoot?"

He looked at the print but said nothing for a long moment. "Don't have to be no Bigfoot."

I nodded. "That's right, Ranger Holliman. In fact, I'd bet it isn't. I'd bet your chickenshit salary that this footprint is part of a hoax."

An aroma far closer to last night's than Ranger Holliman's Brut passed between us on the breeze. We both turned to see a furry head disappear behind a tree.

"That look like a fucking hoax to you?" Holliman asked, eyes wide. "Give me my gun and let's go bag the son of a bitch!"

I didn't even take time to glare at him, I just took a step in the direction I had last seen the Bigfoot; but before I got far, I caught a glimpse of the beast to our left. It was sprinting to outflank us, get behind us. It looked bigger, taller, than the one we had encountered the night before, though at this distance, over uneven terrain, it was hard to tell. I wheeled and took off straight for the animal with Holliman lagging behind me, when it slipped into a shadow and disappeared again. By the time I got to the shadow, there was no sign of Bigfoot. This thing was a hell of a lot better at playing hide and seek in the woods than I was.

Hanging onto a tree, Holliman gasped for breath, his face nearly as crimson as my own. "What the hell was that?"

I shrugged. "I don't know, but it didn't move like a hoax. It just disappeared."

After unloading the clip from his gun, I returned Holliman's pistol and went back to the motel. Stephanie was waiting for me at my door when I arrived.

"How's Walker?" I asked.

"I called earlier but they didn't have much to say. He's still under sedation."

I nodded, unlocked the door and held it for her as we entered. "I saw it again . . . sort of."

She whirled back toward me, blond ponytail swinging. "You did?"

"It looked different in the daylight, but I couldn't catch it. If it's a real Bigfoot, it's faster than I would have believed. What'd you find out?"

"Some of the local farmers said they've seen tracks, broken corn stalks, things like that. A couple even claimed to have seen the Bigfoot."

I nodded.

"And there was one . . . "

"Yeah?"

"One even claimed that he once caught a glimpse of a Bigfoot baby with its father."

"What?"

She plopped onto one of the two double beds in the room. "That's what he told me. Said he was coming home late one night and this thing was in the middle of the road, got caught in the farmer's headlights, and dove out of the way at the last second. The farmer slammed on his brakes and stopped, but he couldn't find the Bigfoot or the baby."

"Some story. You believe him?"

Stephanie shrugged. "No reason to think he'd lie or make it up."

"Not even to see his name in the *National Inquisitor*?"

She considered that for a moment. "Nope. Not the type. What's our plan?"

I fell onto the other bed, stretched, and thought about that. Something still didn't feel right about this. "You game to go back into the park tonight?"

Smiling, Stephanie said, "I thought you'd never ask."

We parked the car in the same place as the night before, but this time we got there earlier. The sun sank behind the treetops and darkness enveloped us, though that was of little concern to me, since we were already hunkered down in position.

Three hours later, our legs cramping, and the chill of the May air infiltrating our bones, I saw the beast climb the hill. I tapped Stephanie, who lay next to me, and I looked through the night-vision lens of Walker's camera.

Bigfoot scanned the horizon, looked our way for a second, didn't spot us, and resumed his reconnoiter. As I continued to watch and occasionally snap a picture (I figured it was the least I could do considering what Walker had been through), Bigfoot reached into a furry hip pocket and produced a walkie-talkie.

I snapped three rapid pictures, thinking this boy had nothing on Kubrick's apes in *2001*.

"We just might have a fake here," I whispered.

"Let me see," Stephanie whispered back.

I handed her the camera, and she peered through the lens, saw him say something into the radio, and return it to its hiding place.

"Stay here," I said.

"Where are you going?"

"To end this," I said. "Get pictures, if you can do it without moving."

She nodded.

I edged out of our hiding place and around the base of the hill, the stale animal aroma from our last visit reassaulting my nostrils. Bigfoot had his back to me. I got as close as I dared and sprang at him. He must have felt me coming because he turned just as I leapt, and instead of hitting him square in the back, I smacked him in the side, glanced off, rolled, and came up face to face with the giant.

He let loose with his most menacing roar and I grinned at him.

"That'd be good if you weren't just a seven-foot asshole in a Bigfoot suit."

"Fucker!"

Apparently Bigfoot spoke English.

He lunged at me. I threw an overhand punch with my stone right hand that hit him full in the chest and dropped him in his tracks. I was about to press my advantage when the mechanical sound came again and dust and leaves rose all around me. In the cup-sized clearing on the far side of the hill, a helicopter sat down quietly. Three men sprinted out of the woods, unloaded some crates, and melted back into the blackness of the woods as the chopper lifted, hovered a moment, then disappeared into the night as well.

I turned back to the fake Bigfoot as he rose to his feet. I took a step toward him and froze when I heard a shell get racked into a shotgun. Turning, I found myself face to face with Ranger Holliman and his twelve gauge. I kicked myself for not noticing the aroma of his cheap cologne.

"You damn freak. I knew you'd screw up this deal."

I tried to appear nonchalant. "What's in the crates, Ranger? Your monthly Brut delivery?"

Holliman grinned. "No harm tellin' you since you'll be dead in a minute. It's chemicals. Me and some of the local farmers found out that there was a lot more money in Ice than there is in corn."

Ice, I knew, was the newest of the designer drugs. It behaved like Ecstasy but kicked like a mule. In short, it made crack look like Mountain Dew. "So," I said, "you talked them into going into the recreational-drug business."

Holliman shrugged. "Gotta keep the wolf from the door. Even a red-skinned freak like you oughtta understand that."

He was beginning to piss me off again.

Bigfoot lifted my pistol and stepped over by Holliman. I had no chance to jump both of them, and if I went for one, the other would get me. This felt a lot like trouble. I was just figuring out which one of them I was going to take with me when I noticed a small movement in the bushes behind them.

Stephanie—shit!

She hadn't had sense enough to stay in the hole and get enough pictures to convict these assholes, and now she was probably going to die with me.

I took a deep breath, probably my last one, and prepared to jump. Then the bushes parted and a dark shape half a foot taller than the ersatz Bigfoot stepped into view. I gulped and leapt toward Holliman as the shape grabbed Bigfoot by the neck.

The ranger's gun exploded, the bright light nearly blinding me as the buckshot whizzed past my ear. I grabbed the barrel in my stone hand and yanked it from Holliman's grasp. In the next instant it became the club I used to pummel him to the ground.

I heard the fake Bigfoot scream as the shape lifted him and threw him like a toy. He crashed into the trunk of a tree with a sickening crunch, and then all was quiet. I looked up, and under the moonlight, I found myself face to face with a real Bigfoot. A nearly eight-foot-tall beast whose face was far more animal than human. Yet the eyes held something I couldn't quite put my finger on. His gaze held me in an understanding that I've seen on the faces of only a scant few humans.

For a moment there, we understood the beast in each of us.

We both turned when we heard a noise and found Stephanie struggling up the hill. "I got it all on film," she said. "We're gonna be rich. This is the scoop of a lifetime."

"I'd rather you didn't do that," a female voice behind me said.

I whirled around to see a strong-boned woman of around thirty, dressed in animal skins, holding a baby. Her dark hair shone in the moonlight.

Stephanie turned too, her mouth agape.

"You're Pam Cervantes, aren't you?" I asked. She looked so much like Anastasia Bransfield that I had to will myself not to embrace her.

She nodded.

Stephanie stepped forward and peeked at the baby, part Bigfoot, part human. "It's a boy," Pam said.

Grinning, Stephanie said, "He's beautiful."

Pam looked hard at the reporter. "He won't be if you show the pictures of his father to the world."

"Pam!" Stephanie said. "Do you realize what a story like this could mean?"

"Sure—'I Had Bigfoot's Baby!' Just another *Inquisitor* story."

"Not this time," Stephanie said, holding up her camera. "Not with real proof!"

I took the camera from her. Stephanie watched wide eyed as I smashed it with my stone hand. "You don't have to worry about us, Pam—your family is safe."

Bigfoot, the real one, stepped forward and wrapped me in an awkward embrace. Then he released me, held out a hand to his wife, and the family disappeared into the woods.

"Shit," Stephanie said. "There goes my Pulitzer."

I grinned. "You've still got a good story about the drug-running park ranger."

"Yeah, but no art."

The camera lay in pieces at my feet. "Sorry."

She shrugged. "Still a good story, I guess."

"Look at the bright side," I said. "You can go tell Walker he's not nuts."

Stephanie laughed. "Just because there really is a Bigfoot doesn't mean Walker's not nuts."

Though his meeting with the tree had taken the fight out of him, the fake Bigfoot seemed to be all right. Holliman already had a nasty lump on his face from the shotgun stock, but he too would live. I handcuffed them together and marched them to our waiting car.

I returned to the BPRD office with a copy of the latest *National Inquisitor*. The headline read, "Bigfoot Deals Dope, Busted by Inquisitor Reporter." Turned out Stephanie had used more than one of Walker's cameras and had some pictures of the fake Bigfoot both with his suit and without. There were no pictures of the real thing, and she went out of her way to say that Bigfoot was a hoax, and that most scientists doubted the existence of such a creature.

Though I didn't much like the story, I knew she had a job to do too, and that she had done her best to protect the family that still lives somewhere deep within Palisades State Park.

Abe saw me looking at the *Inquisitor*. "You reading that trash again?"

I shrugged.

"Didn't you learn anything on your wild-goose chase to Iowa?"

I thought about that a moment and tossed the paper into the garbage. "I learned," I said, "that there are lots more things in life more important than Bigfoot."

Abe stroked his chin. "Like what?"

I didn't bat an eye. "Pizza. And it's your turn to buy."

I wish to acknowledge Matthew Clemens for his contribution to this story.

THE NUCKELAVEE
CHRISTOPHER GOLDEN & MIKE MIGNOLA

The old man had a shuddery way about him, a fidgety, near-to-tears aspect to every glance and gesture that said he'd jump at every shadow, if only he had the strength. If only he weren't so damned old. But his eyes weren't old. His eyes were wild with terror.

It was a cold, clear evening in the north of Scotland, and the sky was striped with colors, from a bruised blue on one horizon to the pink of sorrow or humiliation on the other. The rolling hills that surrounded the crumbling stone estate had no name save for that of the family which had resided there for more than five hundred years: MacCrimmon.

"That's it, then. Just as I said. It's dry as kindling, now, and ne'er will run again," said the old man, whose name was Andrew MacCrimmon.

He was the last of them.

MacCrimmon's wild eyes darted about like those of a skittish horse, as though he waited for some shade to steal upon him. Night had not quite fallen, and already, it seemed the man might die of fright, heart stilled in his chest so as not to be heard by whatever he feared might be hunting him.

Whatever it was, it had to be horrible, for the old man stood on the slope of the hill beside a creature whose countenance would give a hardened killer a week of restless nights and ugly dreams. Hellboy carried himself like a man, but his hooves and tail, his sawed-off horn-stumps, and his sheer size spoke another truth.

There were those who thought him a devil. But Andrew MacCrimmon would have sought help of the devil himself if he thought it would have done him any good.

"You'll stay, then, won't you?" the old man asked. "You must."

Hellboy grunted. He stared at the dry river bed, gazing along its path in both directions. It didn't make any sense at all to him, but he hadn't been there more than fifteen minutes. Just a short way up the bank of the dry river was a small stone building. When the water had still run through there, it would have stood half in, half out of the river.

"What's that?" Hellboy started off toward the stone structure.

"Ye don't understand," the old man whimpered. "Ye've got to help me. I was given to understand that ye do that sort of thing."

As he approached the small building, Hellboy narrowed his eyes. The thing was ancient. Older, even, than the MacCrimmon place, which stood on the hill behind them. The place couldn't be called a castle. Too small for that. But it was too big to be just a house, and too dilapidated to be called a mansion.

But this other thing . . .

"What is this?" he asked again.

"It's as old as the family," the old man told him. "Been there from the start. My grandfather told me he thought it was the reason the MacCrimmons settled here."

Hellboy studied the structure. The ancient stone was plain, but overgrown with ivy save for where the water would have washed across it before the river had gone dry. Centuries of water erosion had smoothed the stone, but Hellboy could still make out the faintest impression of carving. Once upon a time, there had been something drawn or written on that stone surface, but it was gone now.

Curiously, he clumped down into the dry river bed and around the other side of the edifice. His hooves sank in the still damp soil. There was something else on the river side of the building. Set into the stone, there was what appeared to be a door.

"How do you get in there?" he asked.

The old man whimpered.

There were no handles of any kind, nor any edges upon which he might get a significant grip. Still, Hellboy tried to open the door, to no avail.

"Please, sir, ye must listen to me," MacCrimmon begged.

Hellboy paused to regard him. The man's long hair and thick, bristly beard were white, and his face was deeply lined. He might have been a hermit, a squatter on this land, rather than its lord. Of course, "lord" was a dubious title when it referred to the crumbling family home, and a clan which no longer existed.

"Go on."

"The river was here before us, but the legend around the doom of Clan MacCrimmon was born right here on this hill. When the river goes dry, the legend says, it'll mean the end of Clan MacCrimmon. I've no children, ye see. I'm the last of the clan. Now that the river is dry, death will be coming for me.

"I knew it right off," the old man said, becoming more and more agitated. "Took three days for the river to run dry. Three days, you understand?"

Hellboy grunted. "Not really."

It was then that he noticed that the river wasn't completely dry. A tiny trickle of water ran past the door, past the building. It wasn't more than three inches wide, and barely deep enough to dampen the earth, but it was there. Hellboy reached down to put his finger into the water, and MacCrimmon cried out as if in pain.

"No, you mustn't! It's the doom of the MacCrimmons, don't you see? When the water stops running, the doom of my clan will be released."

"That's . . . interesting." With a shrug, Hellboy stepped up onto the slope again. "So what do you expect me to do?" he asked, massively confused by the old man's babbling. "Some legend says you're gonna die, I don't know how I'm supposed to deal with that."

The old man clutched at Hellboy's arm with both hands, eyes flicking back and forth in that disturbing, desperate twitch.

"You'll stay for dinner," he said, but it wasn't really a question. "You'll stay, and you'll see."

It was a very long drive back to anywhere Hellboy might stay that he wouldn't be shot at by local farmers or constabulary, so when Andrew MacCrimmon urged him on, he trekked up the hill to the crumbling manse alongside the old man. It was a gloomy place, a testament to entropy, with barely a whisper of the grandeur it must once have had.

Once they had entered, Hellboy saw that he had not been entirely correct about its origins based on his initial observations. While the manse itself was no more than three hundred years old, it was built around an older structure, a cruder, more fundamental tower or battlement, that must once have served as home and fortress for whomever had built it.

MacCrimmon Keep, someone at the BPRD had called it. Hellboy hadn't understood before, but now he saw it. This was the keep, and the rest of the place had been built up around it.

When they had settled inside, the old man brought out cold pork roast and slightly stale bread. There was haggis as well, but it looked like it might have gone over somewhat. Not that Hellboy was the world's greatest expert on haggis, but there was a greenish tint to it that made him even less likely to eat it than if he'd been trapped for a week on Everest with nothing to gnaw on but coffee grounds and it was a choice between haggis or his fellow climbers—which was pretty much the only way he would've eaten haggis even if it were fresh.

"Sorry I don't have more to offer," MacCrimmon muttered, a mouthful of questionable haggis visible between what was left of his teeth as he spoke. "The cook and t'other servants left three days ago, when the river started to slow. They *know*, y'see. They know."

When the meal was done, MacCrimmon seemed twitchier than ever. The manse was filled with sounds, as every old building is—a sign of age like the rings in a tree stump. The old man must have been familiar with most of those sounds, but now they frightened him, each and every one. He seemed to draw into himself, collapsing down upon his own body, becoming smaller. Decaying already, perhaps, at the thought of death's imminent arrival. Or imagined arrival.

"Cigar?" he asked suddenly, as if it were an accusation.

Hellboy flinched, startled. "Sure."

MacCrimmon led him to the library, which was larger than the enormous dining room they'd just left. Two walls were lined floor to ceiling with old, dessicated books, but Hellboy's eyes were drawn immediately to the other walls. To the paintings there, above and around the fireplace—where the old man now built a roaring blaze—and around the windows on the outer wall. Clan MacCrimmon came to life on those walls, in the deep hues and swirls of each portrait, but none of them was more vibrantly powerful than the one at the center of the outer wall. It hung between two enormous, drafty, rattling windows, and seemed, almost, a window itself. A window onto another time, and another shade of humanity. For the figure in the portrait was a warrior, that much was clear.

"Clan MacCrimmon?" Hellboy asked, glancing at the other portraits on the wall.

The old man seemed reluctant even to look at the portraits, but he nodded his assent as he handed Hellboy a cigar. With wooden matches, they lit the sweet-smelling things and began to smoke. After a short while in which nothing was spoken between them, the old man looked up at the portrait of the warrior that hung between the windows.

"That'd be William MacCrimmon. A warrior, he was, and fierce enough to survive that calling. Old William lost his closest friend in battle in 1453, and promised to care for the other warrior's daughter, Margaret."

Hellboy took a long puff on the cigar, then let the smoke out in a huff as he studied the old man. MacCrimmon was warming to the story of his ancestor, clinging to it as though it were a life preserver. It might only have been a way to pass the time, but Hellboy wondered if, in some way, it was the old man's way to keep his fears at bay, just for a while.

"Though already quite old for his time, William fell in love with Margaret, and married her. It was a sensible thing, perhaps the best way to care for the girl. Trouble was, Margaret was a Christian. William had to make some changes. He wasn't from the mainland, ye see. But from the isle of Malleen. Margaret wouldn't hear of living on the island, for there were stories, even then, of the things which thrived on Malleen."

Hellboy raised an eyebrow and scratched the stubble on his chin. "Things?"

For the first time since he began the story, MacCrimmon looked at him. The old man grinned madly.

"Why, the fuathan, o' course. Ye've never heard of them?"

Hellboy didn't respond. Considering the job, he didn't study nearly as much as he should have. The old man didn't seem to notice, his attention drawn back to the portrait of his warrior ancestor.

"Old William had known the people, the fuathan, since he was a bairn, ye ken. Shaggy little beasts that might be men if not for the way nature twisted their bodies. The legends say they hated men, but not so, not so. They were the servants and allies of the islanders, and held malice only for those from the mainland.

"Still, when William married Margaret, and chose to remain here in the north country, rather than return to the island, the fuathan had no choice. They came along. It were they who built the original keep, and that pile out in the river bed. It were they who made the river run, so the legend goes, for the fuathan were ever in control of the water.

"What it was built to house, the legends dinna say, but the story has it that they raised it in a day, and the keep itself in a week, all the while, making certain Margaret MacCrimmon would never see them. There's a circle of stones in the wood over the hill that were used for worship. The fuathan lived there, in the wood around the circle, and the clan grew with both the new religion and the old faith."

Hellboy shivered. He'd heard similar stories dozens of times, about the encroachment of Christianity into pagan territories, one family at a time. But in this case, with the results crumbling and gloomy around him, it seemed far more tangible. Honestly, it gave him the creeps. The clash of old and new faiths could not have been a healthy one. He had to wonder what it had done to the offspring of that union, down across the centuries.

The old man seemed to have run out of steam, though he still stared at the portrait of the warrior. And there was something odd about that portrait, something that held the eye. Hellboy tore his gaze away, took a puff of his cigar, and turned his attention on the old man again.

"So you live here alone, now? I mean, except for the servants who ran off?"

"Last of the clan," MacCrimmon agreed, apparently forgetting that he'd told Hellboy that already. "Alone here since my brother died."

With the fat cigar clenched in his teeth, the old man moved to the stone fireplace, the blazing light flickering over his features. There were faded photographs in silver frames on the mantel, and MacCrimmon pulled one of

them down and handed it to Hellboy. In the corner, a dusty grandfather clock
ticked the seconds by, its pendulum glinting with the light of the fire as it swung
back and forth.

In the photograph, two young men flanked a beautiful girl, whose raven hair
and fine-china features reminded Hellboy of a woman he had once known. He
pushed the thought away. The two men were obviously MacCrimmon and his
brother. Though Andrew had grown old now, though his face was wrinkled and
bearded, the eyes staring out of that photograph were the same.

Wild, even then. And Hellboy had to wonder if the man had ever been sane.

He handed the photograph back to the old man. "Who's the girl?"

MacCrimmon set his cigar on the stone mantel, and stared at the photo, a
dreamy look relaxing his features for the first time since Hellboy had arrived.

"That'd be Sarah Kirkwall. She was here all that long summer. This photo
was taken the day before me brother Robert announced that they were to be
engaged." The old man frowned, and rubbed distractedly at his forehead. When
he spoke again, his voice was lost and far away. "They lived here, with me, until
Robert . . . died. I told Sarah she could stay, that I'd care for her, just as Old
William MacCrimmon had taken care of Margaret five hundred years ago. That
she could . . . marry me."

The anguish in the old man's voice was horrible to hear, and Hellboy felt the
sadness in that old stone dwelling creeping into his bones.

"So you married?"

The old man shook his head, still staring at the photo. "It were Robert she
loved. When he died, she . . . went away. I never did marry. Sarah was the girl for
me. There never were anyone else."

MacCrimmon looked even older now, shrunken, staring down at the photograph
as though trapped, now, in that other time, back when. Hellboy thought again of
the portrait of the warrior on the wall, how it looked almost like a window on
another time, and seemed to draw you in. The photograph in the silver frame had
the same effect on the old man.

Hellboy scratched the back of his neck, where what hair he had was tied back
in a knot. "How did Robert die?" he asked.

The frame tumbled from the old man's hands and shattered on the stone in
front of the fireplace. Hellboy prepared to catch MacCrimmon, thinking he must
be about to collapse, but the old man just stared at his hands, the spot where the
frame had been. Slowly, he reached out and took his cigar from the mantel, and
pulled a long puff on it.

"Ten years ago, this very night," MacCrimmon said.

He seemed almost calm, and then a shudder ran through him and he turned
and looked at the grandfather clock. When he spoke again, his voice cracked with
a panic he could no longer hide.

"Ten years ago tonight," he repeated. "He died at three minutes past nine."

Hellboy glanced at the clock. It was only a few minutes before nine then, half a dozen minutes to go before the dreadful anniversary.

With that edge of panic still in his voice, the old man continued. "He was three days sick, dying, before he went at last. Just as the river was three days, drying up. Now it's almost time. The last trickle will run through the dry bed out there, and he'll come for me."

Minutes ticked by, and Hellboy just watched the old man in silence. The cigar burned in MacCrimmon's hand, but he made no effort to smoke it. Then, suddenly, the old man glanced at the burning weed in his hand, and he narrowed his gaze, as if seeing it for the first time. With a tremor of disgust, he threw the cigar into the fire, which by now had begun to burn low. The flames flared up inexplicably, tendrils of fire lashing out at the stone masonry, then dying down again.

The grandfather clock chimed nine.

Andrew MacCrimmon dropped to his knees before Hellboy, tears beginning to slip down his craggy features.

"Save me!" he pleaded.

Hellboy only looked at him dubiously.

The clock continued to chime.

As if he'd been startled by some sudden noise, the old man turned his head and glanced about, eyes more wild than ever, hands on his head as though he might hide himself away.

"Did ye not hear that? It's the doom of the MacCrimmons!"

"It's just the clock," Hellboy told him.

The old man rushed to one of the wind-rattled windows and threw it open. He leaned out, but Hellboy knew that from that angle, there was no way MacCrimmon could see what he was looking for—the river bed, of course, and that little stone building the man had insisted was built by horrid little fairy creatures.

"Not the clock! Don't you see? It's him. It's *it.* The stream's gone dry, and it's coming out. Battering down that door. It's coming up the lawn now, coming for me!"

The old man turned from the window and fell again at Hellboy's feet.

He clutched the bottom of Hellboy's duster and buried his face in it, whimpering, muttering.

Hellboy frowned. "Did you bury your brother in that little building out there?"

"You saw that place," the old man stammered. "There's no way to open it from the outside, but . . . from the inside . . . no. Robert's cremated and his ashes are in a niche at St. Brendan's, where they ought to be. But . . . "

MacCrimmon gripped his jacket even more tightly, his voice barely a whisper. "There, you *must* hear it. It's coming for me. His ghost has set it free. There! It's broken down the door. Can't you hear it on the stairs?"

Hellboy heard nothing. He looked down at the old man and felt a little sorry for him, though he had a strong suspicion what had driven him so completely mad.

"You killed him."

The old man wailed. "Robert has loosed the doom of the MacCrimmons on me for murderin' him. I fed him poison and sat by those three days while it killed him. I did it for her, I did it for the girl, and it wasn't ever me that she wanted . . . "

His voice trailed off after that. He fell quiet, listening. Then the old man jerked, suddenly, as if he'd been pinched.

"It's there now!" he screamed, voice raspy and hoarse. "In the hall, just outside the door. Please, help me. Take me with you. Kill me! Anything. Just don't let that thing take me!"

Despite the old man's mad cries, however, the room was silent save for his blubbering and the ticking of the clock. On the face of that antique timekeeper, the long hand had moved inexorably along so that it was now four or five minutes after nine o'clock. The anniversary of Robert MacCrimmon's death had come and gone.

"Don't have a heart attack or anything," Hellboy said. "Look, I'll show you."

He reached for the doorknob, shaking his head ruefully. But just as his fingers touched it, the door came crashing down at him, tearing off its hinges and slamming Hellboy to the floor.

"Jeez!" he shouted in surprise.

As he tried to get out from under the heavy door, a sudden and tremendous weight was put on it from above, pinning him there. Hellboy grunted in pain, struggled to move, and could not. There was a horrid stench, like nothing he had ever smelled before, death and rot and fecal matter, blood and sweat and urine, matted horse hair and putrefying fish, and something else, something worse than all of those disgusting odors combined.

Then, without warning, the weight was removed. Something stepped off the door and into the room. Hellboy summoned his strength and his anger, and tossed the shattered door off him. He glanced around, and then he saw it, one of the most horrifying monstrosities he had ever laid eyes on. It was like a huge, equine creature that might have been a horse if it had any skin. Instead, there was only naked, purple muscle, and white tendons, and swollen, black veins. Growing out of its back was a human torso, also stripped of skin, with a head that swung about wildly as if there were no bones in its neck. Its huge mouths, both human and horse, gaped open and that stink poured out, almost visible, like breath in winter.

Its long arms snaked out and grabbed hold of old man MacCrimmon, and hauled him up onto the back of its horse segment. Hellboy started to roar, started to lunge for it, but a hoof lashed out and cracked against his skull, and he went down hard on the floor of the library, not far from the blazing fire.

By the time he shook off the blow, the creature was gone, the old man's screams echoing through the house and down the hillside. Hellboy rose, ready to give chase, but the fire flared again, and he turned to see that it was blue now. Tendrils of blue flame shot out of the blaze and seemed to touch each of the portraits in turn, ending with that of William MacCrimmon, founder of the clan.

Blue fire seemed to seep into the portrait, becoming paint, becoming one with the history in that window on that past. It truly was a window now, and through it, Hellboy could see the old warrior moving, turning to glare into the library with a stern countenance, cold and cruel in judgment. Tendrils of blue flame jumped from portrait to portrait, and the painted images of the warrior's descendants were somehow erased from their own frames, to appear behind the original, the founder. That portrait seemed to grow, with all of them standing therein, arms crossed before them, glaring down like inquisitors.

Then the portrait burst into flame, and Hellboy heard an enormous crack. The keep, the part of the MacCrimmon homestead that had been built so long ago by the fuathan, began to fall, to collapse down into the remainder of the house. The shelves and books in the library were set aflame, but the flame was nearly snuffed out as the walls collapsed, tumbling toward Hellboy.

He ran for one of the huge windows, not daring to look at the burning, living painting, at the ghosts of the clan MacCrimmon, for fear he might be sucked into that collective past. Hellboy crashed out through the window and fell twenty feet to the hillside below. The walls were crumbling in on themselves, but several stones came falling after him, and he rushed to avoid being crushed or buried.

He could hear Andrew MacCrimmon screaming, down the hill, where the riverbed was now completely dry. Hooves pounding the grass, Hellboy gave chase. Where the river had run, he saw hoof prints from the beast in the soft, damp earth. As he passed the structure that stood on the river's edge, he saw that the stone door he had found impossible to open now hung wide. Seconds after he crossed the dry riverbed, he heard a kind of explosion, and turned to see that even that stone structure had been part of the chain reaction. It was nothing but rubble now.

The doom of the MacCrimmons had come, all right.

There came another scream. Hellboy glanced up the opposite hill and saw the beast disappearing over its crest, looking like nothing more than a large horse bearing two riders. But the way its raw, skinless form glistened wetly in the moonlight . . . it was no horse.

When he reached the top of the hill, however, neither beast nor man were anywhere in sight. Hellboy crouched in the spot he had last seen them, and found a trail. It was relatively easy to track; the beast was so heavy that its hooves left prints in the hardest, dryest ground.

Hellboy followed.

Hours passed, and he made his way across farms and estates, through groves and over hills, and finally he came to a town on the north coast, the tang of the ocean in the air, the sound of the tides carrying through the streets. It was after midnight, and most of the residents had long since retired for the evening. In the midst of the town, on a paved road, he lost the trail. Hopelessly, he looked around for someone who might have seen something. After a minute or two, he spotted a portly man slumped in a heavy, old chair on the porch of what appeared to be some kind of mercantile.

"Hey, wake up," Hellboy said, nudging the portly man with the weight of his stone hand.

The man snorted, blinked his eyes open, and let out a yell of surprise and fear. The odor of whiskey came off him in waves.

"Quiet," Hellboy snapped. "I'm just passing through."

"Thank the Lord for that," the man said in a frightened whisper.

"You see anything strange go through here?"

The man stared at him as if he were insane.

"Anything *worse*?" Hellboy elaborated.

"Depends on your definition of strange, I suppose," the man said. "Two men came through, not long ago. Two men riding the same horse. Only one of them wasn't riding. He was the horse. That's pretty strange."

"You see where it went?" Hellboy demanded.

"Down to the rocks," the man replied. "Down to the sea. And that old one screaming all the way. Weren't a surprise, though. I'd scream too, that horse, and the whole thing smelling like a fisherman's toilet."

His voice trailed off and he moaned a bit, and fell back to sleep, or into unconsciousness. The whiskey had claimed him again.

Hellboy scratched his chin and looked along the paved road to the rocks and the ocean beyond. He could heard the waves crashing, and he started to walk toward them. At the end of the road, he stopped where the rocks began. There was a cough off to his left, and he turned to see an old woman standing on the front stoop of her home in a robe that was insufficient for the chill ocean breeze.

"It was a Nuckelavee," she told him.

Hellboy looked at her oddly, but she didn't even turn her face to him. She just stared out at the ocean.

"When I was but a wee girl in the Hebrides, my father told me a story. He were coming home late one night, and a Nuckelavee come up out of the ocean and chased him. He only escaped by jumping over a little stream of fresh water. The monster roared and spit and with one long arm snatched off me father's hat, but he got away clean save for a pair of claw marks to show off to prove the truth of it."

Now she looked straight at Hellboy for the first time.

"He was luckier than that old man tonight. That's certain."

Hellboy nodded and looked out across the waves again. He could see a dark hump in the distance, out on the ocean.

"What's that?"

The old woman hesitated. At length, she spoke, her voice low and haunted. "'Tis the Isle of Malleen. But don't ye think about goin' out there. It's not a place fit for man, nor e'en a thing such as yourself. There's only evil out there, dark and cruel. If that's where the Nuckelavee was headed, no wonder the old man were screaming so."

Hellboy considered her words, staring at the island in the distance.

"I guess maybe he deserved it," he said after a bit. "I'm starting to wonder if maybe all it did was take that old man home. And I think there'll be hell to pay when he gets there."

The wind shifted, then, and for a moment, it seemed as though he could hear a distant scream, high and shrill and inhuman. But then the waves crashed down again on the rocks, and it was gone.

A NIGHT AT THE BEACH
MATTHEW J. COSTELLO

I had been to Coney Island twice—and I thought I'd never have to visit it again. The first time? 1952. Golden years in the good old USA, and Coney was America's beach. Miles and miles of relatively pristine beach front, an endless boardwalk, and the post-war boomers all baking into lobsters. Not that red isn't a nice color . . . Kinda made me feel okay.

And why was I there? Oh, nothing too dramatic. One person on the board of the Bureau had a house in nearby Brighton. I probably didn't know it at the time, but I was still in the process of being checked out.

Everyone searching for an answer to the big question . . . who was I?

Not that we ever answered the question. We have just all agreed to move . . . past it.

And my second visit? 1975. And Coney was no longer anyone's playground. The big amusement parks like Steeplechase were long gone. Now the empty, haunted rides sat dark while the Atlantic slurped at the nearby coast. When I went, Coney looked like Berlin circa 1946. I actually had to step over a dead dog on the sidewalk wondering . . . how long before someone comes and removes it? Or maybe they wouldn't? Maybe the dog would just lie there until it withered away, until it was just a pile of canine bones on the cracked pavement.

That time I had gone to Coney to talk to someone who had links to a Santeria cult in Manhattan that had turned, as Darth might say, toward the dark side. Alphabet City was turning into death world, and there was a former member in Coney who might help.

Or could have. I found him . . . on his wall, pinned like one of the stuffed prizes from the boardwalk. I'm pretty sure he wasn't completely dead by the time the last giant four-inch nails had been hammered through him and onto the cracked plaster wall.

But he sure was dead by the time I got there.

Made stopping the cult that much harder.

But stop it I did. It's in the Bureau's files. Under "Ritual Murder" . . . or maybe "Demon-Directed Serial Killing." Not sure . . . they've changed filing methods so often. Not my job, as they say.

And I thought I'd never revisit Coney Island again. Place left a multiple of bad tastes in my mouth.

But I was wrong.

I was due at least one more ride on the big Coney coaster.

It started with a grim-faced Abraham Sapien calling me into a small meeting room at the bureau. Now "grim faced" is nothing new for Abe. But even for him, he looked unusually *concerned*.

"Sit down," he told me.

"I'm fine standing," I said. I've broken enough chairs in the joint to opt to stand unless I was mighty sure of my perch.

But Abe sat and opened up a manila folder . . . from which all these clippings slid out.

"Know about these?" he said.

I looked at the clippings, most from the *Daily News*. A few disappearances, kids, a teenage girl, a postal worker who didn't come home. But then there were two stories of . . . drownings. People found with their clothes on who drowned. I checked the locations . . . Manhattan Beach, Brighton Beach, Sheepshead Bay, Coney Island.

The Brooklyn Riviera.

"Yeah, so . . . ?" I said.

"That's not all, Hellboy. These are what the paper's got. Here's the other stuff . . . "

And then he dumped . . . the other stuff. Police reports, photos, audio tapes . . . I only had to skim the material to see what was missing from the *Daily News*'s recounting.

The drowning victims had strange lacerations all over their bodies as though they had been in the cage with a pack of starving wolves. The pictures—even for me—were hard to look at.

The police reports on the missing people had eyewitnesses saying how they heard sounds by the shore, people running, screaming, the sound of splashing water.

In five minutes I could see two things: That all the stories were probably linked. That was a no-brainer. But another element also emerged. Something mighty strange had happened to these people. Strange—and horrible.

"The drownings," I said looking at the pictures, ". . . they're people who tried to . . . escape from . . . whatever?"

"Yes. Except we don't know anything about the 'whatever.'"

I looked at the photos again. One of the bodies was found within sight of the Cyclone rollercoaster. The police photographer went for an art shot. Here's the lacerated body, and here's the decayed amusement park. I put the evidence down.

"You have your work cut out for you, Abe." He looked up. His eyes narrowed. "I mean, it's obvious that you should take the lead on this. With the water tie-in and everything. Your show all the way. I'll be there for back-up, of course. But—"

He held up a hand.

"No. I knew you'd think that. Maybe there's a water connection. Seems obvious, I know. But—"

Abe hesitated. There was something going on here that he didn't tell me.

He looked back up at me. "I don't know how to tell you this, Hellboy. It's not easy to admit."

The air in the room felt close, claustrophobic—as if we were underwater.

"Partly it's intuition. Partly it's making a few conceptual leaps from these photos. But this has something to do with the sea, something in the ocean that's growing in power, feeding off these people. If I go . . . I'll meet them in their world. Which is precisely what they want. You—on the other hand—"

I laughed. If there's one thing I knew about Abraham it was that he didn't scare easily. So I believed what he was saying . . . that this possible water-related investigation might be better done by me.

"Coney Island," I said.

Abe nodded. "I'll do back-up, and I have a few leads for you to follow. And I've asked Kate to help."

I nodded. I wondered if Dr. Kate Corrigan was still annoyed with me. When we were in the Appalachians my overeagerness triggered a whole room full of folk texts to explode into flames. That the books were bound in skin didn't deter her academic's interest in their documentation of three centuries of rural cannibalism.

"She's up for it?"

"Yes, as long as you think a nanosecond before blowing anything up."

"Deal. And the lead?"

"Just this one . . ."

Abe handed me a slip of paper.

I rolled my eyes. "You gotta be kidding me . . ."

But he wasn't.

Kate Corrigan had an office on the campus of New York University though I had never seen it.

"You'd create quite a scene," she said.

"In the Village?' I said. "Give me a break."

There were days I traveled below Eighth Street and I felt as though I fit in just fine. In New York City you could be anything . . . even a Hellboy. The village could be mighty tolerant. Still, she met me at the Used Book Cafe. I didn't exactly disappear, but this meeting of old books and fresh coffee had enough of a bizarre charm that I felt okay.

"So what's up?"

"What?" I said. "No 'Hello, Hellboy—how are you doing'? How's life in the fast lane?"

She smiled. "I have thirty minutes before my urban-legends seminar. If I could only tell them half of what I know . . . "

"And scare the hell out of them? Not a good idea."

She looked right at me. "So—"

I told her what Abe had been talking about, the murders, the disappearances. She sipped her latte.

"I've seen the stories."

"He thinks . . . *we* think . . . that they're connected. Something's happening at Coney Island. And I wouldn't mind an urban-legend expert coming along. After your next class, of course."

"And I'd be very annoyed if you didn't ask. Besides, I haven't been to Coney Island in ages."

"A Nathan's hot dog on me . . . "

She laughed.

We wouldn't be laughing for long.

"Christ—it's like a war zone. Do people actually have fun here?" I looked around at the landscape. Sure there were rides, and games to play, and junk food galore. But everything was a bit . . . *off.* The stuffed prizes in the booths—the plush toys—were unrecognizable, as though we had beamed down to some alternate planet filled with totally unfamiliar cartoon characters. No Donald or Daffy here. No, but you could get a stuffed Demented Duck if you wanted . . . if you could win the game.

We stopped on Surf Avenue right near the Cyclone roller coaster.

"That's supposed to be one great coaster," I said. "Not that I know from personal experience, not that they'd ever let me ride." On cue, a line of cars went screaming above us, the sound echoing down to us. Happy screams, I imagined. The sound of fun.

Was it the danger that provided the thrill? In which case, the riders might be flirting with more danger than they knew.

We passed a carousel.

"That's open all year," I told Kate. "Even in the dead of winter, you can come and try to get some brass rings."

"The operator looks like a happy soul."

The man feeding the rings into a long arm had a haunted expression as though he was operating some infernal machine from the bowels of Dante's hell.

The thumping carousel music filled the car . . . then faded, like the rich smells wafting on the wind, the sweet smell of sausage and hot-buttered corn and—of course—Nathan's famous.

"Still the best hot dog," I said.

"They're off my list of edible food. Still, maybe on the way back I'll test fate."

I nodded. What were we looking for here? Some hidden link that would tie the disappearances together, the missing bodies, the drowned bodies. It was purely instinct, but I thought that someone here must know something. This might be a great place for secrets . . . but nobody can keep secrets forever.

"Turn here," I told Kate. "All the way down to the end."

To our one lead.

She turned, and the boardwalk was ahead. The sun was going down. Less chance for me to cause a stir, I thought.

But I needn't have worried.

The beach was oddly deserted. Here it was, a warm summer day, sun not quite gone, and there were few people in the water, and fewer still on the beach.

"Strange, hm?"

"Business looks a little slow on the boardwalk, too."

Everything looked open . . . just not terribly busy.

"It's the *Jaws* phenomenon," I said. "Something is snatching people around here, and all of a sudden other recreational activities start to look more attractive."

A young man on rollerblades flew by us.

"'Course, if you're really fast . . . maybe you don't get afraid."

"There it is," Kate said, pointing to a small building that sat at the middle of the boardwalk. The building, painted white, glowed a burnished orange in the setting light. Big puffy red letters announced, "The Coney Island Museum of Oddities." It was our one lead from Abe, a good place as any to begin.

"Wonder if it's open . . . "

On cue, a thin, weasel-looking man slunked out of the museum, looked left and right—he couldn't have acted more furtive—then he dashed away.

"We're in luck," I said. "Let's hope the oddities don't disappoint."

I walked up to the white door and turned the handle. It didn't open.

"That's . . . odd . . . ," I said. "I could have sworn we just watched someone come out this very door."

I jiggled the handle. Then Kate knocked, rapping hard.

"Hm, maybe it's—," I pushed hard, and when the door didn't budge, I pushed harder. The sound of splintering wood told me that the Museum of Oddities probably had a termite problem.

The interior was dark, musty . . .

Kate hung by the doorway.

"I don't like this," she said.

"And I do?"

I took another step in, and she followed. Gradually my eyes adjusted to the light and I saw some of the more obvious specimens in the collection. There, floating in a jar of murky water, was a two-headed baby. It looked real enough, but I doubted that it could be. Otherwise, where were all the two-headed humans? A mummy sarcophagus sat in the corner. The paint looked a tad fresh—but then maybe the proprietor re-touched it.

"Get a load of this," Kate said.

And I turned to see a hand.

"Says here . . . that this is the Crawling Hand that strangled the Count Weingrin of Austria . . . after he had his romantic rival tortured and put to death."

"Crawling hand . . . looks pretty still to me."

Kate read from a card. "'The Count had his rival's hands and feet cut off and tossed into the Danube. Later that night, this hand crawled out of the river, found its way to the Count's bedroom and strangled him.'"

"Oh, it's that famous Crawling Hand."

"Ahhh!"

Kate let the hand fall to the ground.

"What is it?"

"I felt . . . something . . . "

"Oh give me a break. Just pick it up and—"

She knelt down.

"Hellboy." Her voice was quiet, still. One of those sounds that's inversely proportional to the alarm she felt.

"Yes."

"I—don't see it. Dropped it here, and now—"

"Just stop fooling around . . . It has to be right there."

"Stop!"

From the darkness, the musty back rooms of the Museum of Oddities, I heard a voice. The proprietor, I thought. I turned slowly. I wondered if he'd ever seen anything as odd as me.

"Tell me," he whispered, holding a rifle, "why I shouldn't just shoot you both now. Breaking and entering. Would be no problem with the police."

Despite the gun sitting inches away, I could have mentioned one reason might be that I could smash him so fast with my hand that he'd go flying out the back of the building.

I heard him wheezing, sniffling.

A member of the coke generation.

I decided to try verbal communication first.

"Just this. We're here . . . because we think you might know something. That maybe—," I took a stab at something. My batting average was anything but perfect, but,— "Maybe you know something, and you're scared and hey—it might all impact your business."

"You mean my museum?"

I laughed. "You wish. I mean your drug business. You're dealing. Keeping Coney high on whatever they want."

He rubbed his nose.

Kate came close to me. She whispered: "I still couldn't find the damn hand."

I whispered back. "Well, you know those crawling hands. Can't keep them down . . . "

"You dropped the crawling hand?" the proprietor said. The tenseness in his voice gave me pause. Maybe bantering about the thing wasn't a good idea.

"I think . . . , " I said slowly, " . . . it sort of . . . scurried away . . . "

The man's eyes darted about. And in that rather surreal moment, I brought up my right had as fast as I could and smacked the man's gun hand. I had hoped that the pain would make him release the gun. Instead he held tight and pulled the trigger.

"Idiot," I said, and now I slammed a backhand to the side of his head.

He was on the floor, out.

"Good one," Kate said. "He'll be great to question now."

"Oh, we'll just wait," I said. "Give us time to find your lost hand—before it finds us."

Richie came to. That was the guy's name, according to the material on his desk—the unpaid bills and the pack of rubber checks he planned on paying then with. Richie Tryp. Sounded like a good name for a fifties crooner. Ladies and gentlemen, Richie Tryp!

Richie sat on the one chair in his office space-cum-garbage dump.

"W-what do you want?" he asked.

The little smash to the head had convinced him that we should make peace, not war. Besides, Kate had his gun.

Kate took the lead.

"You know about all the disappearances, the bodies . . . "

"Yeah," I added, "the way Coney just isn't any fun anymore."

Richie nodded.

"We were wondering . . . you live here . . . maybe . . . you know something."
He turned away.

"Don't know a thing."

"Richie," I said. "Richie, Richie, Richie . . . you don't want your drug business to go bust, now do you? Who will supply all of Coney's campers?"

"If you know something," Kate said, "for God's sake tell us. What makes you think . . . that whatever it is won't get you?"

"Or maybe some of your customers," I said.

No one laughed at my bit of black humor. I turned and looked at the door, still open a crack. Except now the light had faded. The sun was down. Coney at night.

Why did I look back there, I thought. Was it a feeling that something was . . . there?

"Tell us what you know," Kate said. "Before this place becomes a ghost town."

Now Richie Tryp looked up, his bloodshot eyes, so sad and haunted.

"I—I don't know . . . "

No. There was nothing at the door. Just my nerve endings a little hot-wired. Something was up tonight. And Richie was about to reveal all.

Well, almost all . . .

A surprisingly cold breeze blew off the water.
I hummed a bit of a classic song.

I mean, we were, after all, huddled under the splintery boardwalk.

"Enough, Hellboy."

"Just trying to lighten the mood."

The beach was deserted. Nobody as far as we could see in either direction, and nobody on the boardwalk.

"Think Richie screwed us?"

"Doubt it. I don't think he wants me knocking on his door again. Funny, the oddest thing in his museum . . . is the proprietor."

A sudden gust. I heard Kate shiver.

"Not exactly a nice summer night on—"

I stopped.

A sound, voices in the distance . . . carried by the wind, then blown away.

Kate moved. "Steady," I said. "Let's stay hidden as long a possible."

She moved close. I whispered to her, "Hey, maybe you'll get a new urban legend out of the evening."

"Maybe . . . "

The voices grew in volume, excited noises, and then a muffled sound. And finally I saw the group streaming down from the east, from the roller coaster and the aquarium.

"Amazing everyone knows to stay off the beach, eh? The word must be out."

We didn't move. Didn't have to . . . since the merry band was making its way to us.

Carrying someone. A girl—I saw her struggling, arms holding tightly to each limb.

"Let's go," Kate said.

I put out my hand out to stop her.

"One more minute. Maybe it's just a clam bake."

The girl's struggles suddenly freed her head, and she screamed, a chilling sound on the empty beach. But someone quickly covered her mouth again.

I had this thought.

Where are the cops?

Unless—they're *there*. Part of the little party. The crowd looked about twelve strong.

"Richie Tryp scores . . . , " I said. "Have to give him my regards."

The crowd reached the shore. I could barely make out the girl being pinned to the sand, . . . just at the water's edge, . . . when the low keening began, a bizarre moan. A Hawaiian luau this wasn't.

"Now," Kate said.

I nodded.

We got up, the damp sand sticking to our bodies.

"Going to need a nice hot shower when I get home," I said. "Don't you just hate it when the sand gets in all those little cracks and crevices?"

"And you have such . . . big crevices."

"I thought you'd never notice . . . "

We walked to the crowd at the shore, the moaning rhythmic. I spotted the thin sliver of a waning moon in the sky, like a weird grin, as if planet Earth was really one very amusing place.

Lots of laughs.

Especially here, especially now.

Kate and I picked up the pace. My hand was close to my gun . . . not that I was sure I'd need it.

Someone in the group turned and saw us, but the chanting sound went on. They weren't going to let a little Hellboy visit interrupt them.

Kate broke into a run—probably thinking that they might do something quickly to the girl. But I didn't see any weapons glinting in the pale light.

But then, beyond the group, I did see something.

Did you ever see those classic movies in the fifties . . . you know, the ones about the gillman? Not bad effects for the time, old Ricou Browning doing a pretty convincing job as the creature.

Beyond the group, I saw something come out of the water.

Now imagine—if you will—that the gillman . . . was totally convincing. Imagine that he looked as real as some slimy slug in your typical suburban garden.

Not only that, give him an extra pair of arms and mouth of teeth that would put a great white to shame.

Now imagine that after you see the first one, six more pop their ugly heads out of the water.

Only meters away from the girl.

Abe didn't want this. A little too close to home for him.

How nice of him to pass it on to me.

The sea things trudged towards the girl. Their bodies may have been made for speed in the water, but walking in the shallow surf seemed a tad hard.

I reached the crowd.

I backhanded the first few . . . worshippers, and sent them flying like bowling pins. The girl began screaming.

She was looking at me.

"It's okay," I said. "We're here to help."

Then Kate jumped on two of the other beachcombers and the girl was nearly free. But not before I saw the sea things almost at her.

One cultist wouldn't let go of the girl's arm.

I pulled out my gun and fired right at the place his arm joined his shoulder. Suddenly holding the girl didn't seem like such a priority.

"Kate, take her . . . get going."

She looked at me. In her eyes, I could see she knew she was leaving me in one very bad situation.

"Get her out of here . . . "

Kate nodded, and pulled the girl away.

The sea things opened their mouths in unison.

"What are you boys gonna do . . . ," I said, "sing?"

And as if in response, they all hissed at me, so loud and long that I could smell their foul breath.

"What the hell have you guys been eating? No . . . don't answer that."

I formulated a defense plan. Basically, shoot and bash.

One creature leaped at me, but his footing was lousy and he landed on my shoulder. My stone fist smashed down on his head. I heard a soft, pulpy sound. One down . . . five to go.

Another came running, jaws opened wide, like some demented humanoid shark, snapping at the air.

"You wouldn't like the way I taste," I said—and shot him in between two curved incisors.

The shot set him flying back.

But then one landed on my leg and I felt its teeth bite down. Another jumped onto my shoulder, and then—a moment I dreaded—I felt myself being pulled by these things into the water. And despite my size and all my strength, I felt the water on my legs, saw my blood swirling around the milky moon-lit sea water . . . deeper, even as I fired at this creature and tried to smash the other.

I knew once they had me in the water, it would be no contest.

Deeper, until I felt them all around me—were there more? And the water at my chin. Then—I tasted the too-salty water of the Atlantic.

At least the water made the pain better.

The teeth chomping down didn't feel so horrible anymore.

I struggled in the murky water, zero visibility, my arm slowed by the water so even my best attempts to smash the creatures failed. They were all around me.

Then I felt one creature . . . ripped off me.

Then another. Now I could grab one and crush one slimy head between my biceps and chest. I didn't hear the satisfying crack . . . but I felt it.

I grabbed the creature hanging on me and knocked its jaw straight up so that its mouth was now re-located close to the top of its frog-like skull.

Then I thought . . . breathing! Air might be nice. What a good idea.

I shot to the surface.

What had pulled them off me?

A few seconds and then something broke the water.

A familiar face.

Abe.

We treaded water there for a moment.

"I thought this was my case . . . I thought . . . you were worried?" I hurt all over—and I'm sure the blood from my wound was driving the blue crabs below crazy.

Abe grinned.

"Hey, didn't anyone ever take you fishing, Hellboy?"

I looked at my friend. "What?"

"What do you need when you go fishing . . . ?"

Some of the dead sea-things bobbed to the surface. A bunch of them . . . all of them? Time would tell.

"Fishing?"

Abe was grinning, looking demented in the rolling surf, the white moonlight hitting his eyes.

Then I flashed on it. And I laughed.

"Right . . . " I shook my head. I owed him one for this. "I was the bait."

Now Abe laughed, and he looked around at the bobbing sea-things even now rolling towards the shore. "And look how well you did."

"Yeah," I said, turning, starting to swim back to the shoreline. I saw Kate on the boardwalk, waiting. "Catch of the day, don't you think?"

And Abe laughed again.

BURN, BABY, BURN

POPPY Z. BRITE

The girl waits by the side of the road, just past Lolita age but obviously still jailbait. She wears a pair of ragged denim cutoffs and a grubby white T-shirt bearing the logo of John Lennon's Plastic Ono Band. Her dark hair hangs stick-straight and lank to the middle of her back. July 1976, and she's pretty sure she is somewhere in New Jersey.

When a green VW bus comes along, she sticks out her thumb and watches it roll to a stop. The rear doors swing open; hands help her in. Pot smoke. Young male faces, their tufts of attempted beard and mustache like scattered weeds, barely hiding the zits. King Crimson or some other ponderous art-rock band blaring from a stereo that's probably worth way more than the van itself.

"What's your name, baby?"

"Liz."

"How old are you?"

"Seventeen," she says, adding three years. The boy looks skeptical, but Liz can tell he doesn't really care.

They offer her liquor, which she declines, and pot, which she cautiously tries because it smells so good. The end of the joint glows red as she tokes on it, so smooth, doesn't make her cough at all. She holds the twisted cigarette before her face, focusing her eyes on the small, lurid point of fire.

"Hey, babe, quit bogartin' it," says another boy. "Less a'course you want to work out a trade."

The driver swivels in his seat, making the van swerve on the road. "Gas, grass, or ass, nobody rides for free." They all laugh uproariously. Liz feels a hand on her leg, then two more encircling her wrists, not squeezing yet but letting her know they are there. Letting her know she's trapped.

They wish.

Liz hasn't hurt anyone in a long time. The images that come back to her when she does it are too unbearable. She's been learning to focus her ability, to put her power into things that don't scream and hurt and die when they burn. But she is Elizabeth Anne Sherman from the Kansas side of Kansas City, and she is still a virgin, and she's damned if she is going to lose her cherry getting raped by a bunch of stoned hippies.

Among other things, she is afraid her parents might look down from Heaven and see it happening.

So she lets the heat well up from the place deep inside her, somewhere just below the center of her chest she thinks it is, and it arrows out of her in a thin, pure ray. It's spilling from her eyes, her fingertips, and it doesn't hurt her at all, it feels good—

The ratty boys are scrambling away from her, away from the little corona of flames around her. Liz smells scorching hair, knows it isn't her own. She gathers all her strength and reins it in, sucks it in. It has taken the better part of four years, but she can control it now, and she doesn't want to kill these stupid boys.

"Fuck!"

"She musta dropped the fuckin' doob—she's on fire—"

"No, man, it's comin' out her hands! Get the bitch outta here!"

The VW screeches to a halt and Liz hops out before she can be shoved. She stumbles on the shoulder of the road, steadies herself, spins, and manages to shoot them the middle finger before the doors slam shut and the van takes off again.

A hundred yards down the road, she sees it stop again. The back doors open and a blanket is cast out, flaming merrily.

Liz laughs.

It first happened when she was eleven. She'd always hated the ugly ginger-haired boy who lived next door. Her big brother Steve usually made the kid leave her alone, but on this sunny Saturday afternoon Steve was in his room desperately trying to finish some chemistry project that was due on Monday. Liz was playing with her Matchbox cars in the front yard when the ginger kid showed up. He wasn't smart enough to entertain himself, and when none of his equally nasty friends were around, he got off on tormenting Liz.

He leaned over her, stuck his face right in her face. He seemed all freckles and mean, squinty eyes. "Hey, Lezzy," he sneered. "Betcha think you look pretty with that stupid-looking hairstyle." Liz's mother had fixed her hair in ponytails that morning, crowning them with shiny purple holders that looked like grape-flavored candy.

The kid kicked dirt at her, overturning several of the little cars. "Fuck off," she said.

"Hey, fuck you, bitch! Girls ain't supposed to talk that way—so I guess you ain't much of a girl!" He grabbed one of the ponytails and yanked hard. She felt her pretty hair ornament snap, saw it tumble into the dirt. Fury swelled inside her, pure and hot.

She looked up at the ginger kid, her eyes shimmering with what felt like tears, and he grinned. "Awww, look at the little *bay*-bee—"

Then flames were coming from his mouth instead of words. He fell to his knees, clawing at his throat. Liz saw the fire take his hair, sizzle his eyes. He was burning and she was glad. He was a ball of flame, spreading to the lawn, the bushes, the house. Her rational mind was gone now; she did not know she was burning her own home and could not have stopped it if she had. She was nothing but a conduit for the beautiful, deadly fire.

The fire raced through the neighborhood, destroying her house, the ginger kid's house, more. Thirty-two people died that day, including Steve and Liz's parents. Firefighters found Liz wandering in the blackened wreckage, filthy with soot but unscathed. No one could figure out how the fire had started, though arson was suspected. No one knew how Liz had survived. She didn't know either. Though it was in her future to make fried calamari of an Elder God, Liz had no idea how great her powers were.

No one around her understood anything at all until the man from the Bureau finally came to visit.

Some nothing town called Plainville, and she's sitting in front of a cold cup of coffee in a diner when the black girl starts talking to her. "You okay, girl? You want one of these doughnuts? You don't have to pay for it—they're day-old."

Liz accepts gratefully. She hasn't eaten anything since sometime yesterday. She's also never actually spoken to a Negro before. None had lived in the spanking-new Kansas City suburb her parents had chosen so carefully (and which she had lain waste to so easily). A few had gone to her school, but the two races kept themselves separated so completely that desegregation may as well have never happened. And there are none at the Bureau, not yet. She's a little nervous, but after some of the freaks she's met in the last few years, one black girl not much older than her isn't so scary. "Thank you," she says. The doughnut is stale, but Liz doesn't care. She makes it disappear in a matter of seconds, and the girl silently slides another one onto her plate.

"Runaway, huh?"

This isn't the first time she's been out on her own, and she knows how obvious she is, a fourteen-year-old wolfing down free food like some starved stewbum. "Throwaway," she says, though it isn't strictly true.

"That's rough."

Liz doesn't know what to say. She stares at her plate, then looks back up into the girl's friendly face. It's been a while since she saw one.

"My name's Mahogany."

"I'm Liz."

They shake hands. Liz notices that Mahogany's palm is a dusty rose-pink, not brown as she would have expected. The hand is strong, the knuckles slightly swollen.

"You look so tired," Mahogany says. "If you need a place to rest for a few days, I have one."

Liz Sherman's first rule of the road: take what you have to, rides and food and such, but trust no one. "That's okay," she says. "I mean, it's really nice of you, but there's someplace I have to be."

They both know it's a lie, but Mahogany nods, says nothing more until Liz gets up to leave, and then just a soft "You take care, now."

"You too. Thanks."

Liz pushes open the greasy glass door of the diner and sees rain sheeting down. She hates the smell and the feel of rain. She wavers for a moment before realizing that she just can't make herself go back out there yet.

"You said maybe I could stay with you a few days?" she says, turning back to the counter. Mahogany smiles, and Liz feels an upsurge of something she hasn't known in years. It takes her a few moments to realize this feeling is hope.

The man from the Bureau had the kindest, saddest eyes Liz had ever seen. They sat out on the stoop of her current foster residence and he asked a lot of personal questions, including whether she had begun to menstruate yet. (She had, just three weeks before the conflagration that killed her family.) She wouldn't have answered such questions for anyone else, but she felt some undercurrent of empathy with this man, something she couldn't quite identify but couldn't ignore either.

"How's it been for you with the foster families?" he asked.

Liz shrugged. "The Svoradys were weird. They wanted me to act like I was five years old or something. When some little kids came in, they kicked me out. Then I came here, to the Fletchers'. They were pretty nice at first, but . . . well, you know what happened. I guess that's why you're here."

"The accident."

Liz stared at the floor. "Yeah."

"It wasn't really an accident, was it, Liz?"

She threw herself off the stoop, trembling with anger. "I didn't set the fire! I didn't! I know everybody thinks I did, 'cause I was fighting with Donny right before it happened, but I thought maybe you were different—"

"I don't think you set the fire."

She stopped raging. "You don't?"

"Not with matches or a lighter. Not in a way that other people can set a fire. And I don't think you meant to do it. And, hey, nobody got hurt, just a little smoke and water damage. But the fire came from you, didn't it, Liz?"

She looked up at him. He didn't seem angry or scared, just certain. "How do you know?" she whispered.

Instead of replying, the man reached into his pocket and pulled out a dollar bill. He held it in the air between them, and she saw something shimmer from his eyes.

The bill began to burn.

They watched the small flames lick at the paper for several seconds before the man let the bill fall to the ground and smothered the fire with his foot.

"I can do it too," he said simply.

A hundred questions rose up in her. "What—how do we—why—"

The man held up his hands in a placating gesture. "Plenty of time for all that and more. But first I have a proposition for you. Liz, what you have is called a 'wild talent.' Instead of being shuttled around to foster homes, would you like to live in a single place, a home, with other people who have wild talents? Would you like to learn more about yours, and how you can control it?"

She didn't have to say yes; the man could read it in her face.

"It's called the Bureau for Paranormal Research and Defense," he told her.

By the time Mahogany's shift ends, the rain has slackened and the sun is beginning to dry up the puddles on the sidewalk. Mahogany says her house is only a few blocks away. They walk in a companionable silence, having spent most of the afternoon chatting while Mahogany waited on an occasional customer.

The neighborhood looks poor but well kept, the houses painted in pastel colors, no trash in the streets and only a ghostly scrawl of sandblasted graffiti on a wall here and there.

"Two more blocks," Mahogany says. "There's one thing I ought to tell you before we get there."

Liz looks up, guarded, her fragile hope beginning to crumble. This is the part where Mahogany tells her something awful, something about heroin or turning tricks maybe, and Liz will have to turn and walk away from the only person who's been kind to her in weeks. "What?"

"Well, you're not gonna be the only person staying with us. My momma and I sort of help people out, other kids who need a place to go. There's a girl there whose folks threw her out 'cause she's pregnant, and two boys who like each other . . . you know?"

Liz just says, "That's cool," but she could cry with relief, except that she never cries. When they finally come to the house, a solid old two-story deal with bright red trim and a pointy roof covered in multicolored shingles, she almost feels as if she is home.

Just inside the front door, mouth-watering fragrances envelop them: basil, garlic, fresh bread. "Momma!" Mahogany calls. "I've got somebody with me!"

A woman stands at the stove stirring spaghetti sauce. As she turns, Liz sees that she looks old enough to be Mahogany's grandmother instead of her mother.

"Momma, this is my friend Liz. Liz, meet my mother, Zora."

"Welcome, sweetheart. We're pleased to have you here. You hungry?"

"I am now," Liz says.

Zora laughs, and Liz notices that her careworn face is beautiful. "Good. Mahogany, see if you can find David and Patrick. Caroline's feeling poorly; I'll take a tray up to her later. Liz, will you keep me company?"

Mahogany leaves the kitchen. Still stirring the sauce, Zora gazes levelly at Liz. "We don't have too many rules around here, but there are a couple you should know. One, you don't judge anybody in this house. Only God is fit to judge, though I don't believe he does. Two, you're safe here and welcome to stay as long as you want, but if you're in some kind of trouble, I need to know about it."

"I'm not in any trouble," Liz says. "Just on my own and tired." Technically it's true; though the Bureau is probably looking for her, she didn't break any laws by leaving. Her custody is a hazy, difficult matter, and the Bureau is hesitant to stir already troubled waters by hunting her down and dragging her back to Connecticut every time she gets antsy and takes off.

"Good. You don't lie to me, I won't lie to you." Zora turns back to the stove. "Can you lay out those plates for me? Five of 'em."

They eat at a wooden table polished to a golden brown patina, with old-fashioned white lace placemats that remind Liz of a set her mother had. That brings a lump to her throat, but the chatter of David and Patrick, the two boys who like each other, soon distracts her. They are about fifteen, long haired, handsome, and fragile looking. Liz wonders how they ever survived in the real world. By their wits, she supposes; both are as talkative and charming as Siamese cats. They tease Mahogany with great affection, and she gives back as good as she gets.

After washing up, the five of them sit in the living room and talk for hours. At one point Caroline comes downstairs to say hello. The bulge of her pregnancy looks impossible on her tiny frame, but she carries herself with a brittle, formal dignity. No one asks Liz any prying questions, nothing about where she came from or why.

Everything is fine until she goes to bed.

She shares Mahogany's room, which has twin beds on either side of an antique vanity table. The sheets are deliciously soft and cool, especially since she's been sleeping in bus stations and behind minimarts lately. The two girls talk a little longer about nothing in particular, just sleepy scattered conversation like the kind that comes toward the end of a slumber party. Then it's dark, and Liz is dreaming.

She's back in Kansas City, in the front yard of her house. Her Matchbox cars are scattered on the ground before her and the purple ponytail holders are in her hair. The ginger kid is nowhere in sight. She turns and goes up the front walk toward the house. The door to the foyer is partly open, but Liz can't see inside. She has almost made it to the porch when her mother half-staggers, half-falls through the door.

Her mother is in flames. Her face is barely recognizable, her eyes seared shut, her hair burned away. Her mouth stretches open and emits a soundless scream. Her charcoal-claw hands reach out to Liz.

"Mommy!" Liz screams. She rushes to the burning woman, trying to smother the fire with her own body, but it is too late. The flames don't burn Liz, but her embrace crumbles her mother's body and the charred pieces fall away.

She wakes to the sound of screaming, but it is not her own.

The bed is on fire. She sees Mahogany through the curtain of smoke and flames, reaching frantically for her, shouting her name. The covers are destroyed, the mattress beginning to smolder, but Liz feels nothing. She scrambles out of the bed and rushes to Mahogany, who grabs her. "Are you hurt?" Mahogany asks, and it twists Liz's heart a little that this should be her first question.

"I'm fine! Help me put this out!" Liz spins wildly, searching for clothes, covers, anything that might smother the flames.

"We can't, Liz! Look—" The fire is halfway up the wall, exposing joists and wires. Blue sparks fly as it spreads into the electrical system. The girls run from the room, down the hall, yelling and banging on doors.

Everyone gets out alive. That is her only consolation, the only reason she doesn't just throw herself in front of a fire truck. The house and everything in it are completely destroyed.

When the firemen have gone, leaving only a pile of black and stinking rubble where a home once stood, Zora and the two boys come over to Liz. Zora's arms are wrapped around the boys' thin shoulders; all three faces are streaked with soot and tears. Liz sees Mahogany comforting Caroline on the other side of the street. "The officer knows a shelter we can stay in tonight," Zora tells Liz. "I don't know what we'll do after that, but we'll find something."

Liz can hardly meet the woman's eyes. "That's okay, Zora. You guys have enough to deal with. I think I'm just gonna take off."

"In the middle of the night? Why, Liz, I can't let you—"

"I've got someone I can call to pick me up," Liz tells her.

She sits on the curb and watches them ride away in two police cars. Before they'd parted, Mahogany hugged Liz and gave her the address of some aunt or cousin, asking her to write and let them know she was all right. Liz knows she never will. These people don't need her in their lives, don't deserve what she has already given them in exchange for their kindness.

When the last police car is gone and the street is dark and silent, Liz goes to a pay phone on the corner and dials the number of the BPRD. It only rings twice before being answered by a doctor Liz knows.

"Come and get me," she says, and begins to cry. She hasn't cried since she was eleven. The tears burn worse than fire. And when the long black car that comes to fetch her finally turns into the Bureau's winding driveway, Liz knows that this time she really is home.

FAR FLEW THE BOAST OF HIM
BRIAN HODGE

Grown men, they may have been—and now, post-mortem—but they reminded him of children.

All the slaughter in the world, and here they'd gone out for a weekend's lark to pretend to wreak more. Like young boys playing at war games. All the barrels of blood that had seeped into England's soil, and here they'd gone out for a day of make-believe, pretending to shed it all over again.

Well, that blood was certainly real enough now, wasn't it? And there would be no pretending otherwise, not with nearly three dozen new widows left scattered from London to Newcastle.

At least all were now assumed to be widows by anyone who could afford to be brutally realistic. Only just over half the bodies had so far been found, and as long as there's no corpse then there's always hope . . . but Hellboy could not imagine anyone who wasn't nervously fingering a wedding ring, or awaiting news of a missing father, son, brother, lover, was expecting a single one of those poor dumb bastards to come walking in from the border country here near Scotland.

Divine intervention, it seemed, was always in much shorter supply than diabolic.

"The Battle of Lindisfarne," this fellow was saying. Survivor on account of absenteeism. Trevor Copplestone, his name, or something close to that. "June eighth, 793. That's what we . . . they . . . had come up here last weekend to reenact."

"'Battle' of Lindisfarne? How do you figure that?" said Hellboy. "There wasn't any 'battle' to it. There's no battle when the other side's unarmed."

"Ah—so you know Lindisfarne, do you?"

"I may look dumb," Hellboy said, "but that's just a disguise."

"Well, then . . . battle of ideologies, call it," Copplestone said. Working hard at keeping his stiff upper, but the strain was showing. "The sword of the monks' Lord and savior, matched up against the swords of boatloads of raiders whose sole idea of a guarantee into the afterlife was a good death. Wasn't much of a contest, was it?"

"No. It wasn't. And whatever it was that your friends ran into up here last weekend . . . ? That wasn't much of any contest, either."

You had to imagine that by now Trevor Copplestone was feeling like the luckiest man on either side of Hadrian's Wall. A bad sausage in last Friday evening's helping of bangers and mash at a pub near his Northumberland hotel flattens him for the next twenty-four hours, knocks him off his pins and into bed every moment he's not crouched over his toilet. Certainly in no condition to troop out and play Viking with his friends.

Maybe Copplestone looked more imposing when he had his period gear on, his chainmail or jerkin or helmet or whatever he decked himself out in for these weekend outings, but here and now he did not look the part. A big enough frame, and a well-trimmed beard and a shock of hair that the sea breezes stirred, but inside his jacket he was a soft-looking man. Doughy in the middle, and the beard grown to hide his burgeoning jowls. A man shackled to a desk forty or fifty hours each week who looks out his window, if his office even has one, and dreams of living in an age when the cloud-thickened welkin would've been the only roof that mattered.

And he had not been alone. A historical reenactment society, they called themselves. Study up on their favorite bloodbaths, choose up sides, then pick a weekend to go out and pretend they'd been there. Grand fun, but evidently they'd always come back alive before. Full of beans as they invade the nearest pub, and the worst argument they've got to settle is who buys first round.

All history now.

Hellboy had the feeling that it would be a good long while before Trevor Copplestone felt any urge to pick up his sword again. Some new look of haunt and harrowing in his eyes that wouldn't have been there eight days ago . . . survivor's guilt, or just the fact of everything that had once been academic and safely within the realm of pretense hitting him full in the face, to leave its indelible mark: *This* was what it was like to lose friends and comrades by the score. *This* was what it felt like to walk home dragging their memories like heavy chains. *This* was what it was like when there wasn't even enough left of some of them to bury.

This was history, the genuine article. They'd learned it, and still they'd been doomed to repeat its most enduring lesson.

"This one meant something more to you guys," Hellboy said. "It had to. Otherwise, where's the fun?"

"I'm not sure I follow you."

"Yeah you do. Reenact Lindisfarne, and half of you don't even get to fight. All you get to do is wear a cowled robe and fall down and pretend to die. I don't get that. It's over too quick. And they wouldn't even grant you guys permission to stage it where it really happened, because they found the idea too tasteless. So you stayed here on the mainland and settled for a plot of ground just barely in sight of the real thing. That's an awful lot of trouble to go to for something over so quick."

"So why Lindisfarne," Copplestone said, "when there must be hundreds of other battles better suited to keeping us all busy, and for a longer stretch of the day—that's what you're asking?"

"It might help get to the bottom of what happened."

"I sincerely doubt that. It . . . it was the work of a madman, obviously."

Hellboy simply stared; wouldn't even encourage that one with an answer. How badly Copplestone must've wanted to believe this. The handiest explanation that would restore his world back to order. A madman, yes. Just the sort of thing they do. Brute strength and no restraint and even less idea what he's doing . . . you can take comfort in that. Because you can medicate him for it and lock him in a cell. And if he was able to go tooth-and-nail through twenty or thirty chaps with swords, well then, perhaps he was some form of new, improved madman, and yet, for all that, still no match for the right pharmaceutical company.

Hellboy stared at Copplestone until it unnerved him. Reminding him by sheer presence that there were more peculiar things afoot than lunatics. Skin like red armor and an oversized hand that could crush cinderblocks—what did Copplestone think was standing right in front of him? Just another cop like the pair who'd driven him out to the meadow for this meeting?

"Some of us," Copplestone admitted, finally, "not all, mind, but some . . . we'd got to feeling that more than our interests belonged to the remote past. That maybe the claim reached as deep as our hearts, too."

"And what's that supposed to mean?"

"It means that this land, it wasn't always Christ's. There's plenty who'd be happy to tell you otherwise, but all that goes to show you is how thoroughly they've forgotten who their forefathers really were."

"Which forefathers would those be, again?"

"The Angles and the Saxons, of course."

"So whose land would that make it?" Hellboy thinking he knew already what Copplestone was driving at; wanting to hear him say it, regardless.

"Britain was Odin's too, once. Every bit as much as Norway and Sweden and so on. We woke up to that."

"So this Lindisfarne business," Hellboy said. "You thought you'd come up here on its anniversary, commemorate the occasion, celebrate this awakening?"

"Something like that, yes."

"What'd you think you were doing? Giving the whole place back?"

"To Odin?" Copplestone lowered his gaze, stared down at his shoes. Or the earth beneath them. "Nah. Not really. It's his just about any old time he wants it."

"News flash, Trevor. Odin's dead. And if he was ever out there, he isn't any more. You and me, and those cops in that car over there . . . ? All of us might believe there was a Michelangelo, but that doesn't mean he's coming back to carve another statue of David."

Copplestone's eyebrows peaked. "Ancient faiths, old beliefs? Dried-up riverbeds, is what they're like. All they need's a fresh torrent to bring them back to life, and they run as true as they ever did."

"Dehydrated gods? Just add water? That could catch on."

Copplestone looked wounded. "Are we finished here?" he asked. "Because . . . because you've a madman to catch."

Finished. Yes, they were. There was nothing more he could learn from Trevor Copplestone, and if there was, it was nothing Hellboy couldn't guess and have it serve just as well. We woke up to that, Copplestone had said, and if he wanted to believe in aberrant men with the strength of twenty, let him. It felt far more likely, however, that something else had awakened alongside them.

As he stood alone on the meadow overlooking the sea, the salt air gusts snapped the length of his coat about his cloven feet and tail, and he watched Copplestone's back as the man trudged away in a defeat that neither of them could name. The two officers who'd driven him here let him into the car, then gave Hellboy a nervous glance that said everything he would ever need to know about why they'd kept their distance, all three of them now looking relieved to be driving back toward what they believed to be the normal world.

Because as much as they feared the darkness they didn't understand, they feared as well what stood against it, because they didn't really understand that either.

All right. Lay it out, all of it. The known, the unknown, and the conjecture that bridged them together. It was the only way he knew how to start.

Indisputable facts:

Even by British standards, the Holy Island of Lindisfarne was old. *Old.* Three miles off the coast of Northumbria, it had in the early six hundreds proven to be a prime site for the raising of a monastery. Safe, ruggedly beautiful, protected by land and sea, it was ideal for monks who wanted no more of the world than what they required for survival and contemplation. Like most monasteries of their day, they stored Church treasure, compiled Church history. They buried saints. Late that century from their scriptorum came one of western civilization's most highly cherished illuminated manuscripts, the *Lindisfarne Gospels.*

And a century later it all came crashing down upon their tonsured heads. New technology: the Viking longship, perfectly suited for ocean travel. What had once been thought impregnable was just an easy few days' sail from Norway. The

Norsemen looted the monastery, put the monks to the sword, sent shock waves throughout the horrified whole of Europe: the world has just changed.

Getting to Lindisfarne today was no more bother than driving the causeway that spanned the tidal inlet, just as long as one didn't try driving it at high tide. Big draw for tourists, for modern-day pilgrimages. The monastery was long gone, but the red sandstone ruins of an eleventh-century Norman priory and those of a Tudor-era castle served equally well for seekers of the picturesque. And for modern creature comforts: hotels, cafes, even a meadery. Difficult to imagine the more tweedy buffs and conservators of Brit history entertaining even for one moment the notion of a rough-and-tumble reenactment celebrating that twelve-hundred-year-old slaughter.

Hard facts:

Trevor Copplestone and his group had no choice but to remain confined to the mainland, where they went about their faux pillage and plunder on a pastoral meadow rise from which, if the day was clear enough, they could in the distance see the island where it had happened.

All signs indicated they'd made a good long day of it: scraps of food, spilt bottles of ale, whiskey, mead. Lounging about a pair of evening cookfires, no doubt reminiscing over days they could only pretend they'd lived, they had been caught off guard, under cover of dusk. Something coming out of the night and, turnabout being fair play, massacring them.

No quarter had been given, and no deference shown for the roles they had played. Monk and marauder, all had died the same, protected by neither sword nor cross. When found the next morning, this eerie tableau like a Dark Age charnel field that had slipped forward in time, blood making a muck of the earth where the various and sundry parts of them had tumbled, the first natural conclusion drawn was that these silly bastards had really gotten carried away.

It hadn't taken long to rule that out. Grievous though they'd been, their wounds had not been made by swords, by spears. They were much too ragged for that. Whatever had violated these men, it had come from no forge.

Nor did it appear that all of them had fallen where they'd died. Far and wide, they were strewn, on a meandering path inland, as much as twelve miles between one of the stray legs and the hip socket from which it had been torn. And this was only accounting for what had been recovered—nearly half the bodies had yet to turn up. Early on it had been assumed that hounds would be the simplest solution, quickly sniffing out the remains still lying somewhere, awaiting discovery.

But the dogs would have no part of it, Hellboy had heard. They'd tucked their tails between their legs and lowered their ears and slunk away from the fresh scent trail with fearful whines, as though whatever they might find at its end would be worse than the most loathsome excuse for a man they'd ever tracked.

Dogs, in Hellboy's estimation, often showed more common sense than the ones holding the leash. Their reaction, as much as anything, was why he'd been summoned here in the first place.

And so much for the known.

There had been, of course, no witnesses, or if there were, they'd been snatched too, their bodies vanished with the rest. No reports of any missing locals, but you'd figure a tourist or two could disappear for a while without attracting attention.

If there was anywhere in England you could lose someone, this was the place. Northumberland was her most sparsely populated county. Five times as many sheep as human beings, although the sheep's numbers had dwindled a bit of late, too. Farmers rising with the dawn to be greeted by the sight of animals reduced to tatters and mutton. This Hellboy had checked into upon learning that the dead men's wounds looked as though they could only have been left by tooth and claw.

Theories from the civilian population? No shortage of those. Dead farm animals always meant someone, somewhere, would be pointing at the sky and seeing lights. Even now contingents were trying to link the massacre to crop circles, hunting for obscure parallels between the latest patterns in the wheatfields and the haphazard arrangement of the corpses.

And cats. Big cats—it was actually one of the more sensible theories. Hellboy considered its merits as he traversed meadow and field and moor, following the trail of last weekend's strewn carnage—long since shuttled off to the morgue, but something lingered in the air, a miasma of slaughter that the wuthering winds had been unfit to disperse.

The U.K. had big cats, all right, from Cornwall to the most remote reaches of Scotland. Leopards, panthers . . . whatever they were, where they'd come from was a mystery: the Exmoor Beast, and others who'd been bestowed no names. It was no longer a vast and untamed wilderness, this island Britannia, not a place you'd expect big cats to do anything other than get themselves hunted to extinction, yet they were out there, canny black stalkers seen at a distance, even filmed, but it was a rare day indeed when anything but their kills were encountered close-up.

Of course, one alone couldn't wipe out more than thirty men. But suppose, it had been suggested, they were now roaming in packs.

Hellboy'd seen weirder.

Strange place, England, as though by its very antiquity it had been granted license to bend the rules of reality that held more firmly elsewhere. Consider its soil alone, a sponge soaked in the blood of thousands of years of war and conquest and sacrifice; drowned in the psyches of wave after wave of invaders, butchers, tyrants, holy men, madmen. Dig deeper, in the proper places, and you might find crusts of earth stamped with the footprints of giants, while strata deeper still had yielded up fossils seen by fewer than twenty pairs of living eyes, and guarded now with the kind of security usually reserved for national treasuries.

Oh, a place like this, every once in a while you had to expect it to give rise to something that ran roughshod over the laws of nature.

After all, he'd been born here himself, hadn't he? If born was even the proper word. Meaning that whatever aberration this land spawned might conceivably be construed as his brother.

But brothers could be polar opposites.

Been that way at least since Cain and Abel.

Breathe them, smell them, taste them . . . those drafts of otherness that blow through the land in arbitrary gusts. Hear them, watch them, walk them . . . those subterranean currents of other worlds enfolded into this one. These highways and byways known only to the dead.

He fell back on a basic constabulary strategy of searching afield for what had vanished: begin with a nexus of its last-known locale—in this case, the farthest-traveled casualty found thus far—and spiral outward from there. Sure it was time-consuming. But time he had. And he did not tire easily. The arcs of sun and moon overhead did not much weigh on him.

Even in the most desolate meadows and groves he was rarely alone for any span of hours. The land was full of ghosts. Most were bereft of anything resembling soul or mind; they were echoes of what they'd been, sensible enough only to sense how incomplete they were, and to feel the agony of it. They wept vaporous tears; they put their fists through their cheeks while trying in vain to claw at them.

Others, though . . . somehow they had retained themselves. They looked, saw, recognized, knew.

Hellboy came across one such casualty of the past suspended by his neck from a lower bow of an immense oak. A hanging tree, a perversion of Yuletide cheer festooned with its bygone era's accumulation of decayed ornaments, rotted fruits. The fellow was but one of many, and the most aware amongst them all—men, women, children, they spun in slow half-circles, toes reaching for a ground they would never touch. Animals, even. A pony dangled motionless, truly dead, slumping in halves from a thick cable bound around its middle. In contrast, a large wolf whipped its muscled body about and scrabbled its paws at the air, ceaselessly snapping at the cord cinched around its throat.

"You . . . see . . . me," said the hanging man. From behind a ragged veil of hair, his voice was like a creaking door.

"I see a lot more than you, friend."

"Have you come to claim me?" he asked.

"Why do you ask that?"

"Have you seen yourself, sir? There can be only one place whence came the likes of you. 'Tis a realm I always feared to go. So I went nowhere. Am I then to be claimed at last?"

Criminal, victim, suicide . . . Hellboy didn't care what the man had been in life, and certainly didn't care where he chose to spend eternity. Didn't mean he had to tell the truth about it. Death, life—no matter. Fear was still the best inducement to prompt the sharing of secrets.

Hellboy drew his pistol and took a bead on the frayed rope just above the man's head.

"Unless you know of something that'll be more of a challenge for me, looks like you and I have some traveling ahead of us."

And how was it that long-dead eyes could brighten so? Could know hope?

"Such a shabby little prize would I make for the likes of you," he said. "But if it's larger quarry you're after . . . "

Hellboy lowered the gun halfway. "I'm listening."

"I know not what it was, but I believe that I heard its birth. A most monstrous bellowing in the night."

"When?"

The man spread empty palms. "Time . . . is not the same from this vantage. But not long."

"Which direction?"

An arm, trailing shreds of muslin, unfurled from the man's side and pointed to the west.

"Abominable cries, they were, that could belong only to suchlike fiend as passed by thereafter. I could see naught but shadow or silhouette . . . a most dreadful apparition. The likes of it I had never seen before . . . yet it felt in some wise familiar to me . . . as though I should know its form, and had but forgot."

"Have you seen it any more since then?"

"I would not want to. But there have been occasions when I believe I have heard it. It weeps. In the night, it weeps." The hanging man raised his head from the collar of his noose. "Have I fulfilled our contract, sir? You will tell them nothing of me?"

"Go back to sleep. Dream yourself some better company than what you've got now."

"Ah, but they make such willing listeners to my stories. I have so many, you know. So many . . . "

"You and every other dead man," said Hellboy, and pushed onward.

He found it within a couple of hours—if not the end of his search, at least a telling stop along the way. Not like anything he'd ever seen before, but there was no such thing as a finished education, not where matters like *this* were concerned.

It belonged here, in the mists and vapors of the moors. The calendar may have said early summer, but this parcel of land seemed to resist, to cling to starkness and decay. The trees grew more fungus than leaves, and the sun was thwarted in its attempts to brighten.

And then there was the earth itself. The pustule, at first glance, looked like a crater left by a small detonation: a grenade, a mortar shell. On closer inspection it resembled an open wound, as well. A distended heap of earth and membrane that were not separate but somehow intermingled—smooth here, grainy there; in one place a resilient sheet, while in another it clotted and crumbled and smeared.

I know not what it was, the hanging man had said, but I believe that I heard its birth. And right here was the canal.

He hunkered down beside the rim, rolled up his sleeve, thrust his hand into the muddy stew. Fished around until he felt something brush his wrist, and grabbed it, as big around as a boa constrictor. Hellboy stood, put the power of his armored hand into it, and tugged.

It came, and came, and came. There seemed no end to it, as tough and fibrous as a vine, as slick as wet cartilage: an umbilical worthy of a nightmare. Its one end looked raggedly sheared through, bitten; tug as Hellboy might, though, its other end was still anchored somewhere down in the depths of Britannia's earth.

He stopped pulling only when the cord snagged on something near the surface, then brought it up. When the object broke through the soil, Hellboy slung the coils aside and stooped again to inspect the piece and to rub it clean.

It was a helmet, corroded but intact save for the dome, punctured with several elliptical arrangements of holes. They'd not been made in some remote age, however; these holes were fresh, the scarred metal of their edges raw and shiny bright. They looked for all the world as though they'd been left by teeth, gnawing in idleness, out of boredom or frustration or, like human babies with rubber rings, simply to coax the teeth into appearing.

Forget the holes for a moment. He inspected the helmet itself, its form, its design. The flanges around the bottom, the guard that dipped down like a mummer's mask to shield the wearer's eyes.

Hellboy plunged his arm deeper into the hole, a blind search but coming out with piece after piece, find after find: a dagger, a scabbard, a jeweled shoulder-clasp inset with garnets, gold, and glass. He began to suspect that there might be an entire treasure trove here waiting to be discovered, perhaps the greatest find in England since the excavation of Sutton Hoo. The bones of Saxon kings or heroes down there, whose deeds poets had labored to recount in all their rightful glory.

Abruptly he decided to let the rest be. He was no archaeologist, and for the moment had found enough to sate his curiosity, to ignite speculation. The known, the unknown, and the conjecture that bridged them together. He stood at the edge of the hole, staring into it, daring it to deny what must have happened here.

The world was younger then, and wilder, governed by the horizon. They came from the cold forests of Northern Europe, astride the icy timbers of their ships. They came, and they never left, fathering a lineage that still dominated England today, even unto giving the country her name. They came, and buried this Dark Age cache of artifacts, steeped in their blood and sweat and fury and honor.

And somehow the place had become a womb. Seeded by . . . what...?

Belief? Fear?

No such beast as coincidence.

A few days ago he wouldn't have expected it to be so literal, what Copplestone had said about the ancient ways, about old gods awakening to believers who have in turn awakened to them. Dried-up old riverbeds, he'd compared them to, lying in wait for a fresh infusion to come roaring back to life.

Copplestone and his mates, they believed, all right. Said they weren't alone, either, not by a longshot.

And if they'd begun to bring their ancestral gods back home, well, who was to say one or two of the ancestral devils hadn't hitched a ride in the bargain. For aren't those things that mean you harm so much easier to believe in, in the long run, than those which mean you well?

Now that Hellboy had a good idea who he was looking for, it considerably narrowed where he'd have to look.

Spiraling.

Fractal repetition, echoed in scale from infinitesimal to infinite. Twined helix of DNA and spinning sickle starfish-arms of galaxies. Spirals carved in megalithic rock at Newgrange, drawn by shamans in Ugandan dirt. Spiraldance of pagans at revel, round and round and round we go. And somewhere in between, blueprint for the search for the lost . . . this our hub, this our axis.

Involution, evolution. The rise from the swirling waters of birth, the slow drift down into the waters of death. The path deciding all, while the pattern remains the same.

Hellboy couldn't have *not* found this place. The centuries had conspired to spin him to it.

A small lake deep in the moors, its stagnant waters slopped quietly against the muck of its shoreline. With bark leprous and branches gnarled, the surrounding trees looked poisoned, not by substance so much as spirit, as though the soil from which they grew no longer remembered the specifics of some terrible event that had happened here, only the essence of it.

Imagine, then, the heart of the being that would choose to call such a place home.

Imagine having no other choice.

Hellboy found it at dusk, this black oasis, and knew he was in the right place when within a mossy cluster of trees he spotted a great depression in the spongy green, along with a calcium-white heap. Something had rested here, had taken bones of the dead and passed a few idle hours by reducing them to chips and flakes. Grinding them, perhaps. It was said that, in some antiquated Germanic tongue, this was what had given Hellboy's quarry his name.

Even then they had called him a roamer of the night, and it appeared that nothing had changed. Gone for this one already, Hellboy suspected, so he settled onto the cushion of moss to wait. When the moon rose high and the surface of the lake remained undisturbed, that confirmed it: this vigil would last until dawn.

And a lonely vigil it was, the silence here so deep it was unnatural. No frogs, no crickets, no splash of fish from the ebony waters, and when the first soft blush of pink tinged the eastern sky he heard no birds around to greet it. The sole signs of life were those approaching footsteps that had been inevitable, and when their maker at last shambled into view through the trees and the dewy morning haze, Hellboy viewed him over the barrel of his gun.

Grendel stopped, and though he came from an age ruled by another form of steel, seemed to understand precisely what it was.

"Men I know. I do not know what manner of thing you are," said Grendel, "but I see you have learned their lessons well."

"And you know what surprises me?" Hellboy said. "I wasn't expecting you to have the power of speech."

"Why should you have expectations of my ways at all?"

"The man who killed you. Beowulf. Someone wrote about his life. Big, long, epic poem. It's stood the test of time."

"But the poet had no words to give me?" Grendel asked. "Words only for the hero? It is no surprise. Poets save their best words for what they long to be or desire to possess . . . and cannot. And like all men, what they do not understand they fear, and what they fear they find convenient to kill."

"You mean like the way you handled those poor thirty-odd bastards a few days ago?"

"They hungered for a life they never knew. I gave them a brief taste of it. They wanted dragons to fight. I gave them one. It was their yearning that drew me to them. The next morning may have been abhorrent to you, but the night before . . . ? They lived as they had never lived before. They died as few are privileged."

Hellboy hadn't been there, but he had his doubts. Had seen few die with the kind of savage exaltation with which heroes died in the sagas and epics of old. Had they ever, really? They begged, they bargained, they shrieked and wept and bled, and he could not think of a single shame in it.

He imagined that the sight of Grendel would have been more than enough to send them running. Long, muscled, spidery limbs, sharp-tipped and coarse with gray bristles; primal simian face with the shearing teeth of a carnivore, and eyes cunning as a cannibal's. Would bankers stand and fight him; would architects and crossing guards? Never.

Although he was not nearly so large that it would have required four men to carry his head back to Hrothgar's mead-hall. Even then the tales of heroes' exploits had needed help from their tellers, so that their boasts might be better winged to fly down through the ages.

Grendel's speed, though—by any standards it would be legendary.

One arm lashed out, quick as a whip, and Hellboy would not have thought he could reach so far. A slashing blow, and the gun was ripped from his grip, knocked a dozen yards away, where it struck a tree, chipping away loose bark and lichens. And Grendel overhead then, his own limbs merging with those of the oak into which he'd hoisted himself, death from above as he bore down with gristle-flecked jaws. Hellboy reacted out of instinct, dodging and swiping an arc with his huge stone-like hand, and its grip found purchase, and wrenched, and the damage was done before he even realized it: Hellboy, standing there with Grendel's arm dangling from his grasp.

Again, the old wound.

And rain, red rain from emptied socket.

Grendel bellowed into the rising day, launched himself from the branches and into the waters of the lake—a tremendous splash, and then a rapid, rippling calm. For a moment Hellboy watched the wavelets, then retrieved his gun and waded in to follow.

Awash in greenish murk, he swam slowly and, as any good hunter would, followed the threads of blood that swirled and eddied before him. Down and down and down, as the lake was graylit by the first spears of sunlight to pierce its surface, the thinning bloodtrail leading to a horizontal channel dug out of rock and clay. The breath ached against his lungs and an inky darkness enfolded him, total now, and still he kicked onward until a faint flickering orange beckoned overhead.

Grendel's lair. Another land, another eon, but his habits persevered.

Hellboy broke surface, found himself treading water in a small pool ringed by stream-smoothed stones. They had been chosen and placed with obvious care. As if their simple arrangement had been something that had *mattered.*

He dredged himself from the water, stood dripping in a small cavern far below the surface of the daylight world. Its earthen walls crawled with roots; the light from half a dozen torches shimmered on the moist sheen of its rocks and strobed a dance of shadows. In one corner, a heaped jumble of tooth-marked bones.

And upon the walls, suspended from brackets of sticks, hung their swords.

He plucked a torch from its seat of earth and back, back along a corridor where the light was loath to reach, followed the spatters of blood upon the floor. Their size shrunk every step or two, until he could clearly see what they'd led him to.

By all the gods that ever were, he had never seen anything like this.

At first Hellboy thought it was a body sitting propped against the cavern wall, an enormous corpse somehow half-preserved from an epoch when its kind had walked above ground. But no, it had never lived . . . only its parts had.

Bones made from branches—the trunks of saplings for its arms and legs and spine, stout curved branches for ribs. The wool of sheep wound like muscle mass around the makeshift limbs. For a head, a bale of hay stuffed into a large grainsack, with hair of plastered weeds and algae. And skin quilted together from the hides of at least a dozen men, fashioning from them this colossal hag's pendulous breasts, matronly belly, her atrocious face.

It weeps, the hanging man had said. *In the night, it weeps.*

Hellboy understood now whom those tears were for.

His mother. From the only tools at hand, Grendel had remade his mother.

The telling of his slayer's tale had come as news to Grendel. That much was apparent. Could he even know, then, that she too had fallen to Beowulf? Did he wonder, did he suspect? Or did he weep only because he had been spawned once more into a world where she no longer existed?

Hellboy squeezed shut his eyes, able to understand that feeling, his own mother never anything more to him than an echo, a phantom glimpsed in the desecrated ruins of a church in East Bromwich. Old deluded woman at the end of a lifetime shaped by devil's lies.

Or had he only hallucinated her to compensate for what he'd never known, making her outright from the fabric of his need?

At his feet, there issued a turbid flow of blood from the juncture of the hag's splayed and outstretched legs. Hellboy reached forward and, as if opening the flap of a tent, peeled back a drape of leathery skin on the sagging kettledrum of her belly. Behind it, Grendel sat curled double within the hollow, remaining hand clamped over the ragged socket of his shoulder.

The fight now bled from him, Grendel stared back at Hellboy over the muzzle of his gun.

"So plain it is in your eyes . . . " said Grendel. "You do not think I belong in this world or any other."

"I'm hardly alone in that," Hellboy told him.

"Others may look upon you and judge you the same."

"Not if they know enough to judge me by my actions."

"Ah, those," whispered Grendel. "Protecting the very ones who would find you a fearful thing to look upon? Defending them from the rawheads and the bloodybones of a darkness that could not exist if they did not feed it . . . crave it in spite of their piety? Because even a hellspawn is better than their fears that there may be nothing for them beyond this life."

Lifeblood oozed over and between those trembling, spindly fingers. Surely there could not be much more left for his heart to pump. And it was said, Hellboy recalled, that the blood of Cain flowed in him, and this was why Grendel had turned against mankind. He was every man that killed his brother, no matter how loosely one defined the term.

"Answer me one thing," Grendel said. "Will Paradise welcome you any more than it would welcome me? Your heart may be a good one, but will the guardians of the Gate forgive you the birth you must have had?"

He did not know how to answer this. Knew only what he hoped.

"I thought as much," said Grendel. "This, too, is so plain in your eyes." And then he shut his own, and murmured, "Mercy."

Hellboy shook his head. "Even if I was inclined to give it, there's no time and nothing I could do for you."

"You do not understand." Slowly, slowly, Grendel craned his neck forward to bring his skull within a hair's breadth of the gun. "I would not die the same ignoble death twice. So I ask you . . . "

And some part of him—the same part which days ago, this mystery still unfolding as he walked in spirals, wondered if what the land had birthed might not in some way be his brother—didn't want to do this.

" . . . all I ask you . . . "

Oh, but they all wore the mark of Cain, didn't they?

" . . . mercy."

He obliged, and pulled the trigger.

Hellboy waited awhile before leaving the lair. Spent some time sorting amidst the bones for any trinkets that might be recovered for a grieving widow or child, to bring them the tiniest comfort—a necklace, a medallion—but there were none to be found. So he waited until the torches burned themselves out, one by one, and stared at the ruin of this son, this surrogate mother.

Pondering, too, his own fate, his legacy. Wondering if after long centuries anyone, anywhere, might know of him, know the least thing about him, care.

And when the last torch remained, he touched it to those flammable parts of the mother's vast body, the kindling wood and the hay, and when at last they caught, he hoped that it would burn the rest, as any funeral pyre should. And that some of the smoke, at least, would sift its way through the soil, up, up, to be sighed by the earth into the air, spirals of breath and vapor that would rise into the sky to meet the clouds, and linger there, and someday fall back with the rain.

CONTRIBUTORS

STEPHEN R. BISSETTE has been in the comics industry for over twenty years, and writing professionally for over a decade. Along with his award-winning work as a cartoonist and illustrator, Bissette has scripted, edited, published, and co-published a variety of projects.

Bissette is perhaps best known for the award-winning *Saga of the Swamp Thing*, a milestone in comics publishing. Shortly thereafter, he published the Eisner Award-winning horror comics anthology, *Taboo*, which was the birthplace of Alan Moore and Eddie Campbell's *From Hell*. As an illustrator, he has worked on projects by such writers as Neil Gaiman, Joe R. Lansdale, and Douglas E. Winter. As a writer, Bissette's hundreds of interviews and articles have appeared in dozens of magazines. His original novella, *Aliens: Tribes*, won the Bram Stoker Award in 1992, and he has scripted numerous comics. Through his imprint, Spiderbaby Grafix, Bissette self-published *S. R. Bissette's Tyrant*, a rigorously researched portrait of the birth, life, and death of a *Tyrannosaurus rex* in late Cretaceous North America.

He lives in southern Vermont with his teenage children, Maia and Daniel, who also write and draw their own comics and stories.

✠

POPPY Z. BRITE is the author of four novels, *Lost Souls, Drawing Blood, Exquisite Corpse*, and *The Lazarus Heart*; two short-story collections, *Wormwood* (a.k.a. *Swamp Foetus*) and *Are You Loathsome Tonight?*; and a biography of rock diva Courtney Love. She has edited two anthologies, *Love In Vein* and *Love in Vein 2*. Her fiction and non-fiction have appeared in numerous anthologies and magazines.

Brite's interests include Victorian hairwork and mourning jewelry, traveling, gardening, animal rescue, and gourmet dinner with her husband Christopher, a chef. She lives in New Orleans.

✠

MAX ALLAN COLLINS is the Shamus Award-winning author of the Nathan Heller detective novels. He is a leading author of movie and TV tie-ins, including the *NYPD Blue* novels and such best sellers as *In the Line of Fire, Air Force One, The Mummy*, and *Saving Private Ryan*. With artist Terry Beatty, he co-created *Ms. Tree, Wild Dog*, and the miniseries *Johnny Dynamite: Underworld*; co-created *Mike Danger* with Mickey Spillane; and wrote the "Dick Tracy" comic strip for fifteen years. An independent filmmaker in his native Iowa, Collins wrote and directed the cult-fave thrillers *Mommy* and *Mommy's Day*, and recently completed a documentary, *Mike Hammer's Mickey Spillane*.

✠

NANCY A. COLLINS is the author of several novels, including the award-winning *Sunglasses After Dark, Walking Wolf*, and *Angels on Fire*. She has written more than fifty short stories. Her comics credentials include a two-year stint as writer on DC's *Swamp Thing*, and the miniseries *Predator: Hell Come A' Walkin'*, for Dark Horse Comics. She also wrote a comics series based on her fan-favorite character, Sonja Blue.

Several of her novels have been optioned for film.

✠

MATTHEW J. COSTELLO is the author of sixteen novels and numerous non-fiction articles and books. He wrote the script for *The 7th Guest*, the best-selling CD-ROM interactive drama of all time. His latest novel, *Masque* (Warner Books, 1998), has been optioned by Tom Cruise's production company. His upcoming *Poltergeist* novel, *Maelstrom* (PenguinPutnam), will appear in February 2000. His novels have been published worldwide in over a dozen countries.

For The Sci-Fi Channel, Costello co-created and scripted *FTL News*. He is the creator/writer for the Disney Channel's ZOOG-DISNEY, launched in August 1998, and renewed for 1999. Costello is currently writing episodes for the BBC/Disney series, *Microsoap*, and developing a new series for the BBC, with Douglas Adams, called *The Glitch*.

CRAIG SHAW GARDNER has spent far too much of his life around comic books. This has resulted in his management of a comic-book store (the fabulous Million Year Picnic in Cambridge, MA) and his work on a number of media tie-in projects, like the novelization *Batman* (a *New York Times* Best Seller), and *Spider-Man: Wanted Dead or Alive*. Craig has written a whole bunch of other books, from his first, *A Malady of Magicks*, to his most recent, *The Magic Dead* (written under another name that also starts with G).

✠

CHRISTOPHER GOLDEN is the award-winning, *L.A. Times* best-selling author of such novels as *Strangewood* and the three-volume *Shadow Saga*; *Hellboy: The Lost Army*, and the *Body of Evidence* series of teen thrillers (including *Thief of Hearts* and *Soul Survivor*), which is currently being developed for television. He has also written or co-written a great many things—from novels and non-fiction to comic-book series and miniseries—based on the popular TV series, *Buffy the Vampire Slayer*, and its spin-off, *Angel*. Golden's recent comic-book work includes the *Angel* ongoing series; *Wolverine/Punisher: Revelation*; and the upcoming *Batman: Real Worlds*. Golden was born and raised in Massachusetts, where he still lives with his family. He graduated from Tufts University. He is currently at work on his next novel, *Straight on 'Til Morning*. Please visit him at www.christophergolden.com.

✠

RICK HAUTALA is the author of seventeen novels (most recently *The Hidden Saint*, from Berkley) and more than fifty short stories (many of which are published in his new collection, *Bedbugs*, from CD Publications) along with several movie scripts (including *The Jungle Vine*, *Nerve Center*, and *Star Road*) which are currently under option (or they may be in production or option lapsed by the time you read this . . . you know how Hollywood is). He lives in southern Maine, and when he isn't working on his new novel, *The White Room*, can usually be found reading.

✠

BRIAN HODGE is the author of seven novels, the most recent of which is *Wild Horses*, a 1999 hardcover release from William Morrow & Company. He has also written seventy-five or so short stories and novellas, some of which have been chained like galley slaves into the highly acclaimed collections *The Convulsion Factory* and *Falling Idols*. Several times he has been a finalist for the Bram Stoker Award and World Fantasy Award, but so far always a bridesmaid, etc. He also pens book and music reviews, and other non-fiction as the spirit moves, and is currently at work on his next novel.

Turn-ons include movies, wanderlust, *Wallace and Gromit*, collecting weapons (with his medieval war hammer being a particularly intimidating favorite), hearty stouts and ales, and Saint Brendan's Irish Cream. He plays keyboards and the Australian aboriginal didgeridoo, and has begun accumulating recording gear into a cramped but functional collective dubbed Green Man Studio.

✠

NANCY HOLDER is a four-time Bram Stoker Award winner for her supernatural short stories and her novel *Dead in the Water*. She has sold thirty-five novels and over two hundred short stories. Her most recent novels include the science-fiction trilogy, *Gambler's Star*, and a great many *Buffy the Vampire Slayer* novels.

Holder has also written computer-game fiction and manga and TV commercials in Japan. She lives in San Diego, California.

✠

MIKE MIGNOLA, the Eisner and Harvey Award-winning creator of *Hellboy*, has worked in comics since 1983, on many projects, including *Gotham by Gaslight*, *Cosmic Odyssey*, and *Ironwolf: Fires of the Revolution*. He's done illustration work for books and magazines, and design work for television and film, including Francis Ford Coppola's *Dracula* and the upcoming Disney animated film, *Atlantis*.

YVONNE NAVARRO has published four solo novels and three novelizations, plus a whole bunch of short stories. Two of her novels, *Afterage* and *Deadrush*, were finalists for the Bram Stoker Award, and her apocalyptic thriller, *Final Impact*, received two awards. Currently in bookstores is its follow-up, *Red Shadows*, which (as with *Afterage*) has generated countless requests for a sequel. Her novelizations include *Species, Species II*, and *Aliens: Music of the Spears*, and she also published a non-fiction book called *The First Name Reverse Dictionary*.

Yvonne is currently completing *The Willow Files*, a *Buffy the Vampire Slayer* book, and *That's Not My Name*, a solo psychological thriller. She wants everyone in the world to visit her website at www.para-net.com/~ynavarro, where they will be bombarded with subliminal messages demanding they have loads of fun. She currently lives in the Chicago area and plans to relocate to the southwest and get a really neat dog.

✠

Expatriate Englishman **PHILIP NUTMAN** is an award-nominated novelist, screenwriter, editor, and comic-book writer who currently resides in Atlanta. He is the author of the critically acclaimed cult novel *Wet Work*, the forthcoming *Full Throttle*, and has published more than two dozen short stories in anthologies such as *Book of the Dead* and *Splatterpunks*.

In the comics field he has worked extensively for Chaos! penning *Evil Ernie, Chastity, Suspira*, and *The Omen*. He has also written for Marvel and Archie Comics where he produced several issues of *The Teenage Mutant Ninja Turtles* for younger readers. Most recently, he was hired to work on the promotional comic for this year's Madison Scare Garden haunted house. As a screenwriter, he has written a dozen features and numerous treatments. With co-writer Daniel Farrands he recently completed a pitch for the official sequel to *The Amityville Horror* and an adaptation of the Jack Ketchum novel, *The Girl Next Door*.

✠

GREG RUCKA is the author of four novels about Atticus Kodiak—*Keeper, Finder, Smoker*, and *Shooting at Midnight*. He has been writing since the age of eight, and hopefully improving with age. A long-time comics fan, his first graphic-novel series was the suspense-thriller *Whiteout*, published by Oni Press and nominated for three Eisner Awards in 1999. Since that time he has been a contributing writer for DC Comics and an active participant in the *Batman* titles in particular.

Born and raised in California, he earned his undergraduate degree at Vassar College in Poughkeepsie, New York, and his MFA at the University of Southern California. He currently resides in Portland, Oregon. He is twenty-nine years old, has two tattoos, and rides a motorcycle.

✠

CHET WILLIAMSON's latest novels are the three books in *The Searchers* series and *The Crow: Clash by Night* (HarperPrism). Next year will see his first children's book: *The Pennsylvania Dutch Night Before Christmas*, from Pelican Press. Nearly a hundred of his short stories have appeared in such magazines as *The New Yorker, Playboy, Esquire, Twilight Zone*, and many other magazines and anthologies. He has been a final nominee for the World Fantasy Award and the Mystery Writers of America Edgar Award, and a six-time final nominee for the Horror Writers Association's Stoker Award. His work has been adapted for television, radio, and recorded books. Other projects have included a four-issue *Aliens* miniseries entitled *Music of the Spears* and a six-part adaptation of Andrew Vachss and Jim Colbert's novel, *Cross* (both for Dark Horse Comics). He has also written the novelization of the film *The Crow: City of Angels*, and *Hell: A Cyberpunk Thriller*, based on the CD-ROM game.

✠

GAHAN WILSON has produced a few graphic books, but is best known for his regular work in *Playboy* and *The New Yorker*. Something from eighteen to twenty collections of his cartoons have appeared along with a number of works for children and adults. Recently, a collection of his short stories—along with his accompanying illustrations—entitled *The Cleft and Other Odd Tales*, was published to kind reviews. He is presently at work on animated and live-action projects which, he has been told, may someday actually appear in public.

In the meantime, he is glad to be alive.